CANADA IN PIECES

ISBN:
978-0-359-51887-6

DEDICATION

To my beautiful daughters, Emily and Erin Flynn, and to the memory of my late parents, Jack and Barbara Wallace.

CONTENTS

ACKNOWLEDGEMENTS

Nobody can write a book on their own. I certainly can't! There are a number of people I need to thank, without whom this book would never have seen the light of day.

First and foremost, my beautiful girlfriend/life partner Maria Bracalenti. Maria has been a constant source of encouragement from day one when I first thought of the idea of the story until it was done. Maria did a fabulous job proof-reading various edits and providing ideas and support. I love you, Maria.

Thank you to Maria's mom, Nancy Lowell, who assisted with proof-reading and providing ideas and feedback.

Thank you to my editor and childhood friend Laura Brown of Portsmouth, England who did a simply bang-up job editing my manuscript.

Thank you to my very talented cover artist Sarah Quatrano of Warren, Rhode Island. Sarah did the cover art for my 2009 book "The Forgotten Summit". It was wonderful to work with her again.

Thank you to our dear friends Cathy and John Hickson of Grimsby, Ontario. In December 2018 as I was putting the finishing touches on the book Cathy and John were visiting with Maria and I. I was struggling with the title for the book and Cathy came up with the title "Canada in Pieces." John, who is a former colleague of mine from Eastman Kodak, shot the author biography photo.

Thank you to Nick Cheng of Hamilton, Ontario for his invaluable assistance in formatting the book.

Thank you to Richard MacDowell of Basking Ridge, New Jersey. Richard is a former member of the United States Air Force, and who provided me with invaluable information regarding the United States military.

And a final thank you to Sergeant Ng, AH, CD of the Governor General's Horse Guards. Sergeant Ng provided me with very valuable information regarding the Canadian military.

FOREWORD

"Canada in Pieces" began in March 2018. I was the victim of corporate downsizing in my "day job" and the day after my job ended, I began writing what would become this book.

As the author, I have taken certain "liberties." Some of the titles for Cabinet members that I have used are from the past, such as External Affairs Minister, as I felt they more accurately reflect their duties. One perk of being an author is being able to make such changes! I also outfitted the Canadian military with Stinger missiles, which they currently don't possess. Never let it be said that I don't support our troops! The gun battle on the Seaway International Bridge is probably exaggerated with bullets crossing the bridge. But again that is the prerogative of the author!

The main idea of what I hope people will gain from reading this book is; Canada is a very fragile nation and thus this book is a warning – a "shot across the bow" as to what could happen in the near future. As noted in the book the natural trade routes of North America run "north-south." Canada has worked hard to build an "east-west" nation in defiance of those trade routes. Has this been successful? To a point, yes, but there are always cracks in the foundation that make up Canada. Some of them include;

Canada splintered across linguistic lines (English-French) during both World Wars and especially over the issue of conscription. Most French speaking Quebecers did not support Canada's involvement in those wars, or a draft, while the opposite was true in English speaking Canada. There have been other such examples throughout Canadian history. To draw a comparison, in the United States during a serious crisis, historically Americans rally behind their President.

In Canada we split apart.

Canada has always had a very troubled relationship with the "First Nations." We didn't see the bloody wars in Canada that the United States experienced with their indigenous peoples. But to this day, relations between Canada and their "First Nations" are tense and uneasy. "First Nations" peoples make up 26.4% of the Canadian prison population, while they only make up roughly 4% of the Canadian population as a whole. Canadian governments of all political stripes have been guilty of violating treaty rights. We have seen outright violence in such places as Oka, Quebec and Caledonia, Ontario. Previous Federal governments have treated the "First Nations" with disrespect or utter disinterest. The current government in Ottawa came to power in 2015 promising reconciliation with the "First Nations" and a new and more respectful relationship. Neither has come to fruition in the over three years since the last election.

The Federal Liberal Party of Canada is unofficially known as the "Natural Governing Party" as they have dominated Federal politics for close to 100 years. The problem is, under the current Canadian system, two provinces, Quebec and Ontario, dominate Parliament as they have in total 199 seats in the House of Commons (121 for Ontario and 78 for Quebec.) That means a party may gain a majority government simply by dominating these two provinces (there are a total of 338 seats currently in the House of Commons.) This, of course, is a result of these two provinces being the most populated in the country. However, the combined populations of British Columbia and Alberta are higher than that of Quebec. And they have two fewer seats in total than does Quebec.

In the Senate, the situation is worse. Quebec and Ontario have a total of 48 seats (24 each.) The four Western provinces in total have 24 seats. Going back to my previous example, BC and Alberta combined have a larger population than does Quebec – and they only have six Senate seats each.

What this has done is allowed the Liberal Party to focus on the Eastern portion of Canada, which is the Maritime Provinces, along with Quebec and Ontario and to basically ignore the Western provinces. A stunning example of their "Eastern focus" is that in over 100 years, the Liberal Party has never once had a leader from Western Canada. Contrast that to the United States were both the Democratic and Republican parties have had leaders from all parts of the country. In Canada the "West is shut out" in government when the Liberal Party forms the government.

Currently, polls are showing support for separation rising in Alberta and Saskatchewan. This cannot be surprising as currently the Liberals are in power in Canada and as always are led by a Prime Minister from Quebec who appears oblivious or simply uninterested in concerns in Western Canada. This is a very dangerous "time bomb" waiting to explode, in the mind of the author.

LIST OF CHARACTERS

Canada

Federal Politicians and Officials

Pierre Dion – Prime Minister of Canada and leader of the Federal Liberal Party of Canada

Denise McLean – Leader of Her Majesties Loyal Opposition and leader of the Federal Conservative Party of Canada

Gurminder Grewal – Leader of the New Democratic Party

Rocco Mancino – Governor General of Canada

Jean-Guy Blais – Minister of National Defense

Sara Freehan – Minister of Industry and Trade

Dr. Jacquelyn Grant – Minister of Health

Myles Callahan – Minister of Energy and Mines

Stephanie Howatt – Minister of External Affairs

Rogatien Hebert – Minister of Finance

Robert Lalonde – Chief Aide to Prime Minister Dion

Oscar Redstone – Minister of Public Security

Monique Juneau – Attorney General

Maria Russo – Canadian Ambassador to the United States

Provincial Politicians

Karen Van Pelt – Premier of Alberta

Carla Henderson – Premier of British Columbia

Neil Craig – Premier of Saskatchewan

Max Mountjoy – Premier of Newfoundland

Keith Cassidy – Premier of Ontario

Nicole Ouellet – Premier of Quebec

Heidi McNamara – Premier of Manitoba

United States

Katherine Morrison – President of the United States of America

Henry Stillman – Secretary of Defense

Michael Youngblood – Secretary of State

Joel Rafferty – Vice President of the United States

Robert Jackson – National Security Advisor

Lisa Cameron – Secretary of Energy

Jack Stafford – Secretary of Commerce

Dr. Kimberly Tucker – White House Chief of Staff

Hector Lopez – United States Ambassador to Canada

Melissa Calhoun – Secretary of the Interior

Great Britain

King Edward IX – King of the United Kingdom, Canada, etc.

Glenn McMillan – Prime Minister of the United Kingdom

Christine Symington – Minister of Defense

Canada in Pieces

PROLOGUE

Middle East – Sometime in the Near Future
– 3:30am Local Time

Across the borders that Israel shares with Lebanon, Jordan, Syria, and Egypt, the early morning skies turned bright as noon as thousands of artillery pieces began firing. Israeli border posts were vaporized in moments, settlements across the Golan Heights and on the West Bank were almost instantly incinerated. Attack planes from Lebanon, Jordan, Syria, Egypt, Iran, and Saudi Arabia began massive air strikes across Israel, destroying air bases, army facilities, bridges, and entire communities. The Arab nations, for the first time since 1973, were trying to eradicate Israel from the face of the earth.

Israeli defense forces, short-staffed with numerous personnel given leave for Passover, which had begun at midnight, struggled to respond. The Arabs had done a magnificent job moving forces to within the borders of Israel without sparking concern or suspicion. Israeli aircraft were destroyed on the tarmac before they could get airborne. Aircrews were wiped out as they attempted to get additional aircraft into the air. The majority of Israeli government offices in Tel Aviv and Jerusalem were heavily damaged or destroyed in air and artillery strikes. And in an even more sinister escalation, Syrian forces switched to shells and short-range rockets containing deadly Sarin and VX nerve gases and began pounding the Israeli settlements and military forces on the Golan Heights with the horrific gases. Israeli citizens and soldiers staggered out of collapsed buildings and military fortifications and began dropping to the ground, wracked with convulsions from the deadly nerve agents before succumbing to the poisons.

After 45 minutes of massive bombardment, the Arab forces crossed the Israeli frontier. Shattered Israeli border fortifications were easily over-run by the massive armored units of the initial Arab forces. Thousands of T-72 and T-80 tanks rolled into Israel. Following them would be over one million Arab soldiers, intent on revenge for their defeats in 1948, 1967, and 1973 at the hands of the hated Jewish state

CHAPTER I

Around the world, heads of nations were alerted to the situation in the Middle East. In Ottawa, it was 8:30pm as Prime Minister Pierre Dion was reviewing briefing documents on Canadian multicultural initiatives when his private phone buzzed. Dion answered his phone and heard the flustered voice of his Minister of National Defense Jean Guy Blais. "Prime Minister, I'm sorry to have to tell you we have a major crisis on our hands. The Arab states have attacked Israel in a massive offensive and there are some reports they may be using chemical weapons."

Dion sat back in his chair, absolutely appalled. This would clearly be a cataclysmic event for the world.

"Blais, find out everything you can and be prepared to brief the cabinet at 8:am tomorrow. We will need a full update. Also find out what the Americans are doing. Are they going on alert? Have they raised the DEFCON status yet for NORAD or NATO"?

The call ended. Dion dialed the private number for the U.S. President he had never used. He had a very formal, uneasy, relationship with President Katherine Morrison. Morrison, a native of the Elk City Oklahoma region, was a graduate of the University of Oklahoma in history and had a doctorate from the John F. Kennedy School of Government at Harvard. She was the first US President to speak a Native American tongue having learned

1

Cheyenne at home and studied Cheyenne culture at university. She had grown up on a cattle ranch and was still at home riding a horse with a rifle in a scabbard, attached to the saddle and a single action Colt 45 revolver on her hip. More than once she had shot and killed wolves threatening her family's cattle, and in another legendary occasion, a black bear charged her younger sister Christine while the two were out on the outer perimeter of their ranch. The 17-year-old Morrison yanked the lever action Winchester 30/30 rifle from the scabbard on her saddle, and with "ice water in her veins" pumped 7 shots into the bear before it reached her sister.

Her parents had taught her the cattle business, she could read a financial statement, and could accurately judge the price a cow would fetch at auction in less than 10 seconds. She had worked part time to put herself through undergraduate studies at the University of Oklahoma, before landing a scholarship to Harvard for graduate studies. She had then returned home to run her family's cattle business before running for the state senate. After a decade in the state senate, she successfully ran for the Governor's office in Oklahoma and then as the Democratic nominee, she mercifully put an end to the "dumpster fire" that had been the mark of the most recent Republican administration. The National Rifle Association (NRA) had tried to embrace her thinking this was their dream candidate – a female who embraced guns. Instead she fired their rhetoric right back at them saying "guns are appropriate on a ranch. They are not appropriate in cities and not every person should have one." The NRA now viewed her with outright fear and hatred.

There was talk on Madison Avenue at one point on making her the first "Marlboro Woman." Philip Morris through the use of the "Marlboro Man" ad campaign starting in the 1960's had made millions and turned Marlboro cigarettes into the worlds' leading brand. The chance of creating a "modern" such campaign with a woman in it was simply too good to be true. Their hopes were dashed when Morrison, when approached, advised them that she felt tobacco was a "death industry" with no social value at all. The recruiters from Madison Avenue slunk away embarrassed and angry.

She had been married once, shortly after graduating from the University of Oklahoma. That marriage failed during her days in the state senate. Her husband Brian Jones had simply not been secure enough in his own masculinity to remain married to such a brilliant, ambitious woman who very quickly was being touted as "the" rising star in Oklahoma politics with plenty of talk about a national political future for her. The two of them parted fairly amicably and since then, while Morrison had "friends" and at times lovers, her focus was on her career and now her nation.

In less than three years, as America's first female President, she had returned a level of sanity to the White House and had worked hard to restore people's faith in government. She was busy attempting to be the first President to pass a bill that gave every legal resident and citizen basic health care coverage. That was still an ongoing struggle. She had increased funding for education and housing and at the same time through tax increases, and cutting other programs was actually able to balance the federal budget for the first time in generations.

She had the utmost respect for Canada, having studied some Canadian history at Oklahoma and the Canadian government in her studies at the Kennedy School of Government; however, she viewed Dion as an "insufferable pompous egghead with no understanding of finances or business." No male in Congress or business ever underestimated her as they knew she was tougher than most of them, smarter than all of them, and had the credentials to prove it.

Pierre Dion was radically different. He had grown up in a wealthy family and never worked in the private sector. He graduated with a political science degree from Laval University and then went onto McGill University for law. Upon passing the Quebec Bar exam, he joined the Quebec civil service as a lawyer. He became a "household name" in that province when he headed an inquiry into corruption in Quebec politics. As the inquiry moved forward Dion developed the reputation of a brilliant lawyer, with an almost computer like intellect. From there he ran successfully for Parliament, before eventually running for and winning the leadership of the Federal Liberal Party and then the office of Prime Minister. Dion was at home with the wealthy, urbane "Laurention Elite[i]" of Eastern Canada. He was a man who would only listen to arguments that were based on fact and logic. His favorite saying came from his greatest political hero, former Canadian Prime Minister Pierre Elliott Trudeau. And that was "Reason over Passion." Members of his caucus knew they would never sway him with an argument based on emotion. Pierre Dion demanded facts and only facts. And he was ruthless with cabinet ministers whom he felt wasted his time without thoroughly researching issues that they had brought to his attention.

Like his hero, Pierre Trudeau, Dion struggled to understand and be empathetic with the issues in Western Canada. He was also very pragmatic in this regard. He could win elections by gaining a majority of seats in Atlantic Canada as well as Quebec and Ontario. He didn't need support from the Western provinces, and thus felt no particular reason or need to be more aware or sympathetic to Western Canadians.[ii] In fact in the last Federal election his Liberal Party had won but a single seat west of the Ontario border. (That was in Saskatchewan in the riding of his External Affairs Minister Stephanie Howatt.) However, he picked up all 32 seats in the Maritimes, 78 out of 81 in Quebec, and 72 of 121 in Ontario. That gave him a "majority" with 183 seats in the 338 seat House of Commons. The Opposition Conservatives took 90% of Western Canadian seats to no avail. The west was shut out of government – once again.

Dion was content to allow the United States to defend Canada and save Canada that huge expense. However, he, like many Canadians, looked down on most Americans with a sense of moral, even smug superiority. He did not personally care for the American President, finding her brash, and out-spoken and he felt her connection with the US mid-west and its land to be almost beneath that of a world leader. Dion was fluent in French and English, as that was considered "a must" for the role of Canadian Prime Minister and he viewed Morrison's fluency in a "First Nations" language with puzzlement. He could not understand why a world leader would not have exerted the effort to learn a language such as French which is spoken around the world, or even Spanish which is the second most common language in North America.

Dion had married his university "sweetheart" Madelaine Charest after graduating from McGill. Next to his top advisor Robert Lalonde, she was his closest confidante.

Katherine Morrison answered the phone and spoke briefly. "Hello, Pierre, I know why you're calling. I'm about to meet with the Joint Chiefs of Staff and Henry Stillman .When we come up with a game plan, I'll have Henry call Minister Blais. But Pierre – this is huge. If I were you, I'd start thinking about putting your military, or what is left of it, on a war footing."

Dion hung up the phone and buried his face in his hands. That last "crack" from the U.S. President cut deep. Dion was a pacifist from Quebec -a province well known for its' aversion to military conflict.

During world wars, the Korean War and the war in Afghanistan public opinion in Quebec had solidly been against any Canadian (or Quebecois) involvement. That was notwithstanding the superb performance of French speaking regiments such as the Royal 22nd Regiment (the "Van Doos") in these conflicts. The Royal 22nd Regiment in fact, has always been considered one of the most "elite" regiments in the Canadian Army.

Dion had taken the leadership of the Federal Liberal Party of Canada and then the Prime Minister's office by promising a return to the days of Canada being a solid advocate for peace (some would say his platform was solidly pacifist.) The Liberal Party of Canada has been the dominant party throughout the history of the country. It is safe to say that its policies tend to be "centrist" or slightly to the left. It focuses strongly on social justice, but avoids any form of strong ideology. At times the party may "lean more left, or even slightly to the right" depending on the mood of the public. Traditionally it rotated leaders between English and French candidates. It was also "a must" that whoever the leader was they must be fluent in English and French.

Dion's platform in his first election running as Leader of the Liberal Party called for a substantial reduction in the already small Canadian military. He had told the Canadian public, that Canada only needed a military large enough to assist in national emergencies (such as natural disasters) and small peacekeeping missions with the United Nations. Over the strenuous arguments of the Opposition in Parliament and the military itself, Dion's plan had been carried out. The Canadian military was a wreck. And now he may be facing a true emergency.

The following morning, the Canadian cabinet met. Defense Minister Blais briefed the somber group.

"Ladies and gentlemen, we have a true emergency on our hands. At 8:30 pm our time last evening, Arab nations began an all-out attack on Israel. Included in the attack appears to be nerve agents deployed by Syrian forces. Israel was caught totally off guard and their forces at the present are struggling to resist. The Arab forces are making huge advances. As you all know the use of chemical weapons by the Syrians has escalated this conflict far above what would be considered a "normal war" if there is such a term. Israel has nuclear weapons and Secretary of Defense Stillman and I, when we spoke early this morning, fear that with the Israeli defense forces in retreat and the Syrians already using Weapons of Mass Destruction, - well we both feel Israel may very well use their nuclear weapons. Secretary Stillman advised me that the President is moving US forces including their NORAD[iii] forces to DEFCON 3. We will need to move our own forces in conjunction with the US forces."

The room was deathly silent. Not a single Minister in the room had ever contemplated that Canada may be involved in a war while they were in political office. And certainly not as part of a war considering the anti-military campaign that they had run on and won.

Prime Minister Dion stood up, shaking his head. "Ladies and Gentlemen, I'm appalled to have to do this as it goes against all I believe I promised Canadians, and in particular, Quebecers that the days of Canada being involved in international military affairs were over if they elected me. However, we have no option but to follow the American lead here. If we do not follow their lead, all we have to do is remember what our military did when Prime Minister Diefenbaker refused to follow President Kennedy's move to DEFCON 3 during the Cuban Missile Crisis. The military ignored Diefenbaker and went on alert anyway. The chances are that if we refuse to follow the American lead, then our military will do the

7

same thing as they did in 1962 and go to DEFCON 3 on their own initiative. At least this way we can try and control how far we get involved."

Myles Callahan, the Minister of Energy and Mines and Member of Parliament from Newfoundland commented. "I'm not a military expert by any means. But I have to support your thoughts here Prime Minister. We have cut back our own forces so much, that we really have no choice. I am not saying we shouldn't have reduced our forces. But by doing so, we have cast our lot in with the Americans who protect us. We have to support them."

As this was occurring, U.S. President Katherine Morrison was on the phone with Israeli Prime Minister Rachel Katz.

"Prime Minister," the President began. "Please know that the United States stands with Israel. I'm moving U.S. Forces to DEFCON 3 and have advised the Joint Chiefs of Staff to prepare to send American forces to your aid. We have a naval task force close to the Persian Gulf that should be able to send you air support within 12 hours. We have also called for an emergency session of the UN Security Council to deal with this."

There was a brief pause and then the Israeli Prime Minister responded. "Madam President. I appreciate your support as does all of Israel. That being said, we're facing a crisis that threatens our very survival. We are under attack by sworn enemies and even Egypt whom we had a peace treaty with. We can trust nobody except ourselves. Here is our position and you can let our enemies know. Within two hours from this moment all Arab forces will cease their offensive actions against us. Within four hours of this moment, the leaders of Egypt, Syria, Jordan, Iran, Lebanon, and Saudi Arabia will fly unescorted to Jerusalem to face trial for crimes against the

8

Israeli people. If these conditions are not met within these time limits I will order the Israeli Defense Forces to respond to the attacks on our nation by using our weapons of mass destruction. Not to defeat our enemies Madam President. To completely destroy them. To ensure that never again can they ever threaten Israel."

President Morrison reeled back in her chair. She fought to remain calm and replied. "Good Lord, Prime Minister. You can't be serious about using nuclear weapons. That is unconscionable."

The Israeli Prime Minister replied with an icy cold calm. "Unconscionable, Madam President? Really? Was it unconscionable when your nation used nuclear weapons on Japan to save the lives of untold American soldiers? My job is to protect the people of Israel and I will do whatever it takes to do that. I must go Madam President. I have a war to fight and a nation to save."

With that, the phone went dead in President Morrison's ear. She knew she had moments to avert disaster. She quickly called for her National Security Advisor Robert Jackson, Secretary of State Michael Youngblood, and Defense Secretary Stillman. When they gathered Morrison quickly outlined the call she had with the Israeli Prime Minister. When she finished there was a moment of silence then Secretary of State Youngblood began. "We can't meet her deadline. It is impossible. We don't have diplomatic relations with Iran and Syria. We'd have to go through someone like Switzerland or Russia to get their leadership. I can get on the phone right now to our Ambassadors in Egypt, Saudi Arabia, Jordan, and Lebanon. But we don't have enough time to brief them and have them get into see the leadership of those countries and get their military operations stopped. Even if you called their leaders directly right now there isn't enough time."

"What in the name of Christ are we going to do?" President Morrison implored.

Henry Stillman responded; Madam President, there is only one thing to do. You have to get the Israelis to back down and at least give us more time."

Katherine Morrison left the White House Situation Room to return to the Oval Office. She instructed her aid to get the Israeli Prime Minister back on the phone, for an urgent call. The line connected and President Morrison began. "Prime Minister, I've met with my top cabinet officials and while they all join me in offering Israel the unconditional support of our nation, we must implore you to give us more time to approach the invading nations and try to convince them to agree to a cease fire, and then a withdrawal of their troops from Israeli territory."

"Madam President. Thank you for your concern and support. As we speak, my people are dying. The Syrians are continuing their chemical attacks, while the other invaders kill Israeli citizens with conventional arms. No, there will be no extension. Israel and Israel alone will solve this situation and ensure it will never happen again. Good day."

With that, Prime Minster Katz turned to her Defense Minister Moshe Swartz and gave the order; "Initiate Operation Avenge Masada."

Swartz picked up the phone and gave the same order to Israel's nuclear forces. Within five minutes, Jericho III Missiles were launched. Each missile contained a nuclear war head and was targeted at cities in the invading nations. F15's from the Israeli Defense Forces roared over invading Arab armies and dropped tactical nuclear bombs on the advancing columns. Israeli Dolphin class submarines surfaced and launched nuclear tipped cruise missiles. Within minutes, the Jericho III missiles slammed into Cairo, Damascus, Amman, Riyadh and Tehran. In the cities, massive shock and pressure waves destroyed buildings, and then enormous fires storms erupted throughout. The submarine launched cruise missiles tore into the oil fields across the Arab world, sending clouds of radioactive flames thousands of feet into the air. Other cruise missiles had been directed at the invading armies along with the tactical nuclear weapons delivered by the F15's and within moment's entire modern Arab armies and cities simply ceased to exist.

CHAPTER II

The stunned Canadian cabinet met in Ottawa shortly after news of the Israeli nuclear strikes became public. Prime Minister Dion called the meeting to order and asked Defense Minister Blais for a briefing.

"Ladies and gentlemen," Blais began. "Here is what we currently know about the situation in the Middle East. There is currently a cease fire being observed by the remaining combatants. For all intents and purposes Cairo, Damascus, Tehran, Riyadh, and Amman as well as the invading Arab military forces no longer exist. Other smaller cities in the region have also been destroyed. The Suez Canal has been utterly destroyed and we believe every major oil field in the region has been vaporized. Israel even went after oil fields in nations such as Kuwait, Qatar, Bahrain and Iraq. Civilian and military casualties will be in the millions. Radioactive fallout is spreading across the region and that will kill at least hundreds of thousands more. Israel is getting pummeled by it. By resorting to nuclear weapons, they acted in the manner of Samson pulling down the pillars of the temple. By destroying their enemies, they may very well have destroyed themselves.

'As for our forces,' he continued. "Most of our regular forces units are almost at full strength and ready to deploy. All leaves have been cancelled. As of now, with the Middle East in radio-active ruins, there really is no place for them to deploy to. They will remain alert and ready to respond to any issues domestically. We have not started mobilizing the reserves as it would take the Emergencies Act to bring them up to "full speed". That being said I have alerted the defense chiefs of staff to be ready to mobilize them if need be."

Minister of Health, Doctor Jacquelyn Grant interrupted the briefing and asked. "Is Canada in danger from the radioactive fallout?"

Blais responded. "As of right now, no. If the current weather patterns remain the same we should be okay. We will get some here in North America but not enough to pose a true public health risk. I can't say the same though for much of Europe and Africa. As you know Iran shares a border with Russia, and already clouds of radioactivity and fallout are over Russia. It will only get worse.

'My department will work with yours to get information out to the public regarding the concern over fallout. Along with this human catastrophe, we need to talk about something else that will directly impact all Canadians perhaps even more then the Israeli nuclear attacks. On that note I'll turn things over to you, Myles.'

Energy Minister Myles Callahan stood up and began briefing the cabinet. "Outside of this horrific human tragedy, there's something else we need to discuss. The oil fields across that region have been destroyed. The Israeli's deliberately targeted the oil fields in the entire area. Those oil fields are gone. Not damaged, gone. Looking at what our satellites can see through the smoke and flames, I can tell you it will take years to try and rebuild them. And we can't even get crews into the region to the fires due to the radiation. Ladies and gentlemen, we are looking at a total loss of Middle Eastern oil for the foreseeable future. And let me remind you of this, most of Eastern Canada's oil comes from the Middle East. If we had approved and built the Energy East pipeline years ago, we would be self-sufficient on oil from Alberta, Saskatchewan, and the Hibernia oil fields off Newfoundland. But that project died due to our own parties' green policies. I don't have to remind everyone I argued in favor of that project. Now we're in a real mess. Adding to it, oil prices have increased to over $250.00 per barrel since Israel's nuclear strikes and it will keep climbing. It won't be long until we see panic with massive price increases for gas – if it can be found, and other forms of oil. Already gas prices across the country have shot past $8.00 per liter! We are facing a national emergency."

Prime Minster Dion asked. "Myles, do we import U.S. oil? Can that make up for the loss of the Middle East? Or what about sources such as Venezuela or Nigeria?"

"Sure, we can." the Minister replied. "But the world price is going into the stratosphere. I predict we may very well see the greatest economic downturn to hit Canada and the rest of the world, since the Great Depression. People are not going to be able to afford to put gas in their cars. Almost every consumer product is shipped via truck. The price of shipping goods will explode due to the massive increase in oil. That in turn will increase the prices of products to levels I can't even predict. I can't imagine what it will cost to ship say, oranges from California or Florida to Toronto. Or clothing from warehouses to stores. This in turn will prompt demands from labor for much higher wages. We'll return to the days of the early 70's with massive inflation fueled by incredible increases in oil prices. I can't emphasize enough that we have a national emergency on our hands right now."

Dion sat in disbelief. Finally, he replied. "Clearly, we can't allow that to happen. We cannot have the North American economies fall into a state of collapse. I'll call President Morrison today and speak to her. Perhaps, we can create some form of North American oil alliance where we can sell North American produced oil within the continent at a below world market price. I'm just thinking out loud. Any thoughts?"

Minister of Trade Sara Freehan spoke up. "Prime Minister, keep in mind that under both NAFTA and the old Canada-U.S. Free Trade agreements we have to continue to sell oil to the U.S. and Mexico. We may be better off getting out of those agreements to better protect our resources, and figure out how to get Western Canadian oil to the Eastern Canadian markets. I really believe that this is the time for Canada to "hunker down" and protect our own oil and keep it for use by Canadians. I think we will find our partners in the United States doing exactly that. At this time President Morrison will be under tremendous pressure to keep American oil for the use of Americans. I don't believe there's any chance the Americans will be interested in your idea of a North American oil market."

Dion sat silent, then asked. "Sara, are you saying that due to this emergency that we should seriously consider leaving NAFTA and the original Free Trade deal?"

"That's exactly what I am saying, Prime Minister", Minister Freehan responded.

External Affairs Minister Stephanie Howatt spoke up. " Prime Minister, we must be very cautious about thinking of such an action. Under NAFTA we would have to give six months' notice that we were abrogating the treaty. If we were to do that, it would be very difficult to ever negotiate such an agreement again in the future when times are better. And with the six months' notice requirement, I believe the damage to our economy would already be complete by the time the notice was up. We would accomplish nothing."

Later that morning, Dion met with his top aide Robert Lalonde and began talking in French. "Robert, what in hell am I going to do?

16

What is Canada going to do? Have we ever been in such a mess?"

"Prime Minister, I don't think so. We were not directly threatened in both World Wars. Maybe the Cuban Missile Crisis was as bad. I don't really know. What I do know is when we go out in the House today for Question Period the Opposition will be all over you demanding to know what you are going to do about rising gas and oil prices. There isn't a single Canadian who is not going to have their life turned upside down by that. And they expect you, fairly or unfairly to have answers and fix this."

In the Office of the Leader of Her Majesties Official Opposition, Conservative leader Denise McLean met with her closest aide George Braun. The Conservative Party of Canada was traditionally the "second choice" for Canadian voters. It had gone through more than one reorganization in its long history. Traditionally the Conservatives also had a strong social justice platform, although not nearly as strong as the Liberal's, while also arguing for less "red tape" a stronger law and order focus and balanced budgets.

Denise McLean was an unusual choice of leader for the Conservatives. Traditionally the Conservative Party attracted more male voters than female. (Females tended to be more comfortable with the Liberal Party and their stronger focus on social justice and family issues.) McLean was only the second female leader the party had ever selected. She was from Toronto, had completed a Bachelor of Arts in History at the University of Guelph, and then attended law school at the University of Windsor. While at Windsor, she took advantage of the city's proximity to Detroit (the two cities are separated by the Detroit River) to do a combined Canadian/American JD degree through the University of Windsor and University of Detroit Mercy. After being admitted to both the Ontario and Michigan Bars she took a job as a Crown Attorney in

Hamilton, Ontario and became known across Canada for her superb record in convicting organized crime figures. She took that status into politics running for and winning the leadership of the Conservative party. She had focused on her career and declined the idea of marriage but did have a 12 year old daughter. That fact had made her unpopular among the "Social Conservatives" in the party but McLean simply "blew them off" stating "My personal life is nobody's business." She was smart, focused, and possessed an unbending sense of principle and integrity.

The topic of Question Period was first and foremost in McLean's mind.

"Denise," Braun urged, "you can have that bastard Dion on the ropes today. The country is coming apart and people are looking for blood. Dion has no answers and we have to show the country that."

'Jesus Christ, George, don't you think I know that!", McLean sputtered. "The problem is I don't have any answers either. It's great for me to go out there in the House today and be a typical Canadian opposition politician and rip the government to shreds. That is how Canadian parliamentary democracy has always worked. The government members blindly support the government – don't think for their goddamn selves and the opposition does the opposite – no matter what the government says or does we are supposed to oppose it. Hell, if Dion walked across the Rideau Canal today, and told the House he had personally found a cure for all forms of cancer, you would all expect me to roast him for not taking a boat across the canal and then you'd expect me to accuse him of holding back the cure until there was a more advantageous time for him to bring it forward. I ran for office promising to change things and when I took over this role I promised to be a responsible Opposition Leader. I promised to yes, hold the government to account. But, I also promised that if they did something well, I would give them credit.

'My God, we're supposed to be working for the betterment of Canada here. Not just to advance our careers. And right now the mess our nation is facing, demands that we try and work with Dion and try and find a way out this. I don't know if there is one. But we have to try and find one.

'Now George call the Prime Minister's office and tell them I need to see the Prime Minister before Question Period. It is of the utmost urgency."

An hour later, Prime Minister Dion met with Opposition Leader McLean in his office. "Denise, what can I do for you? I was told this was very urgent but I don't have a lot of time."

"Prime Minister, I'll make this quick. I want to talk to you about Question Period[iv] today and what will happen in it."

"The daily circus or feeding frenzy", the Prime Minister wearily said. "Tell me how many different ways will you accuse me of being incompetent, a fool, a liar maybe, perhaps even a traitor, today?"

"Pierre, let me make this more personal", she replied. 'I know our country is in one god-awful mess today. I don't blame you or your government. You didn't create the war in the Middle East. Now I think your own policies and that of the Liberal Party in the past towards our military have been quite frankly disastrous and if I may say so – stupid. But so far Canada has not come under military attack and from what I can see your government did get what is left of our military forces mobilized fairly quickly. So unless that situation changes and Canada comes under direct attack, I will not belabor the point of the state of our military. What I want to talk to you about is this; I will not attack you or your government over the oil crisis we face. I don't believe you have any answers as of yet, and I know I sure don't. In fact, what I want to do is offer you the help of myself and any Conservative Members of the House that you believe may be of assistance. This is one of the most serious crisis's Canada has ever faced and in my opinion now is not the time for partisan politics."

Prime Minister Dion sat stunned in his chair. In Canadian history, rarely did the government and opposition rally on behalf of the country. He gathered his thoughts and said. "Well, Denise, I am grateful for this and commend your patriotism. As you can imagine I am reeling as I am sure you are. I will gladly take you up on your offer and promise you full cooperation and consultation as we try and work our way out of this mess."

Denise McLean paused, then responded. "Thank you, Prime Minister. I have only one request. And that is, don't let me be blindsided by any events. If you want my cooperation, I need to be part of all briefings and I need to be aware of everything going on. In return my party and I will help and of course we will be bound by total confidentiality. And I will go so far as to announce that at today's Question Period."

Dion smiled, stood up and extended his hand. "Denise, that's the best thing I've heard in a long time. Thank you, all of Canada thanks you. I will make sure you and anyone else in your caucus that you feel is appropriate, is briefed on all developments."

Opposition Leader McLean shook the Prime Minister's hand, then said in a quiet voice. "Prime Minister, I don't doubt we can and will work together for the benefit of the country that we both love. However, I wouldn't count on anyone in the New Democratic Party

(NDP) to join us. For years, they've been railing about our dependence on oil and how we need to develop alternative fuel sources. And of course, they're right there and we should have done more. But I predict Mr. Grewal, and his NDP caucus will pounce on you and once they see that we are cooperating on me as well, like a tiger on wounded prey. This is their chance to score points like never before- and the country be damned."

Pierre Dion stared at her for a few moments and finally replied. "Denise, I know you and Gurminder don't exactly drink beer after work together, but I have more faith in his sense of patriotism then you do. I'll speak with him but I am sure he will cooperate with us in the best interest of the country."

Gurminder Grewal, the leader of the NDP entered the prime Minister's office an hour later. The NDP has always been a left of center party. The party has strong ties to the organized labor movement and of all the three major Federal parties in Canada; it has always tended to be the most nationalistic. It distrusts large corporations, has a visible anti-American edge to it, and has always argued to increase taxes on the more wealthy corporations and individuals.

Gurminder Grewal had been born and raised in the Toronto suburb of Brampton. He was a second generation Canadian, with his grandparents having immigrated from India years earlier. He attended York University in Toronto and graduated with a degree in Political Science. York has always been known for many "left of center" professors and Grewal gravitated to their classes and by the time he had graduated, he was a NDP member and had taken a job as an organizer with the Teamsters Union. From there he ran for Parliament at age 29, and lost in that first attempt. Four years later, he successfully won a seat in Parliament and established himself as a loud, at times almost hysterical voice of the left, constantly attacking the Liberals and Conservatives for being too pro-American, or too pro-business. Regardless of what tact the Liberals or Conservatives took, Grewal was opposed to it. Many called him the most effective opposition leader since John Diefenbaker in the 1960's however like Diefenbaker, there were those who felt he was somewhat "irrational" mentally with his over the top rhetoric.

Prime Minister Dion greeted Grewal warmly and invited him to sit down. Grewal sat down stiffly and began. "Prime Minister, you wished to see me."

"I did, Gurminder. As you are aware, due to the war in the Middle East, oil prices have exploded through the roof and we are worried about an economic catastrophe that will make the Great Depression look like a 'walk in the park.' I am hoping we can avoid a lot of unpleasantness starting today in Question Period and work together to try and find some solutions to help our country. Ms. McLean has already offered the support of herself and her caucus. Can I count on you and the NDP?"

Gurminder Grewal glared at the Prime Minister and then practically exploded. "Prime Minister, I can't believe you have the nerve, the gall to come to me with that request. For years, I have been pushing your government and the previous Conservative government to embrace green energy and move Canada away from oil. None of you would listen. All you could think of was the money flowing from the Alberta oil fields and all the tax money you get from the sale of gasoline and other oil products. You saw nothing but money and to hell with the environment and Canada's future."

Dion sat back, shocked. Trying to restrain his anger, he responded. "Mr. Grewal, I have heard you bellowing for years. Myself and every other person in government for the last 10 plus years. What I also never heard from you was what would replace oil? Where would all the people working in the oil fields in Alberta and Saskatchewan work? What would replace the tax revenue and revenues from selling oil? Considering no manufacturer has produced a reliable electric car that can travel more than 100 kilometers on a charge, what are people to drive? I never got an answer from you on these and other questions."

Grewal stood up and pointed his finger at the enraged Prime Minister. "I swear to God, Prime Minister, starting today in Question Period myself and my party will tear you apart. The paint in the Commons will peel off the wall from us. You sold our country down the river to the big oil companies. I'm not surprised McLean and the Tories are backing you. They also sold their souls to big oil. Now every Canadian will pay for the mess that you all created. But I promise you that I will end your career over this. And I can only hope Canada will survive."

Dion stood up and shaking in rage yelled; "You bastard! Get the fuck out of my office now and never come back. Take a run at me and I'll prove to be a very dangerous enemy. Get out now!"

As Grewal left, Dion's chief aid Robert Lalonde rushed in and excitedly in French said. "Good lord Pierre, what just happened?"

"That worthless piece of socialist garbage just told me to my face that we can't count on him or his party for help. He's going to use this crisis, which is amongst the worst any Canadian government has ever dealt with, to score political points. Can you believe it, Robert?"

"Pierre, I'd believe anything negative about that weasel. Denise McLean is a tough opponent of ours, and when she sinks her teeth into something she won't let go. However, I know she'll always put the best interests of Canada ahead of any political goals she may have. Grewal on the other hand, would throw his grandmother down a flight of stairs if he thought it would help him get ahead. The only interest he has is what is good for him."

"I agree, my friend. I can tell Question Period today and for the foreseeable future will be a real challenge. Please get Ed Cooper on the phone ASAP. I need to speak with him before Question Period."

Moments later, Dion, was speaking with Speaker of the House Edward Cooper on the phone. Dion briefed the Speaker of the House on the details of the crisis, and on his conversations with the two opposition leaders.

Ed Cooper, widely respected by most, if not all, Members of Parliament (MP's) listened carefully then responded; "Thank you, Prime Minister. I appreciate the heads up that we will have a most, shall we say, challenging time ahead of us as Canadians, and certainly in the house itself. I will Speak with the Sergeant at Arms and ensure we are ready for anything, be it protests outside Parliament or even within it."

 That afternoon Question Period was the most chaotic, raucous session the Canadian House of Commons had ever experienced. After Opposition Leader Denise McLean asked a simple question of the latest news from the Middle East, NDP Leader Gurminder Grewal stood up and asked.

"Mr. Speaker, I'm sure all Canadians are horrified at the on-going hostilities in the Middle East and the resulting chaos in the energy sector resulting from that conflict. Will the Prime Minister agree now, that my parties' urging over the last 15 plus years to move away from oil was correct, and that the policy followed by his

24

government and all previous Federal governments has been nothing short of disastrous and will he agree right now to resign and call an immediate election?"

Dion's response was buried under the yelling and screaming from the Liberal and Conservative Party members. Speaker of the House Cooper bellowed for order to no avail. The Conservative MP from High River Alberta, screamed "Traitor" at Grewal who responded by storming across the floor, only to be restrained by 3 other NDP MP's. The NDP members wrestled their leader to the floor while across the chamber government and opposition members yelled, screamed, and dared the other to step outside. Seeing the situation spinning totally out of control, Cooper gave the order to the Sergeant at Arms to bring in the Royal Canadian Mounted Police (RCMP) [v] and to restore order. The Sergeant At Arms, along with Mounties carrying riot gear, entered the House. Upon seeing armed police officers carrying riot shields, and wearing helmets with visors march into the chamber, calm descended on the house momentarily. Then, Gurminder Grewal seized the opportunity to scream. "Who in hell is responsible for armed police officers entering the house? This is a violation of Parliamentary tradition and privilege. This is the most outrageous abuse of Parliament in Canadian history! Armed agents of the state have no place in Parliament!"

Speaker of the House Cooper stood, and in a voice many in the shell-shocked media who were present would describe as "eerily, almost dangerously calm" replied. "I say to the member from Brampton West, that it was I who called the Mounties. Never in my life did I ever believe I would witness such a disgraceful scene as I did today. Everyone in this house is supposed to be offering leadership to Canadians. Instead all I saw was a bunch of school yard children. And it was led by you! Sergeants at Arms remove the Member from Brampton West immediately. I'll decide when you can return."

With that the Sergeant at Arms walked up to Grewal, who was disheveled from his tussle on the floor and said. "Sir, please come along with me. Don't make me have to use the police to remove you. I will if you force me to."

The Sergeant firmly grasped Grewal's right arm and calmly led the man out of the stunned House of Commons.

Opposition Leader McLean then rose on a "Point of Order" and suggested. "Ladies and gentlemen, I believe we're all embarrassed and horrified at what took place here. I'll say right now that where fault is to be found for this disgraceful spectacle, I will accept my share of it and for that, I apologize to the people of Canada. I promise I will impose discipline on members of my party who are present and who failed to conduct themselves as honorable ladies and gentlemen. May I suggest that we take the time to adjourn for the day and reflect on what just occurred and how to prevent it as we go forward? Canada is going into uncharted waters as I speak, and Canadians will be looking to all of us here to provide calm, rational leadership.

Prime Minister Dion then rose and said. "Mr. Speaker, I also apologize for the conduct of my party in this deplorable event and urge you to agree to my honorable friends' suggestion of an adjournment."

At that point, Speaker of the House Cooper adjourned Question Period for the day. It was a very somber group of MP's that left. They knew the out of control raucousness of the day would probably take over the front page in the nations media, bumping out the war in the Middle East.

Pierre Dion returned to the Prime Minister's office and was joined by his wife Madelaine, and Robert Lalonde. Madelaine looked at her husband and Lalonde, and said in French. "Well, that sure could have gone better."

"You can say that again," the Prime Minister answered. "With that moron Grewal and his village idiot caucus, I'm not sure if things will improve."

The Prime Minister's prediction was prophetic. Despite the best efforts of himself and Opposition Leader McLean, Question Period turned into a theater of the absurd. Over the next two weeks, the NDP Leader led a constant attack on both the government and Conservative opposition, with his main point being "We warned you to get Canada self-sufficient on energy and away from oil." The Liberal and Conservative caucuses did not always follow the wishes of their leaders and responded with counter-accusations (i.e.; why did the previous NDP government in Alberta keep developing the oil sands, you wouldn't give up all the oil revenue, etc.). On three other separate occasions the Sergeant at Arms backed by RCMP police officers equipped with riot gear entered the House of Commons and shut down Question Period.

Ten days after Israel's devastating response to the Arab attack, Prime Minister Pierre Dion, his aide, Robert Lalonde, Minister of Defense Jean-Guy Blais, Minister of External Affairs Stephanie Howatt, and Trade Minister Sara Freehan, flew to Washington to meet with President Katherine Morrison and members of her cabinet. The Canadians were met at Andrews Air Force Base by Secretary of State Michael Youngblood and Vice-President Joel Rafferty and whisked via motor-cade to the White House. At the White House the Canadians were greeted by President Morrison and ushered into the meeting room set up for them. After the usual pleasantries common with such meetings, President Morrison called the meeting to order. "Ladies and gentlemen, we should get going as we have a lot to cover. Thanks to our Canadian guests for coming. Now Henry if you would please brief us on the military situation in the Middle East, as well as the situation with NATO and NORAD forces."

"Thank you, Madam President," Secretary of Defense Henry Stillman began. "First let me speak to the Middle East. As of right now hostilities have ended. The region quite frankly is a radio active hell. The United Nations has sent in relief forces but they are badly encumbered by all the protective gear they must wear. We're looking at an immediate death toll in the tens of millions, with the guarantee of millions more deaths in the next few years. Overall, cancer rates in that area will be through the roof for the next 20-30 years. Israel ensured the Arab states would never attack them again, by blowing them off the map and basically destroying their own nation as well.

'As far as NATO and NORAD. both are at DEFCON 3. That being said, I would expect both to step back to DEFCON 4 within a week or so. There is simply nobody left in the Middle East who is a threat to us."

"Thank you, Henry," President Morrison said. "Lisa what can you tell us about the oil situation," referring to Secretary of Energy Lisa Cameron.

Lisa Cameron was one of the most respected energy experts in the world. A native of Sheridan, Wyoming, she had graduated from the Montana Technical University with a Bachelor of Science in Petroleum Engineering, followed by a Ph.D. from Stanford. She then went onto a 22 year stint at Exxon Oil before being recruited to join the Morrison administration. When Lisa Cameron spoke about oil and energy the world listened.

"Thank you, Madam President," she began. "Ladies and gentlemen, we're facing the greatest oil crisis in history. As you're aware, the price of oil has passed over $300 per barrel. Nations across Europe and Asia who bought most of their oil from the Middle East are in a panic as the Middle Eastern oil fields are to all extents and purposes gone – destroyed. Other nations such as Venezuela, Russia, and Great Britain with the North Sea oil rigs, Nigeria and others are still selling but it isn't enough. The same is the situation in North America. The US and Canada have a lot of oil. Is it enough for both nations to be self-sufficient? For the US the answer is no. We still require foreign oil. Luckily, Canada is on our border and with our own resources along with Canadian oil we have enough. In Canada, the oil fields of Alberta in particular, along with those in Saskatchewan and the off-shore Hibernia oil fields make Canada totally self-sufficient – if and with all due respect to our Canadian friends present here, they had used better judgment in developing them. Currently, the Eastern part of Canada imports oil as they have never developed pipelines to bring oil east nor do they have the necessary refineries to process what they have. Most Canadian oil is exported to us and refined here in the US and shipped back to Western Canada.

'Now, let's discuss the effect on our economies. The price of gas is now averaging close to $12.00 per gallon here in the US and soaring to close to $20.00 and over per liter in Canada. Of course our Canadian 'friends' tax gasoline far more then we tend to here. And this is only going to keep climbing. I'm surprised it hasn't soared higher. This has led to an explosion in inflation like we've never seen before. Quite frankly, people can't afford to drive their cars and the cost of shipping goods has gone through the roof. I am now hearing reports of illegal strikes at various Big Three auto plants in the US and Canada. Workers are demanding huge wage increases just to pay for gas to come to work! I'll leave the rest of the economic theory to people more qualified than I," she ended nodding to her colleague Commerce Secretary Jack Stafford.

Jack Stafford stood up and addressed the room. "Thank you, everyone, for coming today. As Lisa so eloquently described, we're in the midst of an economic disaster like we have never experienced. Worse than the 'stagflation' we saw in the 70's with the OPEC oil embargoes and even worse than the Great Depression. The US and Canadian economies have ground to a halt for all extents and purposes."

Prime Minister Dion spoke up. "Mr. Stafford, Ms. Cameron, I do appreciate your candor. My question to you and everyone else is, what can we do? The economies of both our nations require oil. Our nations and economies cannot function if people cannot afford to drive to work and companies cannot afford to ship their goods to customers."

"Good question, Prime Minister," President Morrison said. "I'd suggest we put together an executive committee of people in this room to brainstorm and come up with some answers for us. God knows we have enough smart people along with their various departments, we should come up with something."

After further discussion, such a committee was created involving cabinet members of both nations. With that the Canadian Prime Minister and US President along with Robert Lalonde, and White House Chief of Staff, Dr., Kimberly Tucker, retired to the Oval Office to speak privately. The President ordered a naval aide to bring in a bottle of chilled white wine. The aide appeared with the wine, opened the bottle and poured each person a glass and stepped out.

There was quiet for a moment as everyone sipped their wine. White House Chief of Staff Tucker began. "Does anyone have any thoughts on what we spoke about earlier or what we should do? I for one am at a loss. We cannot dictate the price of oil without the government and by that I mean both the American and Canadian governments interfering in the market. I suppose we could nationalize the various oil companies but we didn't even do that in World War Two. God knows what the stock markets would do if we pulled such a thing. It may even make the economic situation worse. But outside of that, I don't know what else we can do."

Robert Lalonde, a native of Montreal graduate of the University of Toronto in Political Science and History, and Pierre Dion's most trusted advisor replied. "I agree with you, Kimberly," Lalonde said in his light French-Canadian accent.

Lalonde had grown up with French speaking parents in a mainly English speaking area of Montreal. He had learned English "on the streets" and after high school decided to attend an English speaking university as he had his eyes on a civil service career and wanted to speak perfect English. He had achieved that. He and Pierre Dion had met during Dion's days as a lawyer in the Quebec government and they quickly formed a friendship that turned into a political partnership. Robert Lalonde was ruthlessly loyal to Dion, but also had the ability to counsel the Prime Minister when or if, he felt Dion was going down the wrong path.

Lalonde continued. "Back in the early to mid-1970's the government of Pierre Trudeau used legislated Wage and Price Controls to try and control inflation. That didn't work very well as they could not legislate the behavior of private companies. If we tried the same thing today we would face the same situation. Mr. Trudeau also created the National Energy Program in 1980 and tried to create a "made in Canada" price for oil. All that accomplished was to shut down the private development of oil in Canada and almost create a war between Ottawa and Alberta. It was a disaster. So, to be honest I think our governments are rather limited in what we can do."

Tucker replied. "It also created very harsh feelings between our two governments, keep that in mind. American oil companies were very hard hit by it. And such a program would not be legal under NAFTA. I think I can honestly speak for our government and say that it would not look kindly upon government action such as that in the North American energy sector."

Prime Minister Dion quickly spoke up. "Ms. Tucker, Mr. Lalonde was simply discussing various ways in which Canada has in the past, attempted to deal with difficult circumstances. He is not hinting at future actions by my government."

"That's good, Prime Minister," Tucker responded. "We need each other right now. I'd hate to see our two nations return to the days of Prime Minister Pierre Trudeau in power when our governments and especially the leaders detested each other."

President Morrison spoke up. "Ladies and gentlemen, I believe we should let our committee work and come up with some answers. God knows we pay them enough for their knowledge. Let them do their job. Are there any other matters we wish to deal with while we are all together?"

General discussion went around the room until they broke up to prepare for a dinner at the White House later that evening. At the dinner that evening both parties put on a brave face with the President and Prime Minister both declaring that they had every confidence in the abilities of their nations to come to a solution to the grave crisis they faced.

The following morning, the Canadians returned to Ottawa. They faced a barrage of media at the airport and Dion deftly made use of the infamous "pivot" (as former US Secretary of Defense Robert McNamara once famously said "Never answer the question that is asked of you. Answer the question that you wish had been asked of you."[vi]) Dion did a masterful job of exactly that. The media left the Ottawa airport scratching their heads. Veteran Toronto Star columnist Tim Butler quipped as he left the airport. "Well, Dion sure subscribes to the old saying that bullshit baffles brains. And my god he can shovel bullshit better than President Morrison can shovel the cow manure on her ranch."

CHAPTER III

After another loud and chaotic Question Period, Dion headed to the Prime Minister's Office. He sat quietly for a period of time, alone in his thoughts. He was facing the greatest crisis in Canada's history which was saying a lot. Canada had survived two world wars, the Great Depression, the "Quiet Revolution,"[vii] two Quebec referendums on possible separation from the rest of Canada, severe recessions, and even some quiet rumblings of possible separation in Western Canada. But never had a crisis of this magnitude arisen.

He called his wife Madelaine at their official residence at 24 Sussex Drive and they spoke briefly. Pierre told her. "I really don't know what to do here."

Madelaine replied in French. "Pierre, nobody expects you to have all the answers. That is why you have people like Robert Lalonde with you and all your various Ministers and other aides. Just remember Canada has always been a very difficult country for anyone to rule. What is good for Quebec and Ontario may very well not be good for Alberta or the Maritimes. You have to make the decisions that benefit the most people. That is what every great Prime Minister has done and that is all you can do."

After a few more minutes talking with her they hung up. He had just begun reviewing briefing papers when his phone rang. It was Public Security Minister Oscar Redstone. "Prime Minister, I hate to make your day even worse but we have a serious problem in Vancouver."

Dion paused and sat back in his chair. He then said. "What do you mean a serious problem, Oscar? What's going on?"

"Prime Minister, riots have broken out in Vancouver, due to high gas prices. There are riots across the city, gas stations in particular are burning and the city police have asked for assistance from the RCMP to restore order. Premier Henderson may request the assistance of the army."

Dion sat there, momentarily shocked into silence. He then reacted quickly. "Get the Premier on the phone right away. Let Minister Blais know and make sure we can get troops into Vancouver if they are needed. In fact, get Blais in here and see if he can bring General Foster (Commander of the Canadian Army Lieutenant General Brian Foster) with him."

Thirty minutes later, Defense Minister Blais and General Foster were ushered into the Prime Minister's office. Dion was finishing a call with BC Premier Carla Henderson and was assuring her of Ottawa's full support, including the military if it was needed. He hung up the phone and turned to meet Blais and Foster.

"Gentlemen, thank you for coming. I know you've been alerted to the situation in Vancouver. I just spoke with Premier Henderson and she is very concerned that the local police, even with assistance from the RCMP may not be able to restore order. She may be requesting help from the army. I know we have the troops mobilized due to the Middle East situation. Can we move troops quickly into Vancouver if need be?"

Defense Minister Blais answered. "Prime Minister, General Foster can give you all the details."

36

Lieutenant General Brian Foster stood up. He was a rising star in the Canadian Army. A graduate from the Royal Military College (RMC) with a degree in Mechanical Engineering, he had joined the Royal Canadian Regiment and quickly developed a reputation as an outstanding combat officer in Afghanistan. Foster, was smart, tough as nails and possessed an outstanding sense of honor and integrity. He began his brief. "Prime Minister, we have the 1ˢᵗ and 3ʳᵈ battalions of the Princess Pats [viii] mobilized at CFB[ix] Edmonton. That is a total of about 1,000 men and women. If we feel we may need more I can also use the Lord Strathcona's Horse Regiment that is also based in Edmonton. They have most of our Leopard tanks and other armored vehicles. Closer on hand, we have the 39ᵗʰ Brigade Group right in the Vancouver area. However that is a reserve unit Sir, and while we can activate it, we cannot order those men into action unless you invoke the Emergencies Act. I can have the Princess Pats ready to move in 12 hours. The armored units will take quite a bit longer as I will have to find air and train transport for their vehicles. We'll probably need to ask the Americans for help there. Now the question will be if we send in the Princess Pats, where do I send them? The bases we have in BC are Comax and Esquimalt, both of which are on Vancouver Island. If I land them there, I need transport to the mainland. Or do I send them to Vancouver International Airport? If so, we need to shut down civilian flights in and out of there and I will need some of the reserve units from the 39ᵗʰ Brigade to secure the airport before the Princess Pats arrive."

Dion sat there shaking his head and then responded. "General, I've two questions. Number one – why on earth would we have to ask the Americans or indeed any other foreign nation for help to move our troops to another area of Canada? And number two – why don't we have a base near Vancouver on the mainland?"

Defense Minister Blais hung his head staring at the table. General Foster, who was known to always follow the saying of "you don't pay me to tell you what you want to hear. You pay me to tell you what you need to hear," answered. "Prime Minister, may I have permission to speak freely?"

Dion responded. "Yes, General please do, although I'm sure I won't like what you have to say."

"Sir, we can't move our own troops easily as we don't have the airlift capacity. The RCAF[x] has asked for years for heavier airlift capacity aircraft and it has always been denied by our civilian leaders including, with all due respect, yourself. And we have never had the funding to open a base on the mainland of BC. Simple as that."

Dion shook his head irritably and responded. "All right, General, I get it. Due to people like me who put a stronger emphasis on feeding the poor, trying to create jobs, the military is struggling to do their jobs. Christ almighty. Get your people ready to move in Edmonton and activate the 39th Brigade. As of right now, the reservists are not ordered to duty, but are being asked to report for duty. I'll pass the necessary legislation if and when it is needed."

 By late the evening, it appeared Pierre Dion's government had dodged a bullet. Vancouver police along with heavy RCMP backup advanced into the streets wearing riot gear, carrying shields and making liberal use of tear gas and rubber bullets. After several hours of street battles, they regained control of the rioting neighborhoods. Premier Carla Henderson had helped by calling for calm and ordering an immediate suspension of provincial gasoline excise taxes and carbon taxes dropping gas prices immediately by over 35 cents per liter. She also threatened oil companies with various legal sanctions if they dared raise gas prices after the massive drop in taxes.

By dawn, the city was still smoking but calm. In a stroke of almost divine good luck, there were no fatalities. Many attributed that to the lack of guns in Canada, compared to the United States. If this had occurred in an American city, the talk was there would have been multiple fatalities. Still Canadians were stunned at the images of police officers in full riot gear on the streets of a Canadian city battling fellow Canadians. The country was angry and politicians were becoming very aware of that.

Later that morning, Prime Minister Dion met with his cabinet. There was one agenda item – the riots in Vancouver. Dion spoke first simply stating his horror of the events and then asked Oscar Redstone, his Public Security Minister to brief the cabinet with the current situation.

"Currently, there is calm in Vancouver," Redstone began. The fire department has caught up with the numerous fires. Police have made over 700 arrests. Vancouver and RCMP riot officers are patrolling the streets. Minister Blais has ensured that we have members of the local militia ready if needed in the armories, but as of right now they have not been required. I don't have any damage estimates yet but it will be bad. Rest assured the various insurance companies will resist paying claims, stating coverage is voided due to acts of war and/or civil unrest. There are a lot of angry people right now in BC and they'll be even angrier when they find out their claims are not being honored.

'Let me say something else, this may well be just the first such civil unrest we experience. People are losing their minds over gas prices. The price of a barrel of oil went up again this morning to over

$340.00 per barrel. People can't afford to drive their cars. Companies can't operate as people can't get to work, and they can't ship their goods. Vancouver blew up first due to the extremely high taxes on gasoline in BC. Premier Henderson got things under control due to her excellent police – they did a great job. But what also helped was suspending gas taxes. That immediately dropped the prices by a lot. But the various provincial and federal treasuries can't afford to lose all that revenue. And gas will only keep climbing. What city is next?"

"Tabernac," Dion muttered a common French Canadian swear word. "I guess we should probably discuss the 10 cents per liter Federal gas tax at some point soon. Problem is," he said staring at Finance Minister Rogatien Hebert, "since we began running deficits again a few years ago, we badly need that revenue. And it is the same with every province, as I am sure my colleague will agree."

Finance Minister Hebert stood up. He was a balding, portly man. A longtime political veteran of Ottawa's political wars he had seen many crises and issues arise and end. He knew though this would be the greatest crisis he would experience in politics. He began speaking. "Prime Minister, you're correct. I would have to argue that lowering the Federal gas tax by any amount is out of the question. We badly need that revenue. The IMF[xi] has already contacted my office with concerns over our debt and possible lowering of our credit rating. And every province, with the exception of Alberta and Saskatchewan are in the same situation. Those two provinces chose to fight deficits and debt and are running budget surpluses. If need be they could lower provincial gasoline taxes and still be okay. I'd also say Premier Henderson is going to have to restart those provincial gas taxes very soon or her books will be even in more of a mess. What she did was done in a panic to try and stop massive bloodshed. It was probably the right thing for the time being. But she can't keep it up. Now, I'd like to make a proposal to everyone here. Minister Freehan and I have spoken about this and we feel it should be heard."

At that moment, Energy Minister Myles Callahan stood up and almost shouted. "Jesus Christ, Rogatien, you are not going to raise that harebrained, idiot idea that you and Sara came up with, are you? Good god, go take another hit on your bong and come up with something more intelligent."

Trade Minister Sara Freehan rose and snarled. "Myles, go fuck yourself. Rogatien and I have given this great thought and we really believe this is the only way out for Canada. I sure haven't heard anything intelligent coming out of your mouth."

Dion then stood and ordered silence. "Good God, everyone get a grip! What the hell are we lowering ourselves to? Myles- what is the crack about a bong? And Sara, I will not allow such profane filth in a cabinet meeting. You are a Minister of the Crown-act like it. And Myles that goes for you as well. I cannot believe what I just heard.

'And now Sara and Rogatien would you care to fill us in on this idea of yours?"

Rogatien Hebert nodded to Sara Freehan who stood up to address the cabinet. "Prime Minister, fellow colleagues first let me apologize for my earlier outburst and use of profanity. It was unprofessional and uncalled for.

'Now here is the idea that Rogatien and I have worked on. And let me say right away – it is very controversial and will provoke a lot of debate. Bear with me before you ask questions or jump all over me. As you are all aware, we have a major crisis in Canada in regard to the price of oil and the impact that has on our citizens. Indeed there probably isn't a nation on the planet who isn't dealing with this same issue. The main problem is the rapidly rising price of gasoline. We've already discussed the impact this has had. Now here is what we suggest should be discussed. I'll be brief as I know there will be a great deal of discussion around this;

First, we believe we should invoke the Emergencies Act. In particular we should invoke Part III – Articles 27-36. That will give the Federal government the power to appropriate property – and in this case we suggest we appropriate the oil fields in Alberta, Saskatchewan and the Hibernia oil fields off the coast of Newfoundland. This may lead to civil unrest, especially out West, so we may also want to invoke Part IV, which is the section that deals with War Emergencies. That would also allow use to mobilize reserve forces.

Once that is completed the next step would be to revive the 1980 National Energy Program, to promote oil self-sufficiency for Canada, maintain the oil supply, and in particular for the industrial base in Ontario and Quebec, promote Canadian ownership of the energy industry, promote lower prices, promote alternative energy sources, and increase government revenues from oil sales through a variety of taxes and agreements.

We introduce Wage and Price Controls to bring prices down and regulate wages. This will help stop the rapid increase we are seeing in inflation currently.

Finally, using the Emergencies Act as a basis for our decision we announce an immediate withdrawal from NAFTA. Currently under NAFTA we must ship oil to the US and Mexico. If we pull out and pull out fast, and introduce the new National Energy Program, we can set the price for oil in Canada and ensure that Canadian oil is only used by Canadians. We won't have to import oil and we will be self-sufficient.

'There is obviously a lot more to this that we need to discuss. But to sum it up we believe that we need to return to the days of a very activist Federal government like we saw during the administration of Prime Minister Pierre Trudeau. And we think these steps are the best ways to get there."

The room was deathly silent. Pierre Dion looked dumbfounded.

Myles Callahan exploded. "Both of you are insane. That's all I can think. No rational person would ever conceive of such utter horseshit. You're talking about nationalizing the oil industry in this country. In other words, stealing the property of international oil companies. Companies that have spent billions of dollars here creating an industry and employing hundreds of thousands of Canadians with good paying jobs. You'd be no better than Fidel Castro for god's sake! And then bring back the most disastrous piece of legislation ever passed in this country with that insane National Energy Program. Good god have either of you considered what would happen if we did this?? We'd be a pariah around the world and we would probably start a civil war with our western provinces. Let me tell you this. I won't have any part of this utter stupidity and will do whatever I have to, to ensure it doesn't see the light of day."

Pierre Dion rose. "Myles, calm down. Sara raised an idea-a controversial one I may say but just an idea. At least she and Rogatien have thought of something. Let's hear an idea from your department before we go off all halfcocked here."

Myles Callahan rose, his face red with anger. "My idea? That's easy. Leave it to the market. Remember when gas prices went through the roof in 2008-09? Gas was selling at $1.30 plus per liter and the sky was falling? And less than 2 years later it was back to under a dollar a liter. The market will correct itself. Leave it alone."

"Leave it alone?" bellowed Rogatien Hebert. "That's like Nero fiddling while Rome burns. The entire economy is collapsing. Good god man, we just had a riot in Vancouver. People can't afford to put gas in their cars – and you say leave it to the market. You are insane!"

Callahan attempting to calm himself raised another point. "Have any of you also considered that some of those oil fields are on First Nations land? And as such maybe they won't be too happy about having their oil taken from them? They worked out contracts with various oil companies and part of that involved those First Nations receiving royalties from the oil. So now you are planning on stealing oil and the resulting royalties from them. Is that it? Have you people lost all your ethics and morals? Or maybe your brains?"

Hebert snapped back. "I don't give a fuck about some savages. They're conquered and they need to remember that."

Callahan responded. "Conquered? Rather like the French after the Battle on the Plains of Abraham?"

Minister of Health Dr. Jacquelyn Grant jumped in. "Christ. Please people let's not get into the whole French/English battle as well as bring in the natives. We have a country that we are trying to save. Let's focus on solving this issue. Right now we are like people in a leaky rowboat. If we all start bailing and grabbing the oars and row we can survive. If we start beating each other over the head with the oars we'll sink."

Callahan snarled in response. "I understand that, Jacquelyn.

However, sometimes people need to be beaten over the head with the oars to make them think!" Once again, Pierre Dion restored calm amongst his cabinet;

"Ladies and gentlemen, enough. I'm not going to sit here and watch us tear each other to bits. We have a huge problem ahead of us. Let's all leave now and as a take away come up with some ideas. The country is counting on us."

Shortly afterwards, Dion met with Robert Lalonde in his office. Lalonde had been a silent observer of the chaotic cabinet meeting. Speaking in French he began. "Pierre, I don't have to tell you that you are sitting on a ticking bomb right now. The cabinet and country as a whole are tearing themselves apart. You have to act fast and decisively. And I believe you should follow the course of action laid out by Sara and Rogatien."

Dion sat silent for a moment and then responded in French. "Robert, I've always respected your judgment. And I see the logic in what Sara and Rogatien are arguing for. But my god, think of the political impact. That would tear the country apart."

"Pierre, listen closely. Canada has traditionally been led by leaders from Quebec. Think about the great Prime Ministers in history. Wilfrid Laurier, Louis St. Laurent, Pierre Trudeau, Brian Mulroney, Jean Chretien. They were all from Quebec. Canadians expect Quebec to lead the country. Add to that the majority of the population of this country lives in Ontario and Quebec. You need the voters in those two provinces to be reelected. Being popular in the West doesn't help you. Pierre Trudeau knew that when he brought in the National Energy Program in 1980. What was true then is true now. The governments of Alberta and Saskatchewan will scream bloody murder at this. They will threaten separation, and then do nothing. They don't have courage like Quebecers do, to actually stage a referendum. They will do nothing but scream. They're like a dog, all bark and no bite. And you know what? They expect Quebec to lead the country! We won the last election with only one seat west of Ontario. And we won a majority government because most Canadians live east of Manitoba. It is basic math. In the next election we will sweep Quebec and the Maritimes and get just enough seats in Ontario to win a majority. Just as we did before, just as Pierre Trudeau did in the 1980 election when he didn't win a single seat west of Winnipeg! And he won a majority government like we did and like we will! Remember what Senator Keith Davey said after the 1980 election. "Screw the West, we will take the rest!" Liberal Prime Ministers from Quebec have always done that, as power resides in Ontario and Quebec. The Maritimes know their economic wellbeing is dependent on keeping Ontario and Quebec happy so they won't fuss."

Dion stared dead ahead without speaking. Finally, he answered. "When we met at the White House with President Morrison and her people to discuss this crisis you mentioned Mr. Trudeau's National Energy Program (NEP) and you called it a 'disaster.' What has changed your mind since then?"

"Prime Minister, what changed my mind was the proposal for the government to nationalize the oil fields. Mr. Trudeau's NEP failed because the oil companies wouldn't cooperate. If we control the oil fields then we control everything about the process. We can't trust the private sector to do the right thing for Canada. We have to do it ourselves."

"I see, Robert. This will cause the shit-storm of all time. Are you sure we have the people who know how to run a massive oil operation?"

46

"I do, Prime Minister. Myles has his ministry stocked with a lot of ex-oil people. Good people who he recruited into government service. They will know what to do."

"Okay, Robert. I've always trusted you, you've never steered me wrong. I can't argue with your history lesson. You're right. Canada has traditionally been led by Quebec Prime Ministers, and when push comes to shove – well we need to take care of our power base. Newfoundland knows they need us. They'll be mad over Hibernia but won't do anything. The West will scream, but in the end they'll do as they are told as they always have done. Get Attorney General Juneau over here to discuss how the legislation should be drafted.

'But, Robert, one thing I need to be clear about. I'm not going down in history as some 'tin-pot' dictator who steals the property of multi-national companies. Make it clear in the legislation that Canada will compensate foreign oil companies for the appropriation of their property. And start figuring out how much that compensation will be. I want to pay fair market value. As well, make it clear that anyone who works in Canada for those companies can keep their job when we take over. The oil companies may hate me. But they won't be able to call me a crook."

"I'm pleased you see things my way. I agree with your thoughts regarding compensation and employees. Once we have the legislation ready to go, I suggest personal phone calls to each of the Premier's in the effected provinces as well as Mr. Cassidy in Ontario and Ms. Ouellet in Quebec. We need to let those two know so they will "have our backs" when we drop this legislative bomb.

'Two more things, Prime Minister. When you begin your conversations with each Premier and the Opposition Leaders, tell them the briefing is being made under the terms of the Security of

Information Act. We cannot risk one of them leaking our plan of action before we execute it. They all need to know that this is top secret.

'And, finally, we must make sure the military is prepared to act if there is any civil unrest. They are still on alert from the Middle East war so we do not have to stir more things up by mobilizing them. We must ensure though that Minister Blais' people are ready to execute orders that you give."

'I agree, Robert. Any leaks would be a disaster. I'll have a word with Jean-Guy. Once the legislation is ready I'll have to meet with Mr. Mancino over in Rideau Hall. I'll need Royal Assent before we can execute. Once I have that everything else is a formality. Now let's get this legislation drafted and get going."

That night in his official residence at 24 Sussex Drive, Dion, with a glass of Johnny Walker Black Label scotch in his hand, he turned to his wife.

"Within 48 hours. I'll either be seen as the hero who saved Canada or the bastard that destroyed it."

"Pierre, is the gas or oil crisis that bad?" she asked.

"It is. The economy is coming apart. Our only hope is legislation that we are working on in secret that will hit the country like a bomb. It will make Pierre Trudeau's announcement of the War Measures Act[xii] in 1970 sound like the announcement for a church picnic."

Madelaine Dion rarely spoke to her husband about politics. She was an intensely private person and avoided the limelight and in fact even refused to campaign with him. The fact that she would never appear publicly with him during "political events" (she would during state events, such as a Royal visit to Canada) ensured the media left her and their three children basically alone. They had met while they both attended Laval University. She had been a steadfast, loyal partner to her spouse, but always "from the shadows."

She replied carefully. "The only thing I can say, is, are you sure you are doing the right thing? History says leaders must make very difficult decisions. The test you should use is to ask yourself – twenty years from now will the person sitting in your chair and looking at the decision you made, agree that you made that decision using all the information that was possible to know at the time and that your decision was logical?"

Dion smiled. Madelaine was exceptionally bright and had a way of taking a tough decision and making it easier for him to decide on it.

"Thank you," he replied. "I do believe that the person who must sit here after me will agree that I made the best possible decision for the most people in Canada."

Madelaine got up, kissed him, left the room leaving Pierre alone with his thoughts and feelings. He was well aware that his government, even more than previous Liberal administrations, would be seen in the most terrible manner in Western Canada. He only hoped that history would prove to be more kind.

Twenty-four hours later, under the tightest secrecy seen in Ottawa since the Iran Hostage crisis when Parliament voted to issue Canadian passports to US diplomats being hidden by Canadian embassy staff in Tehran, the legislation was written. Attorney General, Monique Juneau and her staff drafted it and Dion and Robert Lalonde went through it line by line. Dion then turned to his Attorney General and asked. "Monique, I trust your work, but I need to ask this. Are you positive this is 100% legal? Will it stand up to a constitutional challenge in the courts?"

"Prime Minister," she responded. "The legislation is 'air-tight.' As the Prime Minister you have the right to declare an emergency. I believe that in this case it is an emergency. As such you have the right to decide what the prudent course of action should be. I believe the courts will support this if it is challenged."

"Thank you, Monique," Dion said.

He then turned to Lalonde and said. "Okay, Robert, I went ahead and booked a meeting with Governor General Mancino. I'll head over to Rideau Hall now and brief him. Once I am back we will present this to the cabinet as "fait accompli." This will not be open to any debate. Everyone will be on board. But as we brief the cabinet I will to speak to Mr. Cassidy and Ms. Ouellet. I want to ensure they are behind this 100%. After all this will benefit their provinces the most. As I'm doing that, Monique, you will brief the cabinet and caucus then Ms. McLean and that idiot Grewal. Tell them all I'm sorry I can't do it in person but we're going as quickly as we can. I'm not sure how Denise will react. She's from Toronto, so she'll will know this will help Ontario but she'll be upset over NAFTA being scrapped. And most of her caucus is from the West. It may rip her party apart. Not that that will cause me any tears. But as she has been an ally of ours through this I hope she can manage. Grewal- well he is simply a fool. He will oppose anything we do. Once that is done we will introduce the bill into the House of Commons this afternoon. And, Robert, I am keeping Monique pretty busy. As I am on the phone with the premiers we discussed I want you to get on the phone with the other premiers. Fill them in and make it clear we won't back down."

Robert Lalonde nodded his head. "Absolutely, Prime Minister. I'll take care of that for you."

As soon as he finished speaking, the Prime Minister left his office and hustled to his waiting Lincoln limousine. He jumped in the back while one RCMP body guard slid into the passenger front seat and another joined him in the back. His driver hit the gas and headed out towards the Governor General's Official Residence, Rideau Hall. He didn't expect much resistance from the Queen's Official Representative as Dion had appointed his old university buddy to the role less than two years earlier. Mancino was a native of west end Montreal. He grew up in a blue collar family speaking Italian, English, and French. He was an excellent athlete growing up and attracted the attention of Laval University where he enrolled to play football after he completed CEGEP.[xiii] He also had loose connections with relatives who had ties with Quebec's organized crime world. As well as playing sports, Mancino did "favors" for some of those relatives. He was considered "tough" due to his great football playing abilities – but also due to his "connections."

The two become unlikely friends while they both attended Laval University. One evening in an on-campus pub, Dion became embroiled in a bar room fight. A much larger and drunker male made a number of suggestions to the girl Dion was dating. When Pierre had had enough he ordered his girlfriend's tormenter to cease and desist. The large man declined, more words were spoken, and suddenly Dion was on the ground with blood spewing from a broken nose. As his assailant wound up to hit him again, he was suddenly lifted into the air and catapulted out the door by an even larger member of the elite Laval football team. That man was Rocco Mancino.

From that day forward, Dion and Mancino had a bond that wouldn't be broken. After Laval, Dion moved on to law school where as

Mancino moved into a family real estate business that had been started by his sister Teresa. Mancino also dated and then married Dion's cousin Janelle. That family connection drew the two men even closer. Dion, who was a serious intellect, found he loved spending time with Mancino whom he referred to as a "harmless rogue" and was intrigued by Mancino's "flirtation with the dark side of society." (That was in sharp contrast to Dion's stellar record as an incorruptible public lawyer.) When Dion moved into politics, he brought Mancino into his "inner-circle". At the time Pierre Dion told Mancino. "Rocco, you've been a longtime friend and you saved my ass one time. I have a job for you. But this is what I need from you. I need you to be loyal only to me. To always have my best interest at heart? To tell me not what I want to hear. But what I need to hear. Do that and I guarantee you will always have a job with me."

"You got it, buddy," Mancino replied.

Rocco soon became known as Dion's most loyal aide. And as Dion moved up, anyone who crossed Dion had to face Rocco. And that as the word quickly got out, would be ugly. And at times during various election campaigns Dion was embroiled in, Mancino proved to be very adept at raising money for his old friend. There was talk that some of that money may come from "questionable sources" however Pierre Dion had learned not to ask his friend too many questions. Rocco had his way of getting things done, that needed to be done, and Dion accepted that.

Finally, less than two years ago, Pierre Dion stunned Canada by naming Rocco Mancino to the Governor General's office. People in the "know" were aghast that someone from a blue collar background with alleged ties to the underworld would be named as the Queen's Official Representative. Pierre Dion though was adamant. This appointment was his and only his to make. And he was firm in it.

Rocco Mancino was his choice. When his wife Madelaine questioned him appointing "that lout" Mancino to the role of Governor General Dion replied.

"Dear, think about something. I have a majority government. The only check and balance on my power is the throne, through the Governor General. With Rocco there, if I ever must take extraordinary steps to solve an issue, I know he will have my back. I won't get any pushback from him."

Since taking the role, Mancino had surprised many. He worked hard to avoid any scandals, attended numerous events and by all accounts tried very hard and did a credible job. He was no intellect – nor was he a dullard or simpleton. Rocco Mancino was very street smart. He could face a problem and quickly figure out the solution that was best for him or those he worked for.

Dion, having arrived at Rideau Hall, was ushered in Mancino's office. He rose out of his chair and they shook hands and then the Governor General motioned for the Prime Minister to sit down. "Seeing as it's just the two of us, Pierre we can use first names and dispense with the titles. What can I do for you? Your call made it sound urgent."

"Thank you for seeing me, Rocco. It's very urgent. It's my duty to inform you that this afternoon my government will be invoking the Emergencies Act. Under this legislation the government will appropriate the oil fields of Alberta, Saskatchewan, and the off-shore oil fields of Newfoundland. We will further introduce a new National Energy Program, which will ensure that Canadians are insulated from the wild price swings of the world energy market."

He went on to fully detail all the ramifications of this legislation and then sat back and asked the Governor General if he had any questions.

To say that Rocco Mancino was stupefied would be a gross understatement. Never in his life had he ever imagined that he may be faced with a situation such as this. He also knew he theoretically could refuse to sign the legislation into law when it was presented to him and he could even remove the Prime Minister from office. Those powers he had were very powerful. Yet, if he used them those actions would in themselves create a constitutional crisis. Not since the Byng/King affair of 1926[xiv] had a Governor General invoked their Royal powers to deny a Canadian Prime Minister the course of action they desired.

"Pierre," he began. "Holy shit, buddy, are you kidding me? Talk to me – it is just you and me here. Rocco and Pierre. Outside of the War Measures Act invoked in 1970, there has never been legislation like this introduced in peace time. Have you truly thought this through?"

"Rocco, there's no other way. Our economy is dying quickly. Companies have raised their prices to make up for the increased shipping brought on by the explosion in oil prices. They haven't raised wages. We have many plants across Canada dealing with illegal strikes as the workers are demanding wage increases. Other employees simply are staying home. We cannot function like this. We must take swift action and take control of the entire economy or I fear our nation may be doomed."

Governor General Mancino cursed under his breath. "Pierre, I see your points and am well aware of the mess we are all in. But how will the Western provinces react? Won't they view this as another attempt by Ottawa to take control of their natural resources?"

'Rocco, the oil in Alberta and Saskatchewan as well as

54

Newfoundland belongs to Canada. It should benefit all Canadians."

"I agree. But imagine the situation involved not oil, but electricity and a Prime Minister from Alberta proposed a federal takeover of Hydro-Quebec and the big Ontario hydro plants at Niagara Falls? Would you still make the same argument?"

"Rocco, let's not go there. Quite frankly the majority of Canadians live east of Manitoba. I have to make decisions that will help the majority of Canadians. The West will have to cope. And you need to back me on this. We are going into the greatest threat Canada has ever faced. I need to know you have my back and will support any legislation I give you to sign."

Rocco Mancino smiled. "You got it, buddy. I hope to Christ you and your people have really thought this through."

'Thank you, my friend. I have to go but will be back with the legislation for you to sign once it passes the house and Senate."

An hour later Dion was informed by Robert Lalonde that Ontario Premier Keith Cassidy was on the phone. As Dion walked to his office to speak with the Premier he thought about the Ontario politician. He was one of the Provincial Premiers that he was fairly comfortable with. Cassidy, if he was anything at all, was unique. He was a native of Toronto and had been a star quarterback at the University of Western Ontario, leading the Mustangs to a national championship in his last year and he graduated with a degree in Mechanical Engineering. Many knowledgeable observers from both the sports and business worlds commented on how rare it was for a college football star to excel on the gridiron and in such a challenging academic discipline as engineering.

After graduation, he defied the unwritten rule in the Canadian

Football League that Canadians cannot be pro quarterbacks. He took over the quarterback role in Toronto and led the Argonauts to two Grey Cup victories in six seasons before hanging up his cleats. From there, it was onto a very successful stint in the private sector and then politics. Keith Cassidy had a "rapier quick mind" a superb sense of humor and unlike many intellectual people he had an almost unnatural ability to make any person very comfortable in his presence. His leadership skills, developed on the football field, were legendary. It was said his caucus would follow him to the gates of hell and beyond. He was married to a devoted spouse Jessica, and had twins (a girl and a boy.) Keith Cassidy had also figured out the complex task of being a hard working politician and still be a devoted husband and father. Even his political opponents granted him that.

He had been Premier of Ontario for over five years and was still so popular in Ontario that the joke was he could declare himself "Emperor of Ontario" and not lose any points in the polls. There were quiet rumblings in Ottawa, that if Denise McLean didn't defeat Pierre Dion in the next election, the Conservative Party may very well go after Cassidy to lead them.

"Mr. Premier, thank you so much for taking time out of your busy day to speak with me", Dion began.

"Prime Minister, when Robert Lalonde calls my office and says you must speak with me; I didn't feel I had a choice. And for Christ's sake please call me Keith. I have been asking you to do that for years now," he said with obvious humor in his voice. "So what's so urgent that I had to drop everything to get on the phone with you?"

Pierre Dion shook his head at Cassidy's lack of formality and responded. "Keith, I need to brief you on a significant course of action the Federal government will be embarking on. First though I must swear you to secrecy and I am invoking the terms of the Security of Information Act here. Nothing that you and I discuss on the phone right now can be communicated in any manner to anyone else until I tell you. I have to be totally firm. Are we in agreement on that?"

"Yes, Prime Minister," Cassidy replied.

"Good. I just met with the Governor General and briefed him on a course of action my government will be taking. As we are talking Monique Juneau is briefing the cabinet and later the caucus on the same, and later today we will be speaking to Parliament. Before we go to Parliament I will phone President Morrison and brief her and then I plan on addressing the nation tomorrow night."

"Good lord, Prime Minister, what's going on? What are you announcing?"

Over the next 15 minutes, Dion briefed Premier Cassidy on the forthcoming legislation.

Cassidy reacted as if he'd been shot. He shot back in his chair, his mind reeling. Never in his wildest dreams or nightmares, did he ever consider such an event occurring as Prime Minister Dion was suggesting.

"Keith, what's the position of Ontario on this course of action?"

"Jesus Christ, Prime Minister. I know things are bad, but have you really thought this through? If you nationalize the oil companies you will go down in history as some crazy ass Fidel Castro or Hugo Chavez! And let's take a step back and talk about NAFTA. Sure cheaper oil and gas will be very welcome here in Ontario. But companies have designed their entire businesses over the last generation with free trade in mind. You can't ask a company to redesign their entire business model with no warning. Prime Minister you cannot proceed in this manner. You'll destroy the entire manufacturing base in my province. Hell, even with a lot of notice ending NAFTA would be a terrible blow to Ontario. But no notice at all? You will be pissing away hundreds of thousands of jobs. With so many people out of work and companies who will leave Ontario and head to the US, you'll bankrupt Ontario!"

Dion let that sink in before responding. Then he answered. "Keith, I'm sorry you feel this way. I will keep your concerns in mind and raise them with the cabinet tomorrow. I can't promise that anything will change. But I do promise your concerns will be heard. I am also going to brief Premiers Ouellet, Van Pelt, Craig, and Mountjoy before today is over."

"Well, Prime Minister, let me just say, I know Karen Van Pelt very well. She's going to have your balls for this. You thought Liberal Prime Ministers like Trudeau and Jean Chretien were hated out west? Holy God, this will start a civil war. It won't be safe for you to travel west of Ontario once you announce this."

The call with Premier Cassidy ended shortly afterwards. An hour later, Dion briefed Quebec Premier Nicole Ouellet. Ouellet expressed the same concern over the immediate abrogation of NAFTA but was far more online with the Prime Minister's plans to nationalize the oil sector.

After that, came the most difficult call. Robert Lalonde had arranged a conference call between Dion, Alberta Premier Karen Van Pelt, Saskatchewan Premier Neil Craig, and Newfoundland Premier Max Mountjoy. Dion's dealings with these premiers were mixed.

Premier Karen Van Pelt had a practically toxic relationship with the Prime Minister. She had been born and raised in Calgary, the daughter of an oil company executive. After graduating from her hometown University of Calgary with a Bachelor of Science in Chemical and Petroleum engineering, she joined Imperial Oil (a subsidiary of Exxon) and began working in the oil rich sector of Alberta near the city of Fort McMurray. Possessed with a world class intellect she rocketed her way to the top of a traditionally very "alpha-male environment." She never tried to be "one of the boys "and let her stellar work speak for itself. From there, she entered politics and was now the most powerful person in Canada's wealthiest province. She was called the "Ice Queen" in the media (and quietly in her own party) due to her glacier like blue eyes, blond hair, and intense, almost cold personality. In contrast to Van Pelt, Keith Cassidy in Ontario could make a Nazi SS officer laugh and feel comfortable. Karen Van Pelt would make that same Nazi feel like a humbled child in her presence just with her gaze. She didn't suffer fools easily and her cabinet ministers knew that she probably knew their portfolios better than they did themselves. She was intensely private and very few people knew anything about her personal life. There was great speculation in the media as to her sexual orientation. Nobody knew and as far as Van Pelt was concerned it was nobody's business. Karen Van Pelt was the only person with whom Pierre Dion felt intellectually intimidated by when he had dealings with her. On more than one occasion she had corrected him in a manner that he found chilling. As such, he avoided dealing with her as much as possible.

Neil Craig, the Premier of Saskatchewan, was also intellectually brilliant, although far more approachable than Van Pelt. Born and raised on a massive wheat farm in Saskatchewan, he graduated from the University of Saskatchewan in Saskatoon with a Bachelor of

Science in Agriculture. He majored in Crop Science with a minor in Agribusiness. After graduation he returned home to the family farm. Within twenty years of returning home he had become one of Saskatchewan's wealthiest farmers. From there it was politics and then the Office of Premier. Craig was smart and completely ruthless in business and politics. He could stick a knife in the back of a rival or competitor while smiling at them. His wife Jolene was a professor of Veterinary Medicine at the Western College of Veterinary Medicine which is part of the University of Saskatchewan. They had two sons, and most Friday's found Craig rushing home to Saskatoon from the provincial capital of Regina to spend time with his family.

Neil Craig had a great sense of humor and was very popular in his home province. He was utterly devoted to the people of Saskatchewan and resented the control that Ontario and Quebec seemed to hold over the nation as a whole. Most of his fellow premiers enjoyed his company. It would be safe to say that he and Dion tolerated each other. They both respected the intellect of the other and worked hard at trying to find "win-win" solutions when they were forced to work together.

Max Mountjoy in Newfoundland was entirely different from both Van Pelt and Craig. The child of wealthy parents who made their fortune in fishing, he had partied his way through Memorial University before entering politics. He had survived several scandals involving call girls, drunk driving, conflict of interest, and three divorces. And he always came out on top. The media loved him as he was always quick with a quote and never shied away from the spot-light. He was funny, personable and loved to drink. Many evenings after work he would wander into a pub on George Street in St. John's and quaff a few pints while kibitzing with fellow patrons. His party and its' supporters loved him in spite of his weaknesses, as he spread patronage around for all of them to benefit.

60

And to top it off – despite his personal choices he had proven to be a solid Premier while in office. His government had run modest deficits, unemployment was down and the people of Newfoundland were happy with their "lovable rogue" in power. Pierre Dion personally liked Premier Mountjoy. They worked well together and Dion found Mountjoy's easy going, fun-loving personality to be a welcome respite from dour government business. They were an odd paring - the intellectual French Canadian Prime Minister and the "laugh a minute" Newfoundland Premier. But they did prove to be an effective team when working on a problem.

Dion was at his desk when Lalonde alerted him that the three premiers were on the phone waiting for him.

"Good afternoon everyone. Thank you for taking my call.

'Ladies and gentlemen, before I begin, let me advise you that I am briefing you on a situation of national urgency. What we speak about today is bound under secrecy as per the Security of Information Act. Any breach of confidentiality or leaking to the press or anyone else will be prosecuted to the full extent of the law. Am I clear?"

"Prime Minister," Premier Van Pelt said, "if this is so important why are the other premiers and Territorial leaders not on this call with us?"

"You'll understand in a minute, Premier," Dion replied. He then continued. "As you are all aware, Canada, like the rest of the world, is in the midst of an energy crisis, brought on by the recent war in the Middle East. Our national economy is in dire straits due to the price of oil that has gone through the stratosphere. The cost of all consumer goods has sky-rocketed, inflation as a whole has exploded in a manner not seen since the first Arab oil embargo of 1973, and people literally cannot afford to put gas in their cars. We are facing a national economic crisis of unprecedented nature."

At that moment, Premier Van Pelt, who had an uncanny ability to anticipate "the next move" said. "Prime Minister, I have a very bad feeling that myself and my colleagues here on this call are not going to be in agreement with what course of action you are going to propose to us."

'You may be right, Premier," Dion answered. He then continued. "Therefore, it is the position of the Federal government that a national emergency exists. We discussed many different options. After long debate we feel the following plan is the only option available to help solve this national crisis. As such I will be advising Parliament and the Governor General that the government will be invoking the Emergencies Act. As part of this action we will be nationalizing the oil fields in Alberta, Saskatchewan, and the Hibernia oil fields off the coast of Newfoundland. We will at the same time impose Wage and Price Controls over the entire Canadian economy in order to wrestle this wild inflation to the ground. And finally, we will be withdrawing from NAFTA in order to ensure that Canada's natural resources, in this case mainly oil, remains for the use of Canadians."

There was a deathly silence from the Premiers. Karen Van Pelt broke the silence. "Prime Minister, if this is some sort of bizarre joke, I assure you it is in the very poorest of taste. And if by some chance you are serious, I'd strongly suggest you end this call and return to your cabinet and reconsider this."

Premier Neil Craig added to the dialogue. "Prime Minister let me tell you I support Premier Van Pelt, 100%. The oil in Alberta and Saskatchewan belongs to the people in these provinces. The Federal government has no say over these resources at all."

Prime Minister Dion took a deep breath and then responded. "I agree that this course of action is somewhat extreme. Having said that, we have strong legal opinions that have confirmed by invoking the Emergencies Act, we are able to proceed in this fashion. I am doing this in the best interest of all Canadians."

Premier Mountjoy spoke for the first time. "I will be less formal. Pierre, usually you and I are on the same page on issues. But this time – wow, I have no idea where you and your people dreamed up this abortion. I stand with my colleagues here on this call. This is an outrageous intrusion into provincial jurisdiction and I urge you to step back and rethink this course of action. Maybe you can do it legally – I don't know. I will have to consult my own legal team on this. But what you can do legally and what you should do politically and ethically are very different things. Pierre you will tear this nation apart if you continue down this path."

"Well said, Max," Karen Van Pelt said. "Prime Minister I think you would be very wise to consider his counsel and rethink this disastrous proposed course of action."

"I'm sorry you all feel this way," the Prime Minister said. "However my government is committed to this course of action. We believe it is in the best interests of all Canadians. And we will proceed."

Neil Craig snapped. Prime Minister, you can say that all you want. Let me assure you that we will fight you and your government in every possible manner. You want a war buster – well you just got it! The west is not going to get screwed by yet another Prime Minister from Quebec. You just watch!"

Dion exploded. "Mr. Craig, let me remind you, I am the Prime Minister of Canada. I am not the Prime Minister from Quebec! I speak for all Canadians and represent the best interests of all

Canadians."

"Of course, Prime Minister," Karen Van Pelt answered in a tone cold enough to freeze boiling tar. "You speak for all Canadians – that is why in the last election you only won a single seat west of the Ontario border. In 40% of the provinces in this country, you have one single seat. That is even worse than Mr. Trudeau's 1980 election win. You have no right Sir, to even express an opinion on the natural resources in Western Canada. The people of Western Canada totally rejected you and your party."

Dion snarled back. "I cannot help if most people in Canada choose not to live in Western Canada. Most people live in the east, and they elected me. You are part of Canada and you will do as you are told. I do not need to justify my actions anymore."

The call ended moments later and Dion hung up the phone. He called Robert Lalonde and asked him to come to the office and report on the other meetings that had been taking place. Lalonde entered and in French began right away. "Pierre, we've kicked over the hornets' nest today. Monique says the cabinet is united behind you except for Myles Callahan and Stephanie Howatt. He stormed out and is threatening to resign. She stayed in the meeting but is also talking resignation saying she views this as a direct attack on her home province of Saskatchewan. The rest are concerned about the political fallout but they see the logic behind our plan and support it. I would say we have a mixed reaction with the other premiers. The Maritimes support us, Premier Henderson in B.C. is flat out opposed and says she will support Alberta and Saskatchewan and Premier Heidi McNamara in Manitoba is also supporting the west."

With that, Monique Juneau entered the office. She had sent word that she wished to brief Dion and Lalonde about her meetings with

Denise McLean and Gurminder Grewal.

Dion acknowledged her entry and asked her to proceed with her briefing.

"Prime Minister, Robert, thank you for seeing me, I met with Ms. McLean and Mr. Grewal right after the cabinet meeting. Both of them were stunned at the aggressiveness of our plan. Ms. McLean views it as too strong an infringement on provincial rights and as of right now she and her party will oppose our course of action strongly. She really doesn't have a choice as most of her caucus members come from the west as you know. Mr. Grewal surprised me as he is actually going to support this. Most of his caucus is here in Ontario and Quebec and he only has a few seats out west and they are mainly in B.C. Ensuring the consumers and businesses here in Eastern Canada are guaranteed affordable oil will keep them happy."

"I see," Dion responded. "Well we have one other test before we meet with Parliament this afternoon and that is my call with President Morrison. Let's see how she reacts. Monique and Robert stay with me during this call please

CHAPTER IV

Years from now, the history books will call the exchange between Prime Minister Dion, and President Morrison the "frostiest" in US-Canadian history. President Morrison had an excellent intelligence network and knew exactly what was going on and what Dion would say to her. Along with Chief of Staff Dr. Tucker, she also ensured that National Security Advisor Robert Jackson, Secretary of Energy Lisa Cameron and Secretary of Commerce Jack Stafford were with her in the Oval Office for the call. When the call came through President Morrison answered. "Hello, Prime Minister, I have been expecting your call. Just so you know, with me is Dr. Tucker, Mr. Jackson, and Secretaries Cameron, and Stafford."

Everyone on the call heard the strict formality in the manner with which President Morrison had addressed the Canadian Prime Minister. They all knew this would not be a pleasant call.

'Thank you Madam President. I also have Attorney General Juneau and Mr. Lalonde with me. I must advise you of the following upcoming actions of my government.

I am invoking the Emergencies Act which will give my government sweeping powers to deal with the current situation brought about by the war in the Middle East.

We are proceeding under terms of this legislation to nationalize the oil industry in Canada. By that I mean we are taking over the oil fields in Alberta, Saskatchewan, and the off-shore Hibernia oil fields. That means as well we are taking over the oil companies. I assure you that Canada will compensate the oil company's fair market value for their property. But Canada simply must control its' own natural resources.

Canada is withdrawing from NAFTA immediately or as soon as reasonably can be done.

After a brief pause Commerce Secretary Jack Stafford spoke up. "Prime Minister, what you're saying is your government is stealing the property of American oil companies, and other nations' oil companies as well, and that you are prepared to pay fair market value for that property. Do I have that right?"

Prime Minister Dion responded. "Theft, Mr. Secretary, is the wrong term. I made it very clear, and you admitted that you understood that Canada will pay fair market value. No company is having their property stolen. They are being forced to sell, that is true but there is no theft."

"Tell me Prime Minister," Stafford snarled back. "What is the difference between your proposed actions and if I broke into your home and stole all the family heirlooms that you hold dear and the police caught me but simply said all I had to do was pay fair market value for your property? I didn't have to return your property. Would you feel that is just?"

President Morrison broke her silence. "Prime Minister, I cannot believe I am hearing this. Your actions may be legal under your law – but they are outrageous. I urge you to immediately reconsider as these actions will cause enormous damage to the relationship between our two nations."

'I'm sorry, Madam President, our decision is final. We'll proceed in the manner I described," answered Dion.

"You will regret this Prime Minister, I assure you. This call is over."

The line went dead and the President looked at her group of Cabinet Secretaries and advisors.

"The crazy bastards are serious," National Security Advisor Robert Jackson exploded. "I simply cannot believe they would do something so stupid. Who will ever sign any trade deal with them after they screw their best friends like this?"

President Morrison looked at her Energy Secretary Lisa Cameron and asked. "Lisa, if they go ahead with this crazy scheme how vulnerable are we in so far as our own oil needs are concerned?"

Lisa Cameron looked around the room and began. "As I told all of you when the war first broke out in the Middle East, we're not self-sufficient in oil. We are much better off than we were in the 70's now that we have been fracking for oil in such states as North Dakota. But we never ever considered we would have an unfriendly nation on our northern border that would cut off oil to us, which I assume they will do. There is no other reason for them to pull out of NAFTA outside of denying us oil or selling it to us at a far higher price than NAFTA dictated.

'I am sure after the Prime Minister announced this I will be swamped with calls from the CEO's of Exxon Mobil, Chevron, ConocoPhilips, and everyone else. They are going to lose their minds and they will demand we do something. The question is what do we do?"

President Morrison responded. "Thank you, Lisa. I think we need to speak with Michael Youngblood and Vice President Rafferty. I am thinking my first step just to show how angry we are is to recall Ambassador Lopez in Ottawa. But before I do that I want Michael to speak with him. Now until we decide on a course of action our official position when we are asked, is we are considering our options. That is it. Nothing else until I say so. Am I totally clear?"

Everyone in the Oval Office nodded and she then asked Dr. Tucker to get Secretary of State Youngblood and Vice President Rafferty to her office as soon as possible.

Secretaries Cameron and Stafford left leaving Robert Jackson and Dr. Tucker alone with the President. Robert Jackson quietly said. "Madam President I believe we're in the greatest crisis we have ever faced with Canada. I know President Kennedy and Prime Minister Diefenbaker hated one another, as did President Nixon and Prime Minister Pierre Trudeau. But even in those days neither nation would have ever dreamed of acting in the manner that Dion's government is doing. We need to talk to Michael as this is, his bailiwick but I believe your idea of recalling Ambassador Lopez is sound. That will deliver a message of our extreme anger without doing anything we cannot fix or change."

With that, Secretary of State Michael Youngblood entered the Oval Office. Vice President Rafferty would be later. He was brought up to speed quickly on the discussion with the Canadian Prime Minister and their conversation after the call. Youngblood was a quiet intellectual man. He rarely raised his voice and took pride in making decisions based on objective evidence. He had been born and raised in Florida; his mother was white and his father Seminole Indian. His father was a very wealthy business man and the family had a summer home in the Muskoka Region of Northern Ontario and ensured Michael had the finest education money could buy. He had

70

completed a Bachelor's Degree in History and Political Science at Yale, and then due to his familiarity with Canada as a result of summering there, he completed a Master's Degree in History at the University of Western Ontario.

Youngblood began speaking. "I agree with recalling Ambassador Lopez. It sends a strong message without committing us to a course of action. I'll also make a call to my counterpart Stephanie Howatt in Ottawa. She's a native of Saskatchewan. I can't believe she agrees with this course of action. I suggest as well that tomorrow you summon Canadian Ambassador Russo so that you and I can let her know how damaging this will be for relations between our two nations."

After the meeting, Secretary of State Youngblood returned to his office at the State Department and called US Ambassador to Canada, Hector Lopez, at his residence in Ottawa. The two men talked for about 30 minutes and prepared their strategy for the following day.

As Youngblood and Lopez spoke on the phone, the Prime Minister rose in the House of Commons and announced the Federal government's plan. Almost instantly the House erupted. Conservative Members of Parliament leapt to their feet, banged their desks and screamed in outrage. NDP and Liberal Members rose and roared back at their Conservative counter-parts. Speaker of the House, Edward Cooper, concerned about outright violence breaking out ordered the Sergeant at Arms to once again summon the RCMP Riot Team into the House. Again, as was the case when the Middle East war and oil crisis erupted, helmeted police officers carrying shields and riot sticks entered the House of Commons and restored order. No Parliamentary debate had occurred in the midst of all the turmoil.

That evening Dion and Robert Lalonde sat in the Prime Minister's office sipping scotch. Dion turned to his old friend and in French asked. "Robert, this will work out will it not? We are doing the right thing are we not?"

Lalonde nodded and replied in French. "Yes, we are. We have no other choice. For once, Canada has to control its' own resources. The West and Newfoundland have to realize that they are parts of a nation and most of the people in that nation live in Ontario and Quebec. Therefore, we have to ensure the well-being of the majority of Canadians. As for the Americans, they will calm down and I have no doubt we will negotiate a new trade agreement with them where they get access to our oil, but that access is on our terms."

Dion then said quietly. "Merde[xv]. Myles Callahan sent me his resignation letter about two hours ago. He is resigning from cabinet and from the caucus. He says he has lost all faith in the government and my leadership and also stated we are taking Canada into a disaster that we may never recover from."

Lalonde responded. "Callahan was always a hot head and not a team player. No loss to us that he is leaving."

"Dion answered. "I think we'll miss him. He knew his stuff. Nobody knows oil and the people in that industry better than he does."

"Yes, Myles knows oil and such, Pierre. But he forgot the main rule of cabinet solidarity. We heard him out but once the decision was made to proceed he had to follow it. He chose not to, so good riddance."

Lalonde's cell phone rang. He looked at the number and commented that he had better take the call and then answered. "Good evening, Hector, how are you tonight?"

"Good evening Robert," the American ambassador began. "I am well and I trust that you are. I'll keep this short. I am calling to request a meeting with the Prime Minister, Minister Howatt and yourself tomorrow. It's urgent we meet."

Lalonde responded. "Let me check the schedules here and get back to you. Give me an hour."

"Very good Robert, I await your call."

Lalonde called back within the hour to book a meeting between the parties the following morning at 10: am.

As that was occurring, the phone rang in the residence of the Canadian Ambassador to the United States, Maria Russo. When Russo answered Secretary of State Youngblood greeted her politely and invited her to meet with himself and President Morrison the following morning. Russo accepted the invitation and knew in the pit of her stomach that this wouldn't be a pleasant meeting.

That next day would go down in history as a black moment in US-Canadian relations. Russo arrived at the White House at the appointed hour. She was escorted into the Oval office and found President Morrison and Secretary of State Youngblood waiting for her. They looked grim.

"Thanks for coming, Maria," Youngblood began. "Coffee," he asked pointing at a thermal pitcher of coffee.

"That would be nice," she responded. "Although I have a feeling something stronger may be more appropriate."

Secretary of State Youngblood glanced at the President when Russo made the comment. President Katherine Morrison began to speak.

"Thank you for coming, Ambassador. Normally, I would have my Secretary of State Mr. Youngblood handle this but due to the historical relationship between our nations I thought I'd handle this myself."

Maria Russo stiffened at being referred to as "Ambassador." She had a warm relationship with the Morrison administration and had always just been "Maria" to all of them including the President. She braced herself for what she sensed was coming.

"Ambassador, I want to make it clear that the United States deplores the actions of the government of Canada. We find it totally unacceptable that the property of American companies are to be seized by your government. Despite the fact that your government says they will pay fair market value, we condemn this. We also condemn the actions of your government to leave NAFTA without proper notice. We find both of these acts very unfriendly and we are considering what options are available to us. In the meantime, I've informed our Ambassador, Mr. Lopez, to inform your government that he is being recalled for consultations with the American government."

Ambassador Maria Russo sat quietly for a moment. She herself was appalled at the actions of Prime Minister Dion, however she could not of course say that. She then asked. "Madam President, is it your wish that I leave the United States?"

President Morrison paused and then answered. "Ambassador am I declaring you 'persona non-grata?' The answer is no. I will say that you will find relations between my government and your government will be extremely cool to understate things. You may not find things very comfortable here personally. In fact, I can tell you for sure you will not. Both parties in Congress are viewing this as a direct attack on the United States and possibly our national defense."

Ambassador Russo immediately spoke up to the last point. "Madam President, surely you can't imagine that anything Canada would or could do could possibly be construed as a threat to your national security?"

Secretary of State Youngblood spoke up. "Oh, really Ambassador? The largest source of international oil which is essential to the economy of every nation on this planet has gone up in a massive cloud of radioactive smoke. Then the nation which has always been our best friend just tells us that they are seizing American property and possibly cutting off our access to your oil. How exactly should we view this Ambassador?"

A chill went down Ambassador Russo's spine. This was going off on a very dangerous tangent – a tangent that no Canadian government had ever faced.

"Madam President, Mr. Secretary, I understand your concerns. I will return to my embassy forthwith and immediately convey those concerns to my government."

"Thank you, Ambassador," President Morrison answered. "And please note that you will find a much heavier police and security presence around your embassy. As the media picks up the story of your governments' unfortunate actions I am afraid there will be more than a few protesters out front of your embassy gates. I suggest you beef up the internal security in your embassy-unless of course you have cut that back like you did your military."

With that, Ambassador Russo rose and thanked the President and Secretary of State for their time and took her leave, hurrying to her limousine that would take her back to the Canadian embassy. As she returned to her embassy she asked herself "had any Canadian ambassador ever dealt with an issue this serious before? The only possible one may have been Canadian Ambassador Ken Taylor in Tehran in 1979-80 who had assisted six Americans to flee Iran during the hostage crisis. Maybe that wasn't even as big as this one, she thought.

At the same time, back in Ottawa, United States Ambassador Hector Lopez, sat down in the prime Minister's office with Prime Minister Dion, Minister of External Affairs Stephanie Howatt, and Robert Lalonde.

"Ladies and Gentlemen, thank you for seeing me," the soft spoken Hispanic ambassador began. "My government has directed me to inform you that it deplores your actions regarding leaving NAFTA, and more importantly the illegal seizure of American property."

Robert Lalonde rose to speak, and Ambassador Lopez held up his hand and said. "Please let me finish. I won't take long. My government is reviewing many options to respond to your actions. In the meantime I have been directed to return home to Washington. In my absence the Chargé d'affaires Mr. Sean Dillon will cover my duties. I believe you have all met him. Now I will take my leave. I wish you all a good day."

As Lopez left, he could only shake his head in bewilderment. Did Pierre Dion and the Canadian government really believe that his government would roll over and "play dead"? If so they were crazy.

The room was quiet for a moment after Ambassador Lopez left. Then External Affairs Minister Howatt spoke up. "Gentlemen, I've been struggling with this course of action since I first heard of it. Now I have no doubt it will lead to disaster for Canada. For the first

76

time that I know of in history the United States has recalled their ambassador from here. We have enraged the most powerful nation on earth. I am well aware that the western provinces, including my home of Saskatchewan are beyond furious. I believe you are leading us to catastrophe. As such please accept my resignation from the cabinet and the party caucus effective immediately. I will have no part in this and I warn you I will oppose these actions with every action and protest that I am capable of."

With that, she spun on her heels and stormed out of the Prime Minister's office. As she walked back to her Parliamentary office, she thought to herself "I must have been crazy to think that a government with no representation in the west would ever show respect to that part of the country."

As she left the office, Dion turned to Lalonde and commented in French. "Robert, that's our second English speaking cabinet minister we have just lost. First Myles Callahan and now Stephanie. And Stephanie had our only seat in the west. This isn't good."

Lalonde answered. "Pierre, don't worry. The math still works for us. Most people in Canada live east of Manitoba. We only have to keep them happy and if we do we remain in power."

In First Nations communities across much of Canada there was visible anger. In the government announcement no mention had been made about the oil fields that were on First Nations lands. It was like they simply didn't exist in the eyes of Dion's government.

At this same time an unprecedented media storm had exploded across North America. In Toronto the nation's largest and traditionally Liberal friendly paper "The Toronto Star" expressed concern over the government's actions. In an editorial the paper said;

"Nobody can accuse the Dion government of taking only half measures in this time of a severe national energy crisis. We applaud the bold thinking of the Prime Minister and his government. But we fear the government may have taken more extreme steps than necessary.

For one, nationalizing the oil industry and seizing (even with payment) the property of foreign (mainly American) oil companies is too extreme. It would have been better to sit down and negotiate with these firms and find ways that would better benefit Canada. Now in the future foreign companies will be very leery of investing here for fear their property may be seized.

Along with this action comes a serious diplomatic crisis with the United States. The American government will be under serious pressure to protect the American oil companies who have operations in Canada. We don't know yet how they will react – but we are deeply worried that Canada will be hurt by their response.

And finally, we cannot help but be worried about the national unity implications for these actions. The Western provinces are furious. Not since the days of Pierre Trudeau's National Energy Program of the early 80's have we seen such a rift between Ottawa and the West. This action may very well lead to calls from some Westerners to break up Canada."

The more business friendly Globe and Mail and National Post newspapers were more critical of the government and in particular, the nationalizing of the foreign oil companies operating in Canada. Like the Toronto Star, these papers predicted that few foreign companies would invest in Canada going forward.

The biggest "eruption" came from the Edmonton Journal;

"Once again, a majority government in Ottawa, led by a Quebecer and supported mainly in Ontario and Quebec has moved to expropriate the property and wealth of Alberta, and the West. If it wasn't clear before today, it is clear now. The West will never receive justice or be treated as an equal partner in Canada as long as Central Canadians insist on voting for parties led by leaders from Quebec.

The path before Alberta and indeed all provinces west of Ontario is clear. We must seriously consider secession from the Canadian federation and form a new nation with no economic, political or any other ties to the former Canada except that that has been negotiated with and approved by our own legislatures."

The American media was in a rage. The Washington Post published the most "blistering" editorial perhaps in its existence;

"Since the end of the 19th century, Canada and the United States have enjoyed one of the closest relationships of any two nations on earth. There have been occasions when one side or the other was irritated by the actions of the other, but at no time was this close relationship ever truly threatened.

Until now. The actions of the Canadian government led by Prime Minister Pierre Dion are outrageous, mean-spirited and yes, a threat to our national security. Despite his pledge to pay our firms fair market value for the property the Canadian government is expropriating, the fact of the matter is, American property is being stolen. If someone doesn't wish to sell their property, one does not make it acceptable if you simply seize it and then pay for it. It is still theft.

By ending NAFTA without giving the appropriate notice is also wrong. We feel as do most in the American government that this has been done to avoid the obligations to sell oil and gas to our country. Instead Canada would rather see Americans possibly suffer in the cold to ensure they have enough energy. Is this the mark of a friend?

President Morrison must view these actions as a true national threat and respond accordingly."

As the media storm erupted across the continent, Premiers, Heidi McNamara of Manitoba, Neil Craig of Saskatchewan, Carla Henderson of British Columbia, Max Mountjoy of Newfoundland and Karen Van Pelt of Alberta all gathered in a meeting room in the Alberta legislature building in Edmonton. . There were only a few trusted political aides to take minutes. No official photographers to memorialize this meeting. Just the premiers of Canada's beleaguered (in their eyes at least) energy producing provinces or in the cases of Manitoba and British Columbia aligned with such provinces. Premier Mountjoy was yawning and obviously exhausted from his last minute cross Canada flight. Premier Van Pelt called the meeting to order. "Thank you for coming. I am sure you'll agree this meeting simply couldn't wait. I'll get to the point. Here we have the leaders of the three oil and gas producing provinces along with you Carla, who brings all of BC's natural resources to the table and you Heidi, who I know has always viewed Manitoba as part of the West. Once again we are being persecuted by a hostile government in Ottawa. It is clear to me, and I hope to all of you, that there is no longer room for us in a Canada dominated by a federal government with their tunnel vison obsession with Quebec and to a lesser extent Ontario. Just as we saw in the late 1800's with Sir John A. MacDonald's National Policy which forced our farmers to buy more expensive and in many cases, inferior farm machinery from manufactures in Ontario and Quebec, to Pierre Trudeau's infamous "why should I sell your wheat" to his giving the finger to protesters in BC to his takeover of our oil with his National Energy Program of the early 80's, and finally Brian Mulroney screwing Manitoba with the CF18 contract. Central and Eastern Canada only want our oil, gas and money. They will never give us respect or share power with us. Let me ask you all this. When was the last time the Liberal Party of Canada had a leader from Western Canada?"

With that question, Premier Van Pelt looked around the room. Her fellow provincial leaders looked baffled. Premier Heidi McNamara briefly locked eyes with Van Pelt.

Heidi McNamara was the youngest and newest Premier in Canada. She had been born and raised in Winnipeg. Her mother was a high school biology teacher and her father a Winnipeg police officer. An excellent athlete McNamara played hockey for the University of Manitoba while she completed a business degree majoring in Human Resources. From there it was 11 years in the private sector working in Human Resources, than she ran and was elected to the Manitoba legislature as a member of the governing Progressive Conservative Party. She quickly gained the reputation as being smart, ethical, and had a quick grasp on major issues. Fellow members of the legislature on both the government and opposition sides respected her as she never postured or heckled and always tried to be fair.

Three years into her new career, the Manitoba Premier Jerome Caldwell was killed in a car accident and Heidi ran for the party leadership as a "dark horse" candidate. She shocked political pundits by winning the leadership and thereby being named Premier. After a year as Premier she called an election and was reelected in a massive electoral sweep across the province. Now at age 37 she was considered a rising star in Canadian politics. In her private life she had a common-law husband and no children.

Staring back at Karen Van Pelt, whom McNamara viewed as mentor among all the Premiers, the young Manitoba Premier spoke up. "Karen, the answer is never. The Federal Liberals have never had a leader from the west. Yes Prime Minister John Turner ran in a BC riding when he returned to politics in 1984 but he was an easterner. Most of his political he life he ran in ridings either in Montreal or Ottawa. He was born in England and lived in BC and Montreal as a young person. Their interim leader after Paul Martin, Bill Graham spent part of his childhood in BC. But point well taken – the Liberal Party is not particularly friendly to the interests of Western Canada."

"Thanks, Heidi," Karen Van Pelt answered. "You're right. And while it's better for us when there is a Conservative government in Ottawa, it isn't always great. Brian Mulroney remember was a Conservative and he screwed Manitoba royally with the CF 18 deal back in 1986."

Max Mountjoy spoke up, asking. "What was that all about?"

Before Karen Van Pelt could answer, Heidi McNamara jumped in. "I'll answer this one. Back in 1986, the Federal government put out a tender for the maintenance contract on the CF 18 fighter planes the RCAF uses. It came down to Bristol Aerospace in Winnipeg and Canadair in Montreal. By everything I know and have seen, the Bristol Aerospace bid was technically far superior and it was cheaper than the bid from Canadair. Mulroney, a Quebecer, overruled the process and awarded the contract to Canadair. Prime Minister Mulroney defended his decision by saying it was better that the technology involved remain in Canadian hands as Bristol Aerospace was owned by Rolls Royce of Great Britain. Mulroney didn't talk about how superior the Bristol Aerospace bid was technologically speaking, nor how much cheaper it was. So yes, Manitoba doesn't think much of Federal Conservative governments either."

"Jesus Christ," muttered Max Mountjoy. "I'd have strangled the bastard myself if he did that to Newfoundland."

"There was probably talk about something similar to that effect in Winnipeg at the time," responded McNamara dryly.

Karen Van Pelt then brought the meeting back to order.

"We could go on all day and night, talking about examples of how Ottawa has screwed each and every one of us and how it favors in particular, Quebec. The questions we need to ask ourselves are, are we going to keep bending over and taking it? Or will we fight back? If we are going to fight back, how do we do it?"

"I'll tell you how we do it," Neil Craig of Saskatchewan said. "We take a page out of the book of Quebec and we get a great separation campaign going. And by that I mean all of us together – we threaten to leave Canada as a block and form our own new nation. To use the term from Alberta in the early 80's "Let the Eastern Bastards Freeze in the Dark."[xvi]

Karen Van Pelt responded. "Neil, you read my mind. But if we do this, I don't want to threaten and then back down. We need to be ready to put our money where our mouths are – and that is leave Canada. Hell, as far as I am concerned, the Dion government has left us. We owe them nothing. I think we make a public statement tomorrow with all of us together that we are staging a referendum on leaving Canada and that we will also resist any attempt by the Federal government to seize oil company property in our jurisdictions."

Carla Henderson of BC spoke for the first time. "Let's take a step back here. Are we not discussing treason? I mean, I know the Dion government is overstepping its bounds – just like so many other Federal governments have done so when it comes to Western Canada – and of course now Newfoundland as well. But good lord, we are talking about resisting Federal government actions that, while we strongly oppose, may be legal. And add to that leaving the country. Are we sure about this?"

Neil Craig responded. "Carla, I can tell you I'm sure. I'm sick and tired of my province and everyone else here bankrolling Central Canada while they continue to shaft us. Remember back when Prime Minister Harper added seats to your province, Alberta and Ontario? Quebec pissed and moaned that their proportion of seats was now dropping in the House of Commons, so Harper gave them more! More seats than their population called for. We can never get ahead even if the majority of the population at some point lived out in the west, the whole "game is rigged." Provinces can't lose seats so Ontario will keep their massive lot and we all know that no Federal government will resist giving more seats to Quebec to ensure they always have about 25% of the total number of seats in the House of Commons. Even if they don't have 25% of the population. No, I am with Karen here. It's time to call enough, enough."

Max Mountjoy asked. "I'm with you and Karen, Neil, in theory. Although the logistics of having Newfoundland be part of some "Western Republic" or some such thing will be difficult. However, let's all be open here. Are we willing to negotiate with Ottawa? If the answer is no, then let's all stage our referendums and if we get a yes from our people, then get the hell out of here. But are we willing to talk before we stage a referendum?"

Karen Van Pelt answered. "I think we can talk, but I have my doubts that it will go anywhere. But we owe it to the people in our provinces that we try."

Heidi McNamara added her thoughts. "Manitoba doesn't have the natural resources that all of you have."

Max Mountjoy quickly countered. "Oh, bloody hell, Heidi! What do call your winter winds and all those mosquitos in the summer that are large enough to carry a baby off? No other province has anything like those. They seem like resources to me."

Premier McNamara laughed. Nobody could break up a tense group with a quick joke better than Max Mountjoy.

"Thank you, Max, I hadn't really until now appreciated such natural resources that we in Manitoba have! But on a serious note here. I agree with negotiations but we need to set some ground rules. What I think we should do is make it clear that we will not negotiate with anyone associated with the Liberal Party of Canada. The Progressive Conservative Party of Brian Mulroney doesn't exist anymore so we have no beef with them. The Conservative Party that we saw under Stephen Harper wasn't always as helpful as we would have liked. But it wasn't hostile like the Liberals. So we say that we are willing to negotiate – but not with anyone associated with the Liberal Party. That should be enough to bring down the Dion government and destroy the Liberal Party forever. Let the people in Central Canada really 'stew over that.' And then they can make a decision as to whether they want to elect a government that actually represents the interests of all Canadians. Or stick with the Liberals with their tunnel vision of only representing Quebec and to a lesser extent Ontario. And finally, we say if the negotiations are not successful then, we are staging a referendum on separation from Canada and make it clear that this will be a total separation – we are not looking for something like 'Sovereignty Association.'[xvii] No, we are talking about complete separation from Canada and if Canada wants our oil and other resources they can line up to buy it. Like any other nation.

'As far as treason is concerned. Nobody ever charged people like Rene Levesque or Lucien Bouchard with treason when they planned and staged the two Quebec referendums. The precedent has been set here in Canada that provinces can leave. So I don't believe that is a real concern for us."

Carla Henderson was the first to respond. "Well, that would certainly be taking a position, saying we won't negotiate with anyone associated with a particular political party. But isn't that somewhat undemocratic? I mean I am no fan of the Federal Liberals either, but they are a legitimate party with a lot of political support in parts of this country. Can we say we simply won't negotiate with them if the majority of voters in an area select them?"

Heidi McNamara answered quickly. "Carla, it's the only way we can do this. We need to make it clear to the people in Central Canada that the days of them dominating the west through the Liberal Party, and at the same time expecting us to pay the bills through equalization payments are over. [xviii]"

Carla Henderson, while clearly uncomfortable, said. "I'm not 100 percent comfortable with this, it's so radical. But that being said, I am with you all. We need to stick together."

For the rest of the meeting, the premiers worked on the wording of their announcement and had their press aides contact the various Canadian TV networks and news agencies requesting air time the following morning at 9:00 am Mountain Time. They also used this opportunity to bring in their top legislative aides and after swearing them to secrecy, briefed them on the upcoming course of action. Without exception all of them were left shocked and very uneasy.

Standing up to Ottawa was one thing, they could all understand. But potentially breaking up the country was something not one of them had ever conceived of.

Steve Bradford, Neil Craig's top aide slipped away after the briefing and moved to an empty office and placed a call to his friend Samantha James, who was a top aide to Energy Secretary Lisa Cameron in Washington. They had become close friends while working on their Master's degrees in Political Science at Harvard. Since graduation they had remained close. James glanced down at her cell phone and seeing who it was quickly answered. "Hey Steve, how are things? Are you coping with the chaos up there okay?"

"Hey, Sam, I need to give you a quick heads up as a bomb is going off tomorrow morning that will impact the US. You are going to have to alert the right people at your end."

"Okay, Steve what's going on?"

"Tomorrow morning at 9:00am local time here in Edmonton, the premiers of British Columbia, Alberta, Saskatchewan, Manitoba, and Newfoundland will announce that they are staging referendums to ask their citizens for permission to separate from Canada. They are also advising the oil companies in Alberta, Saskatchewan and Newfoundland not to cooperate with the federal government's attempts to nationalize the oil fields."

"Holy shit," James responded. "Are you freaking kidding me?"

"This is no joke, Sam. These people here are deadly serious and as of right now Ottawa has no clue."

"I've got to tell Lisa right away," she answered. "This goes way beyond oil. We are talking about the breakup of our closest ally and having a potentially unstable country or countries on our northern border. Steve, I have to go."

With that, she hung and dialed her boss. Lisa Cameron answered. "Good afternoon Samantha. What's up?"

"Madam Secretary, I have some urgent news. I must see you immediately."

"Okay, Samantha. Come over to my office. I'll be waiting."

Moments later, Samantha James was admitted to Lisa Cameron's office. There she quickly briefed the Energy Secretary on her phone call with Steven Bradford. After she finished Cameron asked. "Are you sure about all this, Samantha? How well do you know this Bradford guy?"

"I met Steven while we were both at Harvard. He's a good friend. I've never known him to be untruthful. In the past, he's told me how angry Western Canadians are towards Ottawa so I don't think this is totally out of the realm of possibility."

"Thank you, Samantha. You were right to come to me immediately with this. I'll need to tell the President and we will need to start making preparations for possible unrest and chaos on our northern border."

Meanwhile, in Ottawa, Prime Minister Dion met with Robert Lalonde, Trade Minister Sara Freehan, and Attorney General Monique Juneau.

Dion asked. "So, what's this I'm hearing about a big meeting with the various premiers in Edmonton? What do we know about this?"

Lalonde answered. "Prime Minister, we're not hearing anything.

Normally there would be leaks but not this time. I suspect they are planning on some kind of response to our actions. Probably a challenge to the Supreme Court or some other such thing. Any thoughts Monique?"

"I can't think of anything else," the Attorney General responded. "We are 'airtight' legally here. The provinces can scream all they want but they can't stop us. I think for appearances sake that they will go to the Supreme Court and we will win there."

In Washington, Lisa Cameron and Samantha James were ushered into the Oval Office. With President Morrison was her Chief of Staff Dr. Kimberly Tucker.

President Morrison greeted both of them warmly and asked. "What can I do for you both? This must be big as Lisa you have never called demanding to see me immediately."

There was a quiet edge to her voice that said "this had better be really good."

"Madam President, I believe you have met Ms. James before. She brought something to my attention that I believe you need to hear immediately."

"Okay, Lisa. Go ahead, Samantha. Dr. Tucker and I are all ears."

With that, Samantha James began to repeat what she had just finished telling her boss. President Morrison sat "bolt upright" when she heard that Western Canadian provinces were serious about secession from Canada.

" Stop right there. Dr. Tucker get Bob Jackson, Henry Stillman and Michael Youngblood in here ASAP. If they are not in town get them on the phone. I don't care what they are involved with just get them."

Luckily they were all in Washington; within 45 minutes were gathered in the Oval office. At President Morrison's signal, Samantha James carefully briefed everyone in the room. When she finished there was silence and then Defense Secretary Henry Stillman spoke up. "Holy God. This is massive. We could potentially have a very unstable, disintegrating Canada on our northern border. That will be a huge problem."

Dr. Tucker turned to the Secretary of State and asked. "Michael what do you think Prime Minister Dion will do and do you think those provinces may actually leave Canada?"

Michael Youngblood stood up and began speaking. "I know Canada very well. My family has had a cottage in the Muskoka region of Northern Ontario for over 75 years. I spent most of my summers growing up at our cottage in Ontario. I have a lot of good friends who live there that I met as a young person in those summers. I also did my Master's degree at the University of Western Ontario, in London Ontario. So I can speak very well on this subject and to answer your question, yes, they may very well leave. The Western Provinces throughout Canadian history have been looked down upon by the so called political elite of Quebec and Ontario. That 'elite' is often referred to as the 'Laurentian Elite' referring to the Laurentian Mountains in Quebec. When they think of the Western Provinces, they think of red necks, cowboys, ignorant social conservatives and country bumpkins. Even with the population of provinces like Alberta in particular growing, they have never been awarded the number of seats in the House of Commons or Senate that their population would dictate that they should have. Prime Minister after Prime Minister throughout history has chosen to take action detrimental to the best interests of the west in order to keep

90

the east happy. Now those chickens are coming home to roost.

'Let me ask another question to the group. If those provinces do leave and reach out to us to join the Union what is our answer? Not that I think that will happen for sure. Canadians, or at least English Canadians, have never built a true national identity based on what they are. It has always been 'we are not British or American' and historically in Central and Eastern Canada there has been a solid core of Anti-Americanism. That feeling isn't nearly as strong in the West but just don't think they will automatically come running to the USA to 'save them.' They are very proud people and we need to remember that."

President Morrison smiled and answered. "Well, as I remember in my high school history class, our original constitution, The Articles of Confederation, had an open invitation in it for Canada to join our union. That isn't in our current Constitution of course, but if we were asked I don't see why we would say no. Oh I realize that some of our Republican 'friends' in the House and Senate may not at first embrace the idea of several million new very liberal, at least by our standards, voters entering the country. On the other hand I do believe their opinions would also be swayed by the oil and gas fields in Alberta, Newfoundland, and Saskatchewan, the timber and harbors of British Columbia and the stable, well-educated population of Manitoba. I also agree with you Michael that we cannot assume they will turn to us or wish to join the Union.

But before that happens, Michael, what do you think Prime Minister Dion will do? How will he react?"

"I believe he will first try and enforce his state of emergency and declare some form of martial law and attempt to arrest those premiers. He may even try and make use of the military. What do you think Henry," he said looking at the Secretary of Defense.

"Jesus, I really don't know what that crazy bastard will do. His actions already are simply nuts. To think that the provinces would simply roll over and accept this? He is nuts.

'Back to your question. The Canadian military is amongst the best trained and most professional in the world, bar none. They are superb. Their issues lie with a lack of numbers and modern equipment. They can handle one small crisis in one area. They will not be able to successfully handle a large scale crisis across Western Canada if say there is some form of revolt. And if Dion calls up the reserves – well most of the reserves are made up of locals. I am not so sure a soldier in say a reserve unit in Alberta will be too eager to take up arms against his friends and neighbors to enforce the orders of a Prime Minister from Quebec. To add to this there are French speaking Regiments in the Canadian Army as well as English speaking regiments. There are also bilingual regiments. Now I ask you just imagine if you have a Prime Minister from Quebec who may have to order an English-speaking regiment to take action against say an English speaking government in Manitoba. Will the regiment follow those orders? Or what if there is a split between English and French speaking soldiers in a bilingual unit?

'Let me add another concern. What will Canadian native groups do? Let me pause and say that in Canada they refer to what we call natives or Indians as 'First Nations.' Although Canada never had the bloody history of Indian wars that we had, their record of dealing with native groups is not stellar. The courts up there are jammed with lawsuits over treaty rights. In 1990 we saw an armed stand-off between Mohawk Warriors and the Canadian Army at Oka, Quebec that went on for an entire summer. I actually thought there would be heavy fighting there. It was a miracle that there was not. Years later

92

there was another violent clash with the police and natives outside of Toronto in a town called Caledonia. In the 1995 Quebec Referendum, natives in Quebec made it clear that they would not blindly follow Quebec out of Canada and in fact due to their treaties they didn't have to. I suspect we will see violence on Indian reserves in Canada very soon as they will not accept their futures being dictated by white governments. They have had enough of that."

"My God," muttered President Morrison. "Are we really talking civil war in Canada?"

Michael Youngblood quickly spoke up. "That would be a worst case scenario. For all we know the people in those provinces may accept the legal authority of Ottawa and aqueous. I seriously doubt it and I do believe we will see an attempt at secession. I just don't know for sure if Dion will try and use the military and if he does, will they follow his orders?"

Henry Stillman then added. "Madam President. If Prime Minister Dion does attempt to use his military there will be many frightened Americans in border communities. They will be worried that unrest may spread across the border. I'd suggest that we make preparations to activate National Guard units in Minnesota, North Dakota, Montana, Idaho and Washington."

"I agree, Henry," President Morrison said. "Keep it quiet but draw the orders up and perhaps let the Governors in those states as well as the Commanding Officers in the Guard units know that this may be coming. But for god's sake keep it quiet.

'Everyone listen closely. What we discussed in here today is confidential. Canada is a sovereign nation and they have to sort their own problems out. If they want our help we will give it. But they will have to ask first. If American lives or interests are threatened we will act. But I am not going to act like a 19th century Teddy Roosevelt who was trying to enforce Manifest Destiny or the Monroe Doctrine. Canada is our friend and we will support them. But they will have to solve their own issues. Am I clear?"

Around the room heads were nodding.

Morrison turned to her National Security Advisor Robert Jackson and asked. "Bob, you have not said a word since we have been here. What are you thinking?"

"I agree with what everyone is saying. But let me add a point we must consider. If Dion uses the military, things may come apart in Canada very fast. We don't know if all his forces will obey his orders.

'What if French speaking units do and English-speaking troops resist? What if they begin fighting each other? We may have no choice but to send in troops to restore peace. How will that go over with NATO and the UN? I don't know the answer to those questions but we better start thinking about it. And be prepared to move more than National Guard units to the border. I'd move the 10th Mountain Division at Fort Drum, New York up to a higher level of alert. If things blow apart in Canada they can quickly move into Ontario and Quebec and restore calm. Same with Fort Lewis-McChord in Washington. The troops of I Corp and in particular the 7th Infantry Division and 2nd and 3rd Brigades, could be across the border and into British Columbia as fast as we need them to be. They could take control of Vancouver and Victoria the same day. We may wish to have a naval task force off the coast of New England and able to move towards Newfoundland and the Maritimes quickly. Perhaps even arrange for a few ships from the Navy to be 'visiting' St. John's and Halifax Harbors and make sure we have a contingent of

Marines aboard who can seize the harbors if need be. At the same time move some naval units from Pearl Harbor towards the coast of B.C. and make sure they have a large contingent of Marines aboard so if we need to move in quickly and seize the Royal Canadian Navy base at Victoria, we can do so. I'd also suggest ramping up the readiness of the 82nd and 101st Airborne Divisions so they can deploy anywhere we need them quickly. We may also want to think about adding some naval vessels into the Great Lakes. Perhaps have a couple of ships near Toronto and Hamilton, Ontario."

"Wow, Robert are you after my job?" Henry Stillman exclaimed. "You have really thought this through."

" Henry, over the years I have thought ahead and wondered how we should react if there was ever political instability on our northern border. I think we need to be prepared to move quickly and forcefully and enforce stability and calm."

Stillman replied. "The only area we need to be very cautious of is the Great Lakes. Due to the Rush-Bagot Treaty of 1817 we are seriously restricted as to how many naval ships we can have on the Great Lakes. I'd have to look up the exact details but I don't think we can have more than about two. If we start putting naval units in there we will be violation of the treaty and might as well send up a flare or put out a front page announcement saying what we are doing."

"Henry, I agree with Bob," President Morrison said. "I think the steps he is suggesting are wise. And I also agree with your thoughts Henry on the Great Lakes. Let's avoid sending the Navy in there at least for now. As for the other moves do it, and again for god's sake do it quietly. And if there are any Canadian units currently training at our bases make sure they are not tipped off."

"Consider it done, Madam President," Henry Stillman said. "I'll see to it personally."

CHAPTER V

The following morning at 9:00am local time Premier Karen Van Pelt went to the podium in the legislative briefing room in Edmonton. In front of her were journalists representing every major media organization and newspaper in Canada as well as some from international media organizations. Sitting behind her were her fellow premiers showing a united front with her against Ottawa.

"Good morning, everyone. Thank you for coming. I stand here speaking for a group of Canadians who feel personally attacked by the actions of what we see to be an undemocratic Federal government in Ottawa. We feel that the actions of the Dion government to nationalize the oil and natural gas sectors and to seize the property of companies working in these sectors in our provinces are nothing less than antidemocratic. We also feel it is yet another attempt by a Federal government controlled by the Liberal Party of Canada to persecute the provinces of Western Canada and Newfoundland. The history of such actions date back almost to Confederation and have continued throughout the history of our nation. It is therefore the decision of these provinces to take the following actions."

As Premier Van Pelt said the last sentence Premiers Henderson, Craig, McNamara, and Mountjoy stood up and gathered around her in a show of unity.

"We will be staging referendums in each of our provinces on the same date and asking the same question of the people who reside in those provinces. That question will be "Do you agree that the Province of *insert name* should separate from Canada, and form a new and separate nation or join a union with other such former Canadian provinces, and have no legal, political or economic ties with the former Canada except those of which are negotiated after secession."

As you can see this is not an ambiguous, cowardly question as were the ones asked by Quebec in 1980 and 1995. It is clear and straightforward and respects the Clarity Act.

We are prepared to negotiate this however it is our decision that we will not negotiate with any group or party associated with the Liberal Party of Canada. Throughout history that party has proven through words and actions to be unfriendly towards us. Such negotiations would be useless.

And finally, we will not in any way cooperate with the Federal government's attempts to nationalize private and provincial property in our provinces. We will later provide details of how we mean to resist these actions until the results of our referendums are known."

After brief silence the room exploded with journalists' questions. As that occurred a firestorm erupted in Ottawa. Pierre Dion had been watching the news conference with Robert Lalonde, Monique Juneau, Sara Freehan and his wife Madelaine.

"Tabernac," Dion exploded. "How did I not know this was happening?"

Lalonde, Freehan and Juneau both looked ashen. Never in their wildest dreams did they ever believe news of this stature in Canada would catch them off guard. Dion was shaking with rage when Lalonde scrambling to recover spoke up this time in English. "Prime Minister, first we need to try and calm down and to think rationally. Let's take a step back. You have taken a legally correct course of action. There is nothing you have done that is not legal. These premiers are acting illegally. I'd say have them all arrested immediately for treason. After that we can see what else we can throw at them."

"Robert is right, Prime Minister," Sara Freehan said. "We had better nip this little revolt in the bud right now. And we can also remind people of our disallowance powers. We can disallow any provincial legislature – that is one constitutional right the Federal government has. So they will need to pass legislation to stage their referendums. We simply disallow their legislation. Harsh, but Canadians need to know we are in charge."

Dion nodded and turned to his Attorney General. "Monique, I'm not sure what the whole process is, but get the Mounties to arrest those premiers, and do it publicly. I want to crush any sort of resistance right away. There are going to be no referendums for secession on my watch."

He then turned to Lalonde and said. "Robert, get hold of Minister Blais, and tell him that I want troops mobilized all over Canada. I am taking a page out of Pierre Trudeau's 1970 War Measures Act book, only instead of just having troops guard Parliament Hill and the streets of Montreal I want the troops visible all over the country."

Lalonde replied. "Pierre let me get Blais and General Foster in here and we can sit down with them and make rational plans."

"Fine, Robert, but do it fast. Meanwhile Monique, get those arrests made."

Monique Juneau replied. "Prime Minister, let's take this slowly. Give me some time to plan this and see if public pressure makes them back down. No Canadian Prime Minister has ever had a premier charged with treason. Let them go back to their provincial capitals and see what the resulting 'storm of publicity' does. It will also give me time to work with the Mounties to coordinate this. Please, I really need this time."

"Fine," Dion said angrily. "Let's meet back here tomorrow at the same time and we'll go through what is happening and how our plans are progressing. And Robert, we need to think about putting together a cabinet committee to lead the response of the Federal government to these provincial actions."

Later that afternoon, Dion met with Lalonde, Defense Minister Jean-Guy Blais and Lieutenant General Brian Foster, Commander of the Canadian Army. In the meeting Dion and Lalonde spoke to General Foster about their plans and the need to deploy troops throughout Canada but in particular the Western Provinces. When they were done Foster looked horrified and then he slowly spoke.

"Prime Minister, Minister Blais, Mr. Lalonde. I am sure you are all aware that I was born and raised in Calgary. I was afraid of something like this and I wondered how I would react. Now I know how I will react. I am afraid that I will have to follow the same actions that General Robert E. Lee did at the outbreak of the American Civil War. Just as he would not take up arms against his home state of Virginia, nor will I do that against my home province of Alberta. I hereby resign my commission as an officer in the Canadian Army."

Pierre Dion erupted at this statement. "General Foster, I view this as

100

nothing short of treason. I could have you arrested right now."

General Brian Foster stood up straight and glared coldly at the Prime Minister. "Yes, Prime Minister, you could. But ask yourself if you would do the same to a francophone general who refused to lead an armed occupation of Quebec. And trust me here – I will not be the only officer who refuses to carry out these orders."

Defense Minister Blais then stood and said. "General Foster, get out of here. You are done. Finished. You are relieved of your command. Do not return to National Defense headquarters. I will have your office cleaned out and your personal affects brought to your home. You're dismissed."

Robert Lalonde then summoned the Prime Minister's RCMP body guards who escorted General Foster out of the office.

An enraged Dion looked at Lalonde and Blais and stated. "There is no fucking way we can trust the English officers in the military to carry out our orders. Find me a senior francophone officer to promote to run the army and get him in here fast."

Lalonde and Blais did the Prime Minister's bidding and presented a French Canadian officer that evening. However it was not a "he." It was Major General Nancy Drolet. She was ushered into the Prime Minister's office to meet with Dion, Blais and Lalonde. The three men presented their plan and described General Foster's refusal to carry it out. They then sat back and waited for her response. She began speaking in French. "Gentlemen, our country is truly in a crisis now. I must say that I never believed I would be asked by my superiors to possibly take up arms against my fellow citizens."

Prime Minister Dion jumped on that almost bellowing. "General Drolet, are you going to tell me that you are going to refuse my orders?"

"Prime Minister, I've been taught that a military officer does not partake in politics. However as I see my country coming to pieces I will have to disregard that. I believe your actions in regard to the energy producing provinces are unconstitutional. I also believe you and your government like so many other Federal governments have a bias against Western Canada. Tell me – how would you react if say an Alberta born Prime Minister nationalized Hydro Quebec and said he was doing that to ensure all Canadians had cheap and reliable electricity? You and all Quebecers would lose their mind and they would be shouting separation immediately. Well this is the same situation. I believe your actions are illegal and I will not take up arms against fellow Canadians. Plus let me add that no Prime Ministers in the past ordered the arrest of Quebec politicians who were staging referendums on separating from Canada."

Dion glared at her and icily asked. "Have you forgotten that you are a Quebecois and you are receiving orders from a fellow Quebecois?"

General Drolet stared back and responded. "No, sir. I am a Quebecois but I am also a Canadian, and a very proud Canadian. My Canada includes Quebec as one of 10 provinces."

Robert Lalonde, embarrassed that this francophone refused to follow the Prime Minister's orders icily asked General Drolet. "General, have you forgotten about your oath to your Commander in Chief here?"

General Drolet, replied in just as icy a tone. "Mr. Lalonde, I haven't forgotten my oath. But it seems you don't understand that my oath was to Queen Elizabeth II and her heirs which today means King Edward IX. The Commander in Chief of the Canadian military is the King represented here in Canada by the Governor General. Not

102

the Prime Minister. I understand however that my service to my nation has now ended. I will resign my commission before this evening is finished."

With that, Major General Nancy Drolet left the Prime Minister's office, escorted by RCMP officers, where she was taken to her office at the Department of National Defense. There she drafted her resignation, and removed her personal effects from her office before leaving for the final time.

The following morning, Major General Jean-Claude Tremblay met with Dion, Lalonde, and Blais. Unlike General's Foster and Drolet, Tremblay was fully prepared to carry out Dion's orders. When he left the meeting the orders were going out mobilizing Canadian troops across Canada.

Jean-Claude Tremblay was 56 years old. A graduate of the Royal Military College in Kingston, Ontario, Tremblay had moved up through the ranks mainly due to his administrative skills. He had commanded troops in UN peace keeping missions but had not seen combat during Canada's almost decade long fighting in Afghanistan. He was fluent in English and French and most importantly for his own career, he had a knack of making his superiors look good.

At the Ministry of Justice, Attorney General Monique Juneau met with her staff members who were drafting plans to arrest the "renegade" premiers. As she briefed her staff, a young lawyer named Caroline Oulett asked. "Madam Minister, are we sure about this? And what if the Premier's bodyguards resist us? Are we prepared to actually resort to force or possibly violence to do this? That is unthinkable in Canada."

Juneau paused at that question. The image of the RCMP being

resisted by the various bodyguards protecting the Provincial Premiers was not one she had contemplated. She then spoke carefully. "I have to say, Caroline, that's not something I considered. Let me take that back to the Prime Minister."

At the Kahnawake, Quebec, Mohawk reserve, numerous Mohawks discussed the ongoing events. Most of the oil fields were of course in Western Canada; however the Mohawk's had a long, proud history of standing up for First Nations rights. In the eyes of many Canadian government officials, the Mohawks were the most organized, and at the same time, most belligerent of all First Nations groups.

Reg Hill, one of the more outspoken members of the Mohawk Warrior Society snarled. "Look at this. The Federal government is talking about seizing oil fields many of which are on our land. First Nations land! And the western provinces are talking about leaving Canada, and in all of this nobody is talking to the First Nations."

Ellen Abraira, one of the matrilineal elders [xix] commented. "As always, Ottawa either simply ignores us or persecutes us. We had better start making plans to mobilize as things are going to get ugly really fast. And we had better be prepared to protect our people. And at the same time we may have to provide support for our friends out west."

South of the border, the US military was also moving. In armories across the western border states of Minnesota, North Dakota, Montana, Idaho and Washington orders came through activating Army National Guard units ordering them into border communities. At Fort Lewis-McChord, Washington the 7th Infantry Division moved to a higher readiness status. The same was true at Fort Drum, New York with the elite 10th Mountain Division. At Fort Devers

Massachusetts various Army Reserve and National Guard units were activated and put on alert in case of issues in the Maritimes. This was all communicated in a call from Secretary of Defense Henry Stillman to Defense Minister Blais. "Good morning Minister Blais, thank you for taking my call," Stillman began.

"Good morning, Mr. Secretary," Blais answered stiffly. Blais was concerned about the timing of this call with Canadian military units going on alert. "What can I do for you?"

" Minister, I need to let you know that I have taken the liberty of moving some National Guard units up to many of our border communities out west. Many Americans living there are quite concerned that there may be some unrest and of course we need to ensure the safety of our citizens. I am sure you understand."

Blais was caught off-guard. He answered carefully. "I do understand, Mr. Secretary. I appreciate your letting me know and as long as your troops stay on your side of the border there is nothing for me to say here."

Henry Stillman smiled grimly and then responded. "Minister Blais, I quite understand. And just so we both are on the same page the opposite is also true. As long as any issues that arise in Canada stay in Canada, then we will not have any problems. But just make sure you keep control of any issues so they don't become our issues. Am I clear? I will also remind you that back in 1970 President Nixon moved US troops up to the various border areas around Quebec for the same reason. There is precedent for our moves as our government, unlike yours, I am sorry to say, views our most important, indeed our most sacred duty is the protection of our citizens."

Blais reacted angrily. "Mr. Secretary, I resent that comment. What are you implying?"

"Minister, it's simple. We've never relied on another nation for our own security. Since the end of World War II, your nation has disregarded the entire notion of the Canadian government being responsible for the protection of its citizens, for the idea that the United States would do so. I believe you are going to have some major problems now within your borders with the political forces you have unleashed and you don't have the security forces to protect your citizens if things get, shall we say, ugly. I hope that you will be able to prove me wrong. But I don't believe you will be able to do that. That's all I have to say. I wish you the best of luck. Good day."

Blais slammed down the phone. What was so galling to him at this moment was that he knew Henry Stillman was right. And although he would never admit this to Pierre Dion, Blais had no confidence that his military forces could control more than a single isolated incident.

Orders continued to flow out of National Defense Headquarters in Ottawa, and across Canada military units began mobilizing. At Canadian Forces Base Petawawa, in Eastern Ontario, the 1st and 3rd Battalions of the Royal Canadian Regiment, one of Canada's most historic and decorated units received orders to "mount up" and proceed to Ottawa to provide security to Parliament Hill and other government buildings. (The 3rd battalion also consisted of Canada's only active paratroopers.) In Quebec at the massive Val Cartier army base the elite Royal 22nd "Van Doos", Canada's internationally renowned French speaking regiment geared up to move into Newfoundland.

As units across Canada continued to mobilize, Premier Keith Cassidy of Ontario dropped a bombshell. As turmoil exploded across the nation Cassidy decided to sit down with his caucus. He had met with his top advisors beforehand and they were in agreement on the necessary, proposed course of action. In the caucus meeting that followed Cassidy spoke.

"Ladies and gentlemen. I think everyone is shook up at what we are seeing happen in our country. People we consider to be our friends have decided that there is no future for them in Canada. I know we all find that distressing. But we have to decide now, is what we are going to do. The Dion government has basically declared war on the oil and gas producing regions of Canada. But by leaving NAFTA with no notice they are also declaring war on Ontario. Our manufacturing base here will be devastated and will probably never recover. That will mean the loss of hundreds of thousands of jobs here in Ontario. As well by simply seizing the resources that constitutionally belong to those provinces, is anything in Ontario safe from the federal government?

'So, the question before us is what does Ontario do? Do we stick with the federal government and follow them down the path they are embarking on? Or do we take a different road?

'My belief is we take a different road. And that road is we follow our friends in Newfoundland and out west. And yes that means the provinces that wish to leave Canada. I don't wish to be part of a nation where the federal government can simply decide to violate the constitution and take over resources that belong to a province. That is not the Canada I know or wish to live in.

'I must ask what you all think. And let me make something clear. I am not imposing party discipline here. We will proceed via consensus. But one thing I will make clear. If as a caucus we decide to stick with the current Canada under the Dion government, then I will resign and I will move myself and my family to one of the western provinces. I will not raise my family under this government."

The impact on the caucus was equivalent to a nuclear bomb. After a brief silence the room erupted. Comments like "treason," "fuck Quebec," " screw the west" and others ricocheted throughout the room. Finally at the end of it all a vote was held. Of the 96 members of the caucus 68 voted to follow Premier Cassidy. The other either abstained or voted against it.

Cassidy then spoke again. "Thank you, everyone. To those who agree with me, thank you. To those who do not I respect your views and there are no hard feelings. I wish you the very best in the future. As a government we will follow our friends in Newfoundland and out west but I also assure you that there will be a binding referendum on separation and you will all of course have your vote there and the ability to campaign. God bless you all."

After the caucus meeting, Cassidy booked a conference call with the "rebellious premiers." Max Mountjoy was the only one missing as he had been forced to fly back to St. John's to deal with an urgent provincial issue. Mountjoy did join on the call however. When the call went through Cassidy began. "Good evening everyone. Thank you for taking the time to talk to me."

There were murmured greetings back and Cassidy moved into his 'spiel. "I know you're all busy and we're going into uncharted constitutional and national unity waters here. I realize in Canada's history Ontario has always tried to act as an honest broker and bring various parties together. Today though I am taking a different tact. Ontario will not try to mediate any issues here. I want you to know that Ontario stands with all of you against the actions of the Federal government. By pulling us out of NAFTA, Dion will destroy an already shaky manufacturing base here, costing hundreds of thousands of jobs. And as far as I am concerned there will be no Canada, if a government in Ottawa can simply seize the resources and property of any province. When you stage your referendums Ontario will be joining you."

There was a stunned silence before Karen Van Pelt spoke up. "Keith, we are all deeply moved by your support and we accept it fully! On behalf of all of us it's s gratifying to see that Ontario isn't bound up in the control of the 'Laurentian Elite' any longer." I must say though have you the support of your caucus? And even more important the support of the people in Ontario?"

Cassidy paused and then answered. "As far as my caucus is concerned, the answer is yes. While we are all more than concerned about rising oil prices and the impact on our economy here, the truth is the actions of the Dion are simply beyond the pale. You cannot justify it. And if he will do this to your provinces what will stop him when he decides he needs something of Ontario's next? He is as big a threat to Ontario as he is to the west. He has to be stopped or we need to leave."

Neil Craig from Saskatchewan commented. "Keith, welcome aboard. If nothing else by standing up to Dion we will mark the dawn of a new era in democracy here in Canada."

"I agree," Heidi McNamara added. "And if we see that our referendums do get passed it will be nice to have a friendly neighbor on my eastern border as well, Keith."

"Thanks, everyone," Cassidy answered. "Now I have to make a very unpleasant call to the Prime Minister in Ottawa. He will lose his mind when I tell him."

After Cassidy disconnected, Karen Van Pelt turned to the other premiers gathered with her and said. "I think Dion may blow a gasket and do something really extreme after he talks with Keith. In fact let me rephrase that. I am sure he will do something extreme as he will be facing the fact that Canada broke apart under his watch. I would suggest that we stick together here otherwise the Prime Minister may try and have police or military units arrest us individually."

Carla Henderson then spoke up. "Karen, believe me I feel safer with us all together. After all, what's the old saying 'there is safety in numbers.' But are we not more exposed with all of us in the same place?"

"That is a good point you raise Carla," Neil Craig answered.

Heidi McNamara suggested. "Why don't we split into two separate groups? That we are still not alone, but Dion can't send police or the military to one specific location and get all of us."

Karen Van Pelt responded. "These are all good points. I have a summer retreat near Banff. Why don't some of us head there while others remain here? I should stay in Edmonton as the Premier. But Carla and Neil, why don't you both head to Banff while Heidi and I remain here in Edmonton? Max, you are already in St. John's so we are now nicely split up and not one big target for Dion."

Keith Cassidy's next call was to Pierre Dion. Before he dialed the number he briefly reflected on what he was about to do. In the long history of constitutional battles in Canada, Ontario had always tried to be the "honest broker" "or "the big brother" who was watching over the entire family looking out for everyone. It tried to bring everyone together. Now he was taking Ontario and making a leap into the abyss. He hoped to god history would judge him kindly.

When he placed the call, it was, as he predicted, "ugly." Dion took the call in his office with Robert Lalonde present. "Keith, what can I do for you," the Prime Minister asked. "And forgive me here I do hope it won't take long. I am rather busy as you can imagine."

"I'll be as quick as possible, Prime Minister," the Ontario Premier responded. "The reason I am calling is to inform you that I just finished a conference call with the western premiers and Premier Mountjoy."

"I take it that you thoroughly criticized them for their lack of Canadian patriotism," Dion snapped.

"'I'm afraid not, Prime Minister. As I told you when you first informed me of your plan that I wasn't comfortable with it. Now not only am I not comfortable with it, I think it is unconstitutional and quite frankly insane. Totally nuts. I will not support it. Furthermore I pledged my support to Mr. Mountjoy and the western premiers on my call to them today. Ontario will be following their lead and staging a referendum on secession from Canada due to your governments' actions."

Dion, just as Cassidy predicted exploded. "You are a fucking traitor to Canada. You are a disgrace and you disgust me. I'll personally see that you pay for this!"

Dion slammed the phone down and turned to Robert Lalonde and in French snapped. "Get General Tremblay and Blais on the phone now. I don't care what they are doing or where they are. I want to talk to them now!"

Within minutes newly promoted Lieutenant General Jean Claude Tremblay was on the phone. Defense Minister Blais who had been in his parliamentary office had hurried over to the Prime Minister's office.

"Prime Minister, you requested I call immediately" Tremblay said in French on the phone. 'What can I do for you?"

"General and Minister Blais, I'm giving you a new set of directives," Dion said, continuing in French. "Instead of putting troops onto the streets as a 'show of force' backing our emergency legislation I want you to use our forces to seize control of the legislative buildings in British Columbia, Alberta, Saskatchewan, Manitoba and Ontario. If at all possible coordinate this with the RCMP and take the premiers in these provinces into custody. Am I clear?"

"Very clear, Prime Minister. When do you wish me to do this?"

"Within 24 hours. I want to see troops in every provincial legislative building within 24 hours. I don't care what you have to do. Call up the reserves, do whatever you need to do. If I have to sign something send it to me. Just make it happen."

Defense Minister Blais turned to the Prime Minister and said. "Prime Minister I suggest we do call up the reserves. We may face civil unrest as we move on those rebellious provinces and we will need the extra troops. We will require an Order in Council to activate the reserves though."

Dion turned to Lalonde and said. "Robert, get that order drafted and get those reserves activated. We need to make this happen fast!"

Within hours, the Order in Council was drafted and across Canada phones began ringing calling reservists up to mandatory active duty for the first time since 1939. [xx]At other bases "regular forces" (known as Reg Force) gathered to review their orders. Saying there was concern and bewilderment would be charitable.

At Canadian Forces Edmonton it was chaos. Brigadier General Patrick McKenzie, a native of Peterborough, Ontario, reviewed his orders with his senior officers. They were very direct.

"General McKenzie, you will take the 1st and 3rd Battalions of the Princess Patricia Light Infantry as well as the Lord Strathcona Horse Regiment forthwith and take control and secure the Alberta legislature grounds. You will assist with the police in taking the Alberta government and in particular Premier Karen Van Pelt into custody.

At the same time once the legislature and government is in custody you will work with the Edmonton police and RCMP and all other civil authorities in keeping order in the community. More direction will follow ASAP."

General Jean Claude Tremblay

General McKenzie after reading the orders looked around the room and asked. "Ladies and gentlemen, these orders are very clear. Are there any questions?"

"Yes, sir," Major Natalie Witowsky said. "Sir, I joined the army to protect my country. I didn't join the army to arrest the duly elected government of my home province and possibly take up arms against my friends and family here. Are you sure the actions of Ottawa are legal?"

McKenzie paused before answering. He had dreaded this and had the same doubts himself. "Major we have to assume that the orders coming from National Defense Headquarters are legal and proper. It is not up to us to question orders. We simply carry them out. We have all sworn an oath and we have to carry out our duty."

"Well, sir, then I am afraid I can't do that. I swore an oath to Elizabeth II and her heirs. Not to a Quebec based Prime Minister who's acting like a tyrant. As well, I will fight in the streets against a foreign enemy or terrorists. I will give my life to defend my neighbors, my family and any other fellow Canadian. But I will not carry out orders which I believe are illegal. And if I may sir, I would suggest you remember the precedent laid down at the Nuremburg War Crimes trial where the court ruled that 'just following orders was not an excuse.' I do believe sir that anyone following these orders will be acting in an illegal manner. With all due respect, sir, I truly believe that."

Lieutenant Colonel Andrew Renko then spoke up. "Sir, it is my duty to inform you that I feel the same way as Major Witowsky does. I cannot take up arms against my fellow Canadians. Add to that sir, I was born and raised in Ontario and the Prime Minister is ordering the same actions in Ontario as he is here in Alberta. I cannot follow those orders."

General McKenzie felt trapped. He didn't agree with Ottawa's orders however he also felt as a professional soldier he must follow orders. He tried tact. "Ladies and gentlemen, I understand these are shall we say, controversial orders. That being said as professional soldiers we are obliged to carry out lawful orders. We have received orders from our superiors and at least on the surface they are lawful. Anyone who refuses to carry them out, I will have arrested for mutiny. Am I clear?"

Major Witowsky stepped forward.

"Sir, I place myself under arrest then."

Lieutenant Colonel Renko looked around and nodded at his fellow officers and stepped forward beside Major Witowsky.

114

"Sir, I stand with Major Witowsky. I place myself in custody with her."

Around the room over 80% of the other officers stepped forward to stand beside Major Witowsky and Lieutenant Colonel Renko. General McKenzie looked around at the officers before him. He quietly said. "God bless you all. I have no choice but to support you. I'll alert Ottawa to what has occurred and we can wait here for the military police and/or Mounties to come for us."

Similar orders were being received at armories and military bases across Canada. In cities where there were no "Reg Force" bases, reserve units were mobilized with orders to stand by for further direction. The Van Doos had been ordered to "stand down" from moving into Newfoundland and to instead guard the National Assembly legislature in Quebec City and assist the civil authorities in Quebec City and Montreal in case unrest broke out. Ottawa was clear. Federal authority was being used in a manner that had never been seen before in Canada.

Around the country, similar situations that had transpired in Edmonton were also taking place. In Toronto, the 48th Highlanders and Queens Own Rifles, two distinguished reserve infantry regiments refused orders to leave the Moss Park Armory and take control of Queens Park. The same was true across most of English speaking Canada.

The first "spark" of violence occurred in St. John's Newfoundland. There the Royal Newfoundland Regiment had marched out of the city armory, and surrounded the provincial legislative building. However as opposed to taking Premier Max Mountjoy and his government into custody as ordered by Ottawa, they informed Premier Mountjoy that they were present to protect him and his government from the actions of the Federal government. As the troops began setting up defensive positions a convoy of 15 RCMP vehicles approached and stopped at the sight of the heavily armed soldiers blocking their way. The commanding RCMP officer Gilles Boisvert stepped out of his cruiser and approached Lieutenant Yvonne Chadwick. Boisvert glared at her and snapped. "I understand you are here to assist us. Get your people out of the way and be prepared to assist us if the security in the legislature resists us."

Lieutenant Chadwick was practically shaking in her boots. She had joined the reserves thinking it would be an interesting and fun part time job that would supplement her income as a bank teller. But she was fiercely proud of her Newfoundland roots and home and was appalled when her commanding officer had outlined the orders from Ottawa and had no qualms about joining the "mutiny" against Ottawa. She stiffened her back and glared at the arrogant RCMP officer and responded.

"Back off. We're protecting our Premier and our government. You aren't getting past us. We do not believe the orders from Ottawa are lawful and we will not follow them. Please take your people and leave."

Boisvert was stunned. When he had received his orders to arrest the Newfoundland Premier and his government it had never entered his mind that the military may resist him. It was simply assumed they would follow orders from Ottawa and assist his officers. However he had made his mark in law enforcement busting biker gangs and other organized crime. He didn't scare easy and the sight of a young, smaller, female army officer who refused to back down to him didn't faze him one bit. He acted instantly grabbing hold of the officer and trying to twist her around, slam her against the car and handcuff her.

116

He knew the best way to intimidate any gang was the take down their leader and he treated her in the same manner as he would a Hells Angel leader. As he did so, more RCMP officers leaped out of their cruisers drawing their weapons. Lieutenant Yvonne Chadwick may have been scared and only a part-time soldier but she was no coward and she was trained in hand to hand combat. She wrenched herself free with a curse, and drew her own sidearm. Constable Andrew McArthur leaping from his car panicked when he saw her draw her weapon and fired three rounds into her chest. Chadwick was knocked flat by the impact of the bullets but the rounds were absorbed by her body armor. As she fell, her finger in a reflex tightened on the trigger of her Browning 9mm pistol sending a round crashing through the skull of Boisvert who dropped his weapon and smashed face first into the ground.

Immediately, with the sound of the gunfire and two bodies hitting the ground, a firefight exploded. The Mounties were armed with handguns, carbines and shot guns. The police fired first and the soldiers responded back in kind. The young reservists armed with C7-assualt rifles and wearing military grade body armor had a huge advantage in firepower, protection and combat training. Their military caliber ammunition punched through the police officers body armor while their own body armor protected most of them from the police gunshots. In seconds it was over. Eleven Mounties lay dead or dying on the ground. Another 16 were wounded, some on the ground, others huddled in bullet riddled police vehicles. Eight soldiers lay on the ground with head and leg wounds that had avoided their armor.

Lieutenant Chadwick sprang from the ground. Her chest was killing her. Her body armor prevented the RCMP bullets from penetrating into her flesh but didn't lessen their powerful impact. She would later find out she had three cracked ribs as a result. The air was thick with the acrid stench of gunpowder and shrieks of wounded and dying soldiers and police officers.

"Cease fire, goddamn it, cease fire," she screamed. "We need medics here fast!"

Captain Nils Böckmann, Chadwick's commanding officer sprinted over to her. He had immigrated to Canada from Germany when he was 13 and was proud to serve in the military of his adopted nation. He looked at the carnage and in his thick German accent yelled. "Jesus Christ, Lieutenant, what happened?"

"The Mounties fired on us first, sir. We had to defend ourselves. I don't know what else to say."

Böckmann responded. "There will be hell to pay for this. Nobody fires on my troops and gets away with it. These fucking lunatics!"

 He looked at his own dead and wounded soldiers and muttered. "Murdering bastards!"

From there, he ran to assist the medics who were frantically trying to save the wounded. The scream of ambulance sirens were sounding in the air as the medics, covered in blood worked desperately to save the lives of the wounded soldiers and police officers.

As the gunfire exploded in St. John's, Newfoundland, US naval units began entering the harbors of St. John's, Halifax, Nova Scotia, and Victoria, British Columbia. It's common for US and Royal Canadian Naval vessels to visit each other ports so no alarm was being raised at the appearance of the American naval ships entering Canadian harbors.

In Victoria, the Ticonderoga class guided missile cruiser USS Shiloh, followed by the USS Wasp, a heavily armed amphibious assault ship, which contained a detachment of almost 2,000 Marines, and 2 destroyers slowly moved towards piers in order to dock.

In Halifax, the USS Yorktown another Ticonderoga class cruiser, escorted the amphibious assault ship USS Bataan and three frigates into harbor.

St. John's saw the amphibious assault ship USS Iwo Jima, with its' heavily armed Marine detachment enter the harbor along with one frigate and two destroyers.

Each amphibious assault ship carried six Harrier fighter planes, four Super Cobra attack helicopters as well as numerous other helicopters and landing craft designed to get the detachments of Marines ashore and supported quickly.

Closing in on both coasts were two US naval task forces led by the carriers USS Nimitz in the Pacific and USS Harry S Truman in the Atlantic. If President Morrison felt she had to give the orders to seize Canada's naval bases quickly the US Navy was well positioned to do so.

In the Great Lakes, the Freedom class combat ship USS Little Rock glided into Lake Ontario almost like an avenging "Angel of Death." She was familiar with the Great Lakes having conducted her sea trials in Lake Michigan (the only of the Great Lakes which is 100% within the United States) and was commissioned beside her namesake, the WWII and Cold War era guided missile cruiser USS Little Rock which has been docked in Buffalo, New York for years and is now a tourist attraction. The "new" USS Little Rock carried MK31 surface to air missiles, deck guns, attack helicopters and a small assault team of Marines. This "small" US Navy ship had more firepower than anything in the entire Royal Canadian Navy. The Pentagon earlier announced that the Little Rock would dock in Hamilton and Toronto Ontario and be open for tours.

Meanwhile, across Ontario and the four western provinces, "hometown" army reserve units began surrounding the provincial legislatures. Police forces in these cities having heard of the bloody debacle in St. John's backed away from taking any action.

In Ottawa, the first chaotic news of the gun battle in St. Johns followed by the mutinies by English language military units rocked the Dion government. In a scene almost reminiscent of Adolf Hitler's incoherent behavior in the Fuehrer bunker in Berlin April 1945, Pierre Dion ranted, raved, and screamed. "Câlice[xxi], Lalonde, what the fuck is happening? How can military units refuse direct orders? Where is their loyalty? You never told me this could happen – that English language troops would refuse to follow my orders."

Robert Lalonde was dripping with sweat. He had also never considered English language units rebelling to be even a remote possibility. He quickly said in French. "Pierre, calm down. Let me speak with General Tremblay and we will have a solution. I promise you this."

Dion took a deep breath. He turned to Lalonde and asked "We have English troops from Petawawa just outside the door guarding Parliament Hill. Do I need to worry about them launching a coup of some sorts?"

Lalonde, thinking fast and having not considered that now seemingly very dangerous possibility, answered. "Pierre, they've not made a move. I am sure if they were going to they would have done so already. Let me speak with General Tremblay and get back to you. Your RCMP guards are out front. You are quite safe."

120

In Washington, President Morrison met in the Oval Office with Henry Stillman, Robert Jackson, Michael Youngblood and Dr. Kimberly Tucker. Very quickly, Robert Jackson began briefing everyone. "It's just as we had feared. We are getting reports of widespread mutinies among English language military units who are refusing to carry out Prime Minister Dion's orders. As well, there are preliminary reports coming out of St. John's Newfoundland, of all places about a possible gun battle between RCMP officers and army reservists who had surrounded the Newfoundland legislature to protect Premier Mountjoy and his government."

"Christ in heaven," President Morrison muttered. "Michael, you more than anyone in this room know Canada. Are we looking at a civil war or total breakdown in their society?"

Secretary of State Michael Youngblood stood up and began pacing the room. "As I have said before, I know Canada," he began. "I will say it's a very delicate nation. If you look at a map of North America, you'll see that the natural trade routes run north-south, not east-west. Think about this. A fisherman in New Brunswick has far more in common with his counterpart in Maine then he does with a wheat farmer in Saskatchewan. Same goes for a business person in Toronto, they're far more at home in Manhattan then Medicine Hat, Alberta. Canada from day one was fighting the natural trade routes in order to build an east-west nation. Add to that there has always been tension between the English and French. Most Prime Ministers since the mid-20th century have come from Quebec and there has been serious resentment by many in the rest of the country due to that. The Liberal Party of Canada which dubs itself as the 'Natural Governing Party' always rotates between what they refer to as Anglophone and Francophone leaders and have never had a leader from Western Canada. Half the country or at least the west has always been left out of the leadership of that party which forms the majority of Canadian governments."

Robert Jackson interrupted and asked. "Michael, is the Liberal Party anti-Western Canada? Why have they never had a leader from the western part of the country? Hell here in the United States we have had Presidents from New England with Kennedy, New York with Trump, the deep south with Jimmy Carter and Bill Clinton, Texas with Lyndon Johnson and the Bushes, the Midwest with Obama and California with Richard Nixon just to name a few. We don't choose our leaders from basically one state or region of the country. Why does it seem that almost every Canadian Prime Minister comes from Quebec?"

"Good question, Bob," Michael Youngblood answered. "I think the answer is pretty straightforward. There are two big reasons.

'First and foremost, with the party's insistence on full English/French bilingualism for any party leader or possible Prime Minister, well over 50% of the nation is simply not eligible. I mean, the bilingualism part isn't law. It is an unspoken rule. Now French is really only spoken in some parts of Ontario, the entire Province of Quebec and in neighboring New Brunswick which is the only officially bilingual province in Canada. Yes there a few other pockets of French speaking people around the country but they are few and far between and the reality is to survive in say Newfoundland, Saskatchewan or Alberta and only speak French is impossible. You would have nobody to speak with! And even if you take French in school in say Calgary, Toronto, or Vancouver, outside of the classroom you would almost never use it. Unless you were dealing with the Quebec government or say your office in Montreal you simply would have no use for it. You'd be better off learning Punjabi or Mandarin as there are so many immigrants from India and China, or if you deal with American firms, Spanish.

Remember Spanish is the second most common language in North America. Something the Canadian government doesn't like talking about.

'Let's face it. Unless you speak a language regularly you will never be proficient. So, someone outside of the Ontario, Quebec, New Brunswick bilingual regions is never going to be proficient enough in French and therefore will never be considered for the leadership of, in particular the Liberal Party, which has always identified itself closely with the interests of Quebec.

'Secondly, there is a huge cultural issue. In Quebec working in the public sector and especially politics is something people, especially those well-educated and perhaps coming from wealthy families, strive for. It is very prestigious there. That isn't the case in English Canada. The people there are more like us. The brightest and most ambitious enter the business world and want to make big money. Why would you want to be, say the Premier of Nova Scotia or Prime Minister of Canada and earn something like $200-$300, 00 per year when you could be the CEO of a major corporation and make millions? So the end result is the brightest and best in Quebec gravitate to politics and in the rest of Canada they gravitate to the business world.

'Does that answer your question, Bob?"

"It sure did, Michael. Thank you."

"Okay then back to what I was originally speaking about. Could we see Canada splintering or worse 'blowing' apart? I believe we very well could be seeing this. Remember it was only in 1995 that Quebec almost left. The English-French tensions, the entire 'unnatural' trade routes of Canada make for a delicate, even unstable union. And we are seeing the foundation cracking now in a big way."

President Katherine Morrison swore under her breath and then asked. "Thank you, Michael. Now the question is what in hell do we do, if anything? Do we send in troops to help restore order if it gets more out of control?'

Michael Youngblood again spoke up. "Madam President we need to be very cautious about the use of troops for several reasons.

There would be implications within NATO if we did this, without an explicit request from the Canadian government for help. The only way this wouldn't cause major issues in NATO or elsewhere is if we had some form of armed conflict that spread across our borders from Canada. If that happened we would have every right to defend our own citizens and use troops.

As I have said before, Canada outside of Quebec, has never really established a true national identity of what they are as a nation. Their identity has always been based on what they are not – and a big part of that is they are not American. If we just rush troops in we may very well see them stop fighting amongst each-other and start fighting us! And I don't have to tell you that Canada is one big country that would be a nightmare to be fighting a guerrilla war in. We thought Iraq and Afghanistan were bad – well this would be one for the ages. And not in a good way!'

"Thank you, Michael," the President said.

She then turned to her Secretary of Defense and asked. "Henry, where are we in so far as troops go, if we need them in Canada?"

Henry Stillman took Michael Youngblood's place pacing the room. "We have National Guard units now in most of our border communities out west and along the border with Ontario. The Border Patrol has also increased their patrols to assist us making

124

sure any conflict doesn't cross our border. We have naval units that have docked in Victoria, Halifax and St. John's. All of them have an amphibious assault ship with them, all of which contain a detachment of close to 2,000 Marines. As discussed earlier, if need be those Marines could quickly seize the harbors and we would have more than enough firepower to defend and hold on to them. I have sent the USS Little Rock into Lake Ontario and it is making stops in the large harbors of Hamilton and Toronto, Ontario. I may also send it on to Kingston, Ontario. There's not much more I can send into the Great Lakes without violating the Rush-Bagot Treaty that I previously mentioned. Even so, the Little Rock has more firepower available to it then probably the entire Canadian Armed Forces.

'Our forces at Forts McChord/Lewis in Washington, Fort Drum in New York, Fort Custer in Michigan, and Fort Devers in Massachusetts are on a heightened state of alert and can be moved quickly. Rest assured our armed forces are ready to do whatever is needed here.

'May I make a suggestion?"

"Absolutely, Henry," the President answered.

"Thank you," Henry Stillman responded. "Michael made a very good point about the reaction of NATO if we, for whatever reason, deployed military forces in Canada. Here's my suggestion. Canada has very historic roots with the United Kingdom. King Edward is also King of Canada. If we feel the need to deploy into Canada, perhaps a call from the President to Prime Minister Glenn McMillan may 'pave the way.' Canada is part of the Commonwealth. If we give the heads up to Prime Minister McMillan we will have shown respect for those historical ties or roots between the two nations and very possibly pulled the UK onto our side in the case of a major rift in the Commonwealth."

Michael Youngblood quickly spoke up. "Henry that is an excellent idea! At the very least it would show that we are not using unrest in Canada as an excuse to refight the War of 1812, and complete Manifest Destiny."

President Morrison nodded her head and said. "I also agree. I get along very well with Glenn McMillan. He is very level headed and a good friend to the US. He'll listen to me. It also helps that he and Pierre Dion detest one another."

She then turned to National Security Advisor Jackson and asked. "Bob, any other thoughts?"

"Not really, Madam President. I think both Michael and Henry have given you very sound advice. I particularly like Henry's idea of bringing Prime Minister McMillan into the loop if we need to deploy troops into Canada."

President Morrison turned to her Chief of Staff. "Kimberly, how about yourself? Do you have anything to add?"

"Yes, just a thought. I understand the Canadian Forces base at Shiloh, Manitoba hosts a lot of NATO troops for training. In particular the UK ambassador commented to me this week at an embassy party that there are British forces there right now training. Could they be of some assistance if we had to restore order?"

Henry Stillman nodded his head and responded. "Dr. Tucker as always a great idea. If we get to that point perhaps the President can raise it with Prime Minister McMillan and if he agrees I can work out details with my UK counterpart Christine Symington."

126

President Morrison answered. "If you think they would help by all means I will ask Glenn. It may also make out own actions far more palatable around the world if the British assist us."

CHAPTER VI

The following morning Canada awoke to the news of the fighting in St. John's and military mutinies across the country. All was quiet on Parliament Hill. The Royal Canadian Regiment troops continued to patrol the grounds. On Robert Lalonde's recommendation time had been booked with the national media organizations in order to address the nation. At 11am Eastern Time Dion appeared on nationwide radio and TV, and live streaming across the internet. "My fellow Canadians. I speak with you today at a time of great national crisis. As you are all aware my government took some admittedly extreme actions to try and deal with a national and international energy crisis that was impacting all Canadians. I realize that these actions are controversial but they were planned and executed in order to benefit the greatest number of Canadians.

'We are now seeing terrible examples of some disobedience among military units and some very isolated violence. This is all of course totally unacceptable. Let me make things very clear. It is the expectation of this government that all members of the Canadian Armed Forces follow any and all orders from their superiors. As of this minute, any member of the military who failed to carry out their orders, if they immediately report to their superiors and indicate that they will follow their orders, then no disciplinary action will be taken against them. This is a onetime only 'amnesty' for those who failed so terribly in their duty to their nation. Anyone who still fails to follow orders however will face charges under the National

Defense Act.

'So far as the violence we saw in St. Johns last night, I think I can safely say that all Canadians are shocked and appalled by it. The RCMP is investigating this and I fully expect criminal charges will be laid. There is no room in Canada for such appalling criminal actions as we saw last night.

'We have built a great nation. Together "two solitudes" English and French have built a wonderful, bilingual, multicultural nation that is the envy of the world. Let us not throw that away over petty differences. Let us remember that we are all Canadians. English and French, and whatever other cultures we are, and whatever languages we speak. Let us all come together in this time of crisis and remember that we are all Canadian.

'Thank you."

Across Canada some people took comfort in Prime Minister Dion's words. Among the First Nations however anger really boiled over. There had been no mention of the First Nations in Dion's speech. No suggestion at all that the First Nations should or could be part of the consulting process on healing the raw wounds that had opened in the Canadian fabric. No, as always, the Federal government was blind when it came to the First Nations. ·

At the Mohawk reserve in Kahnawake, Quebec, members of the Warrior Society agreed that Pierre Dion needed to remember that long before the English and French came to North America, the First Nations were here. And as leading Mohawk Warrior, Reg Hill commented. "Now is the time for us to start pressuring the Federal government ourselves. All these white people across the country are standing up for themselves against Ottawa. We also have to rise up or we will be left behind and forgotten. Or crushed."

130

That afternoon, during the evening rush hour, the Warriors struck. In a repeat of their "attack" during the Oka Crisis of 1990[xxii], a convoy of Mohawk vehicles rumbled halfway across the Mercier Bridge which separated the Island of Montreal from the heavily populated South Shore suburbs. At the half way point of the bridge Mohawk drivers stopped and then maneuvered to block traffic. As horns began blowing and outraged drivers stepped from their vehicles, covers were pulled off machine guns in the beds of two trucks. Other Mohawks pulled M16's, AK47's, Ruger Mini 14's and other rifles from their vehicles. John Littleton, known as "Black Angel" on the reserve, fired a clip from his M16 over the roofs of dozens of cars, prompting a panicked rush of drivers and their passengers who abandoned their vehicles and ran. In minutes the Warriors had full control of the bridge.

Quickly members of the Surete du Quebec (SQ or Quebec Provincial Police) and Montreal Police, including a SQ SWAT team arrived. Not able to bring their vehicles onto the bridge due to the abandoned commuter vehicles heavily armed police officers rushed forward. Police officers moving forward and taking cover behind vehicles shouted commands in French at the Mohawks. Warrior Joe Lassiter screamed back in Mohawk. "None of your filthy French you white bastards, speak Mohawk. You are on our land!"

For years people will wonder who fired first. That may never be answered. What is known is; moments after Lassiter yelled, shots rang out. Then a full-scale firefight erupted. Police officers fired C8 carbines, semi-automatic handguns, and shotguns. The Mohawks responded with massive fire from two old Vietnam War vintage M60 machine guns as well as numerous other weapons they had been carrying. Bodies on both sides were dropping when M60 rounds burst through the gas tanks of several abandoned vehicles sending fireballs into the air. A scene of absolute horror occurred when 2 police officers were turned into human torches as they were covered in blazing fuel. They ran shrieking and rolling as the flames burned them to death. Other officers trying to reach them were cut down by Mohawk gun fire. Finally, the shattered police forces retreated leaving a scene of bullet riddled and burned out vehicles and numerous corpses littering the bridge.

The horrifying news from Kahnawake rocked the Dion government and people across the country. Video footage of the firefight amidst burning vehicles and the scene of the two burning police officers were seared into the minds of all who saw it.

Montreal radio host Gilles Lapointe was a well know "rabble rouser." A strong proponent of Quebec sovereignty and the need for Quebec to restrict the public use of all languages outside of French, Lapointe launched a tirade on his late afternoon radio show. Without waiting for details, Lapointe "went off" ranting and raving about Mohawks, how they wouldn't assimilate, couldn't speak French, and were a threat to Quebec. He urged the SQ to cleanse Quebec of them and "wipe them out."

A young Mohawk named Peter Russell had been in Montreal during the "Battle of the Mercier Bridge." Sitting in a bar he heard Lapointe's tirade and other people in the bar agreeing with him. Russell had been drinking and a black mood came over him. As he listened further, he fingered the 357 Magnum, Colt Python shoved in the back of his pants. Realizing he was only 2 blocks from Lapointe's studio, Russell left the bar and headed towards it. He entered the lobby and when the security guard by the name of Nicole Savard, asked him in French what he wanted, Russell drew his firearm, and demanded to be taken to Lapointe's studio. Savard, who was a university student and working for minimum wage, was certainly not prepared to give her life for her employer. She quickly led Russell up the elevator and to the studio, all the while begging for her life. Savard who had a master key let Russell into the studio. Russell turned to her and said. "You can live. Get out of here now. Run."

With that Savard sprinted for the elevator. When she reached the lobby, she ran outside and called 911 on her mobile phone.

Peter Russell entered the radio station office and marched right to Lapointe's studio. The show's engineer saw him advancing with the pistol and screamed in French. "Oh my god, we are going to die."

Russell kicked the door open before the engineer could lock it. Lapointe, live on the air bellowed in French. "There is an armed man in my studio!"

The young Mohawk went into the "Weaver stance" and pumped six 357 rounds into Lapointe's head and chest. His skull exploded spraying blood and brain matter all over the wall. Radio listeners across Montreal sat stunned as they heard the murder live. Russell then went to the microphone and in Mohawk and then in English. "I just killed a racist pig who was occupying Mohawk land. Let all Mohawks rise up and drive the French bastards off our land!"

Russell pulled a speed loader from his pocket and reloaded. The engineer who had been cowering on the floor scrambled to his feet and made a run for it only to be brought down with three rounds into the back. Russell then stood over him and pumped three more into him finishing him off. He used his last speed loader to reload as the elevator opened and four Montreal police officers, responding to the 911 call, burst out. The first officer out of the elevator spotted Russell and screamed in French. "Drop your gun now!!"

Russell dropped him with two rounds into his head, before being riddled with over 20 rounds from the other three cops.

In Ottawa, Pierre Dion, a fan of Gilles Lapointe sat stunned in his office. He had the Montreal radio host on as he worked and heard the screams from the radio studio and the gunfire as Lapointe died. Then further gunfire as Russell killed the engineer and then the final gun battle with police. He turned to his left and vomited into his waste basket. As he finished an ashen Robert Lalonde came in. Dion wiped his mouth and said. "So, Robert, we have a country coming apart on linguistic grounds, the military in mutiny, and now possibly a race war. What else could go wrong?"

"My God, Prime Minister, I don't know what to say."

"Is there any news from the military? Have any of them come around to our side?"

Lalonde looked sadly and answered. "No. According to General Tremblay, we have status quo. The provincial governments are 'hunkered down' in their legislatures surrounded by, in most cases local reserve units who are protecting them. Police are refusing to try and enforce the law as they fear, and possibly rightly so, a repeat of what happened in St. John's last night."

Lalonde's mobile phone rang. He looked at the number and said. "It's General Tremblay."

He put the phone on speaker and answered. "Yes, General, I have you on speaker and I am with the Prime Minister."

"Thank you, Mr. Lalonde and Prime Minister. I realize you've both had a very difficult couple of days. I am afraid I'm not going to make it better. With the fighting at the Mercier Bridge and the murder of Gilles Lapointe I am receiving reports of some isolated rioting in

Montreal. I expect any time I'll receive requests from Premier Ouellet for troops to assist in restoring calm."

Dion answered. "General, we already have units of the Van Doos in Montreal so why not deploy them now? Perhaps have them take over from the police at the Mercier Bridge. Maybe the sight of the soldiers will scare the Mohawks there into surrendering. At the least if there is another gun battle the army is far more capable of defeating the Mohawks then the police are."

"Very good, Prime Minister," Tremblay answered. "I'll issue the orders immediately."

CHAPTER VII

In Halifax, the HMCS Toronto, a Halifax class frigate of the Royal Canadian Navy (RCN) was docked within easy view of the small US task force that had entered port the previous evening. Over the last few days news of the unrest across Canada had been the talk of the ship. Despite that, the captain had allowed full liberty ashore for the crew and hadn't worried about increasing the maintenance crew aboard her. The small crew on duty had smuggled bottles of liquor aboard and had drank themselves into a black, aggressive mood.

Able Seaman Ross Hackson took a swig of Canadian Club Rye and snarled. "Our fucking country is blowing apart and look at the goddamn Americans over there – they are here I am sure to take control of us when all the shit hits the fan."

His friend Ordinary Seaman Charles (Chuck) Frame who was also plastered, mumbled. "Ross, you have a mouth like a fucking sewer. It's disgusting."

Hackson belched loudly and then laughed. "I have a mouth like a 'fucking sewer?' Who are you, Miss. Manners? And you know what? We need to do something about those fucking Americans sitting there in our harbor. We kicked their ass in the War of 1811. They should have learned their lesson then."

Frame replied in a boozy slur. "You mean the War of 1812 numb nuts. And so, what do you want to do about the Yankees anyway?"

Hackson had an evil look in his eyes. He said. "Well Chuck, old boy. I just happened to finish refurbishing one of our 50 caliber machine guns in the machine shop. I have some ammo for the 'ole girl' stashed away and we are nicely in range of the USS Bataan. How about we lug her up on deck and squeeze off a few rounds and make the Yanks over there shit their pants?"

Nobody would ever accuse Chuck Frame of being a Mensa Society member. Being drunk however, he was even more "daft" then usual. "Okay Ross, if you think so. That'll be funny!"

The two drunken sailors brought the heavy Browning 50 caliber machine gun plus ammunition up on deck. Less than 300 yards away the USS Bataan was peacefully docked. Hackson and Frame could see crewmembers on the Bataan attending to their duties. The Bataan's commanding officer Captain Francis Fonseca had not been as liberal with liberty for his crew as had the Toronto's commander so he had full contingents of guards and damage control parties aboard.

Hackson and Frame had the weapon set up and Hackson sat behind it and took the safety off and aimed at a Harrier jet parked on the flight deck of the Bataan. With a crazy, drunken cackle he squeezed the trigger. The heavy rounds ripped through the distance between the two ships in a faction of a second and slammed into a fully fueled Harrier jet. It immediately exploded, sending shrapnel and burning fuel across the deck. Beside it another Harrier went up in flames, as three Marine guards dropped to the deck riddled with shrapnel and doused in blazing jet fuel.

Hackson, gripped with a drunken, crazy blood lust and fueled by whiskey began sweeping the carrier deck of the Bataan as more aircraft exploded and men and women dropped. Frame helped him feed another belt of 50 caliber ammunition into the gun. Alarms began screaming on both ships. On board the Bataan, officers on the bridge sounded General Quarters. Men and women already reacting to the explosion and gun fire ran for their battle stations. Damage control parties grabbed their equipment.

On board the HMCS Toronto acting Commanding Officer (CO) Real Lemieux reacted instantly. He screamed. "Who's firing? Cease fire, cease fire!!"

He ran to the sound of the gunfire. Chuck Frame saw their CO run towards them screaming to cease fire. Lemieux totally unarmed, bravely charged the two men. Hackson laughed wildly and swung the heavy machine gun around and cut Lemieux in half, riddling his body with rounds. He then swept the weapon back to the Bataan and continued to hammer her.

As the rounds blasted in, Marine Private Joseph Howahkan, an Oglala Sioux from the Pine Ridge Reservation in South Dakota, raised his head from where he had been seeking cover. He was on guard duty that evening and was fully armed. He, like all the guards, never expected to face attack from a Canadian warship, but he was too well trained not to react instantly. He saw the muzzle flashes from the Browning, aimed his M16 and fired off a full magazine in response. His rounds tore Ross Hackson to shreds blowing body parts across the deck. Chuck Frame was wounded and staggered away from the improvised gun position. As he did so Petty Officer 2nd Class Louise Lacroix who had arrived to see the two crewmen in the midst of their attack, dropped the wounded sailor with a flying tackle. Screaming for help, she held him down until more assistance arrived. Lieutenant Commander Howard Goldstein who now appeared snapped. "Get him to sickbay and put him under guard. Make sure he's secured and can't get away."

He looked over at the burning flight deck on the Bataan and added. "Signal the Bataan and tell them we have the situation under control here and do they need our help. Jesus Christ in heaven, what just happened?"

On board, the USS Bataan damage control teams were fighting major fires on the flight deck. The other US ships in Halifax had now gone to full General Quarters. Weapons systems onboard were being armed and Marine guards had their rifles locked and loaded.

In Arlington, Virginia, across the Potomac River from Washington D.C., Henry Stillman was at home quietly enjoying a glass of red wine with his wife Marian. When his secure phone rang Marian sighed and said. "Oh, dear we so rarely ever get a night to ourselves."

"I know," Stillman replied.

When he answered the phone, he listened and then asked while looking totally dumbfounded. "Would you repeat that, please?"

When he hung up, he looked stunned. Marian looked at him and asked. "What's wrong?"

Stillman answered. "For the first time since the War of 1812 Canada has attacked us. Sorry, I have to call the President."

Moments later, Stillman was on the line with President Morrison. He explained to her what he knew – that is a Royal Canadian Navy frigate had opened fire on the USS Bataan causing major damage and causalities. The "fighting was over" but the Bataan was battling fires on her flight deck and being assisted by damage control parties from the other US warships with her. Assistance had been offered by the Royal Canadian Navy, and had been declined. Stillman finished and President Morrison asked him. "Henry, I know we have ships in other Canadian ports -I believe in Victoria, and St. John's, where there was just some fighting between soldiers and police. Can we expect the same in those harbors? By that I mean do you believe our ships there may be attacked? And what about our ship you sent into Lake Ontario?"

"Madam President, I've no reason to believe this was an act of war. I believe it was an isolated event. But that being said, our ships are 'sitting ducks' in harbor. We can blow anything Canada has out of the water – but they can hurt us badly with an attack like this."

"Okay, Henry. My first responsibility is to protect American lives. And it sounds like a lot of Americans died in Halifax tonight on the Bataan. I am giving you a direct order now. Tell the Marine commanders aboard the amphibious assault ships docked in Canada to take immediate control of those harbors. I want the harbors and every ship in them under our control. Am I clear?'

"Yes, Madam President, totally clear. I take it you will call the Canadian Prime Minister?"

"I'll call him right away. I wish that man would get control of his country. Henry, if the Little Rock is docked in one of those Canadian ports you mentioned on Lake Ontario, get it the hell out of there. Get it back out into the lake and put it on full alert. If any other sort of ship comes near it that they can't identify, have them blow it out of the water. The hell with the goddamn Rush-Bagot treaty anyway. I am not going to have my hands tied by some treaty that is almost 300 years old."

"Madam President, consider it done," Stillman replied.

Pierre Dion had not yet been aware of the "attack" in Halifax. He was reading some briefing papers when his phone rang. Seeing it was the US President he immediately answered. "Good evening, Madam President. This is a surprise."

"Good evening, Prime Minister. This isn't going to be a pleasant call. I have just been alerted by my Secretary of Defense, Henry Stillman, that one of your frigates opened fire on one of my amphibious assault ships, the USS Bataan in Halifax Harbor just minutes ago."

Dion was truly aghast. He responded. "My God, I have heard nothing about it. Are you sure?'

"Yes, I'm sure! And from what I have been told there have been many American casualties and the Bataan is fighting a serious fire on her flight deck."

"Surely to God, Madam President, you don't believe this was a deliberate act by Canada, do you?"

"Prime Minister, you tell me. What do I see in your country now? I see your military refusing to follow orders. I see provinces threatening to secede. I see Canadian soldiers and police officers in gun battles with each other and Canadian Indians fighting with your police. Now one of your war ships attacks an American vessel that was peacefully docked in a Canadian harbor. What I see Prime Minister is you are losing control of your nation and fast."

Dion sat up stiffly and responded. "Madam President, do not tell me how to run my country. You have enough issues in your own country right now."

Prime Minister, you don't see any of my states trying to leave right now, do you? And my warships are not firing on yours. But having

142

said all that let me tell you I just gave orders to the Marines aboard the three amphibious assault ships docked in Canada. Those orders are to immediately take control and secure the harbors in Victoria, Halifax, and St. John's. I will not have another one of my ships attacked by your navy that you clearly have no control over."

"You can't do that. Canada is a sovereign nation. You cannot simply sail into our harbors and then seize them!"

"Prime Minister, may I remind you, that our ships docked in your harbors with full permission of the Royal Canadian Navy. May I also point out that at this moment there are Canadian naval vessels currently docked at our naval bases in Norfolk, Virginia and Pearl Harbor? We have not attacked them, have we?"

Without giving Dion a chance to respond, she continued. "Seeing as you can't control your navy, just as it is plain to see you cannot control your army, I am ensuring that while our vessels are docked in Canada that they are safe. You cannot or will not do that. So my Marines will. We will not bother or put into custody any of your citizens. But those harbors and naval bases are being secured Prime Minister. And quite frankly there is nothing you can do about it."

With that she hung up. Dion threw his desk phone across the room and unleashed a string of French and English cuss words. He then picked up the handset of the phone, and seeing as he had broken it when he threw it across the room, he found his mobile phone and called Robert Lalonde. "Robert," he yelled when Lalonde answered the phone. "I just got off the phone with President Morrison. She says one of our ships attacked one of theirs in Halifax and she is having Marines seize our harbors there, St. John's and Victoria."

Lalonde was floored – he as well had yet to be alerted to the Halifax incident. "Let me make some calls," he gasped.

Lalonde called General Tremblay who was already on the phone with naval officials in Halifax. As he was speaking to both the Halifax base and Lalonde, the General suddenly heard over the phone connection with Halifax. "I am Captain Robert E. Lee Fraser of the United States Marine Corp. Hang that phone up now!"

The Canadian officer said to Tremblay. "General I have two Marines pointing M16's at me and an officer is aiming his sidearm at me. I believe I need to follow their directives sir."

With that, he hung up the phone. Tremblay took Lalonde's call and confirmed he had also heard from Canadian military officials in St. John's and Victoria. In these two harbors as well, the Marines were taking control. One point Tremblay made was. "Mr. Lalonde, I have instructed our people not to resist. I am sure this is some bizarre misunderstanding and the diplomats can get it under control. We don't need a shooting war to break out."

The bad news continued for Pierre Dion. The following morning Mohawks at the Akwesasne Reserve which spanned parts of Ontario, Quebec and New York made their move to show support for the warriors at the Mercier Bridge. A column of pickup trucks and SUVs' carrying Mohawk warriors armed with various semi and fully automatic rifles as well as numerous civilian hunting rifles and handguns, roared up to the Canadian Customs booths at the Seaway International Bridge, of the Three Nations Crossing. Warriors rushed the customs booths screaming at the Canadian border guards to drop their weapons and come out with their hands up. As this was unfolding, many people who had been waiting to enter Canada tried to turn around and return to the United States. Others simply left their vehicles and ran back towards the American side of the bridges. Hearing the chaos from the Canadian end of the bridges, New York National Guardsmen and women who been moved to the border crossings in the last couple of days moved forward onto the bridges and advanced to the mid-way point. They allowed civilians fleeing from Canada to go past them, knowing the border guards would deal with them. When they reached the midpoint of the bridges, they formed lines across the roads blocking any possible entry by the Mohawks onto the US side of the bridge.

On the Canadian side of the bridge, customs and immigrations officials were now sitting on the ground, guns pointed at them and their hands on their heads. Mohawk Ronald Burningsky looked at his captives with contempt. "You gave up without a fight. And you are supposed to be defending your country," he sneered.

He then looked at a sign indicating that people could be served in English and/or French here. He said. "So, people can be served bilingually, here can they? Tell me – which of you speaks Mohawk? C'mon who here speaks Mohawk? "

There was no answer. Burningsky turned to Anthony Tucci, the senior Canadian customs officer present. Burningsky, who by now had a very dangerous, angry look in his eyes said. "Mr. Tucci, tell me. How come you have set up operations on sovereign Mohawk land – but none of you here can speak our language?"

Tucci could feel the cold sweat of terror dripping down his back and chest. Trying desperately not to provoke anything, he commented. "Sir, I don't make the laws. Canada is legally an English-French bilingual nation. That is what we are legally required to offer services in here. I didn't make the law."

"You don't make the laws. I get it. But still, you come and work on our land, and don't bother to learn our language. I think that makes you an ignorant racist."

Tucci responded. "Please understand myself and all my people respect you. But we don't make the laws here."

"Perhaps not," Burningsky said in an eerily calm voice. "But by working here and accepting pay from the Canadian government you obviously support their racist policies. Why haven't you and your people, who make money enforcing white laws on our land, at least show the courtesy of speaking our language?

Tucci, almost panicking now as he could feel the situation spiraling out of control responded. "I am sorry, we all are. We are, and have been insensitive. We can, and will do better. Please allow us the chance to do so."

Burningsky glared at Tucci. Then he casually drew the Smith and Wesson Model 19, 44 Magnum from his shoulder holster and fired two shots into Tucci's head. The Canadian border official toppled over, his skull exploding, spraying gore over several yards. The other captured Customs and Immigration officials began screaming. Burningsky then casually shot another guard in the face all the while shouting for quiet.

As the blood flowed, on the Canadian side of the Three Nations Crossing, Lieutenant Darryl Woodward of the New York National Guard, standing on the American side of the bridge, saw the "executions" through his binoculars.

"Jesus Christ," he yelled. "Holy shit, the Mohawks have started shooting the Canadian border guards."

He radioed his commanding officer, Captain Perry Chapman.

"Sir, the Mohawks are shooting Canadian border guards. May I have permission to take my men into Canada and stop the killing?"

146

"Denied, Lieutenant," Chapman answered. "Do not enter Canada. The Canadians are going to have to sort this one out themselves. We have no beef with the Mohawks. Our job is to keep our country safe. Don't let anyone pass you on the bridge. What happens in Canada is their issue, not ours."

At the same time, an Ontario Provincial Police (OPP) Swat team backed by dozens of "regular" officers, moved in. They had been alerted to the Mohawks seizing the Customs and Immigration posts. As they moved in, their "spotters" alerted them to the killings. With that the orders were given. "Active Shooters! Engage and destroy."

The OPP snipers immediately opened fired on the visible Mohawk Warriors. As the Mohawks began dropping riddled with police bullets, Francois Legault, a 33-year-old Immigration officer leaped up and tackled Burningsky. The two men rolled around fighting ferociously. Finally, Burningsky was able to roll on top of Legault, pulled a hunting knife from his belt and slashed the Immigration officers' throat. Covered in blood that sprayed like a "geyser" from the doomed officer's throat, Burningsky leaped up only to then collapse with an OPP bullet crashing through his skull.

Mohawk Terry Alstock, a fiery 20-year-old with adrenalin and blood lust pumping through his veins, backed away as the police bullets screamed in and sprayed the captives in front of him, emptying the full magazine of his M16. The dead and wounded border guards lay in a heap in front of him. He then hit the ground with the top of his head blown off by an OPP sniper.

Other warriors sought cover and began to return fire. Many of the Mohawks had military experience and they used cover and fire to their advantage. Police SWAT teams rarely engage well trained, well-armed adversaries and now an intense gun battle was raging.

The police were at a disadvantage here as they had no experience attempting to engage an enemy while under automatic and semi-automatic gunfire. After dropping Burningsky, Alstock and another Mohawk, OPP sniper Lloyd Dean cranked the bolt of his rife to fire another round when a Mohawk bullet ripped through his throat and sent his mortally wounded body crashing to the ground.

By now, the entire area around the Canadian Customs and Immigration offices was a scene of horrific carnage. Dead and dying Mohawks and Canadian border guards covered the ground. Mohawk warriors under cover blazed away at the responding police who in turn were pouring fire into the Mohawks position.

Police rounds were also travelling across the bridge into American territory. Private Deshawn Johnson had stood up to get a better view of the fighting on the Canadian side, when a stray OPP bullet tore through his throat. The young African-American soldier writhed on the bridge in agony as medic Corporal Jessica Vanderbrant tried frantically to save his life. Her efforts were in vain though. As she battled to save his life, Lieutenant Woodward crawled over to her. "Jesus Christ, Corporal, can you save him?"

Covered in Private Johnson's blood, which sprayed over her, she looked at her commanding officer, shook her head and answered. "No, sir. The round took out his jugular. Blew it right apart. He couldn't be saved if this had happened in a hospital trauma room."

Woodward got back on the radio to his CO. "Captain, there are rounds coming into American territory and one of my men has been killed. Please let me take my troops across the bridge. We are sitting ducks here."

As he finished, a scream erupted as another American soldier was hit.

148

"Son of a bitch, sir, they hit another of my men!"

Captain Perry Chapman cursed and then snarled to another officer beside him;

"God damn it, the Pentagon said let the Canadians sort out their own mess. But now Americans in our own country are dying."

He paused and muttered to himself. "It's easier to ask for forgiveness then ask for approval. I'm not going to let my men and women get shot down like dogs and not be able to protect themselves."

He ordered a force of 5 M1 tanks forward. He then got on the radio and ordered Woodward. "Lieutenant Woodward, take your troops and advance across the bridge using the tanks as cover. As American troops have come under fire from the area, you may fire at will. Take possession of the Canadian end of the bridge and secure it. Anyone who surrenders is to be treated as a POW until I advise otherwise. Am I clear?"

"Yes, sir," the young Lieutenant answered. With that, he ordered his troops to clear a path for the tanks. As they did so, another guardsmen dropped, fatally wounded from a bullet fired from Canada. Once the tanks formed up, they began to advance across the bridge with the New York National Guardsmen and women following behind.

At the Canadian end, it was the police who first saw the American troops advancing across the bridge towards them. OPP Commander, Inspector Neil Rossiter ordered his officers to cease fire and withdraw.

"We don't need a war with the Americans, to go along with the one with the Mohawks," he said, not realizing his police had already drawn blood in the United States.

The US forces moved in fast. A few OPP rounds bounced off the steel bodies of the M1 tanks before the firing stopped. The Mohawks couldn't retreat as the OPP was behind them. They couldn't advance into the United States and they would be slaughtered if they stood and fought the US troops. They did the only thing possible and that was surrender. Lieutenant Woodward's troops disarmed the warriors, and medics began treating the wounded warriors, border guards, and police officers.

OPP officers approached the American soldiers who had entered Canada and taken control of the bullet shattered Canadian Customs and Immigration building and numerous Mohawk warriors. OPP Inspector Rossiter approached Lieutenant Darryl Woodward. Not recognizing the rank emblem on Woodward's battle tunic, the Canadian police officer began speaking very firmly. "Okay Yank. You're in Canada illegally. Get your people out of here, back to your own country. We'll take control now. Move it."

Wood ward stood there, momentarily aghast. He then snarled back. "Okay, you listen to me, you ignorant Mickey Mouse cop and you listen good. You assholes killed more than one of my men. The shots that were fired came from your direction. The Mohawks were shooting in the opposite direction – at you. Your people fired into my country and killed some of my men. My training tells me that is an act of war. So, if you want to take us on go ahead and let's do it. My people are frigging angry at their friends being killed so they would love to kick your ass. Now if you want to keep things peaceful, then drop your weapon and tell your people to drop their weapons and surrender. You fired at American forces that were in the United States. You and your people were the ones out of line.

150

What's it going to be?"

With that, Woodward aimed his M16 at Rossiter. His troops seeing that action then proceeded to aim their weapons at all visible Canadian police officers. Rossiter realizing, he was on the verge to provoking a gun battle he could not win took a step back and said. "Okay, you win. For now."

He dropped his service pistol and yelled to his officers. "Everyone drop your weapons and unbuckle your duty belts. The US Army is taking us into custody. Don't argue – just do it and do it now!"

The shocked OPP officers unbuckled their duty belts and let them drop to the ground and slowly placed their weapons beside them. National Guard soldiers quickly moved forward to gather them up, all the while aiming their own weapons at the police.

"Wise move," Woodward responded. "And let me assure you we have no intention of entering any further into Canada."

Word of the fighting and the advancement of American forces into Canada reached Ottawa and Washington at the same time. In Ottawa, Robert Lalonde got the word and rushed to Dion's office.

"Prime Minister," he began." I've been advised that at the border crossings at the Akwesasne Reserve, Mohawk Warriors have seized the Canadian ends of the two bridges and have killed several border guards. The OPP have engaged them and while in the midst of a gun battle American troops advanced across the bridge and appear to have taken control of our customs and immigration offices and have disarmed the criminal Mohawks. "

Dion exploded in French at the news. "Tabernac[xxiii] Robert!" Those ungrateful Mohawks strike us again and to add to that we now have

Americans troops in Canada? Get me the President on the phone fast."

In Washington, Henry Stillman was briefing President Morrison on the unfolding events at the Canada/US border. As he went through the briefing, she stopped him and said. "Wait a minute, Henry. First, we had a Canadian naval vessel fire on one of our ships docked in Canada and killing many of our sailors while doing so. Now you are telling me that American soldiers have been killed in the United States by Canadian police or soldiers who fired into our country?"

"Yes, Madam President, that's what I'm telling you."

"All right, Henry. I know the Pentagon has contingency plans to send troops into Canada to restore order. I want to see those plans fast. We also need to think about booking a meeting with Congressional leaders to brief them on our deployment into Canada if we go that route. And if we go that way, I will want to speak to Prime Minister McMillan. I think that was an excellent idea on your part Henry. And finally, I'll speak to that idiot in Ottawa and try and make him see some sense and cool things off."

"I'll take care of that immediately', Stillman responded.

Before he could act, a White House aide came in and announced that Prime Minister Pierre Dion of Canada was on the phone for the President.

Stillman quickly said. "Madam President, don't take the call. We have yet to decide on our response. It wouldn't be wise to engage him now."

"Thanks, Henry. But I will speak to the Prime Minister. But stay here while I speak with him."

152

She walked over to her desk, picked up the phone and engaged the line. Very coolly she answered. "Hello, Prime Minister. I was just thinking of calling you."

"Hello, Madam President," Dion responded. "The reason I'm calling is that I have been informed of an unfortunate incident at the border crossing between Cornwall, Ontario and Massena, New York. Some Mohawk criminals seized our end of the bridge and began murdering our border guards. The police responded and tried to stop the murders. There was a gun battle. I was informed some of your troops who were based at the American end of the bridge have crossed into Canada. I must insist those troops leave Canadian soil immediately and as well that you remove your Marines from our harbors. They are to return to their ships immediately."

"Prime Minister, I'm trying to control myself as I listen to you. I'm going to be totally clear. First, American soldiers who were stationed on the US side of that bridge were killed by gunfire coming from Canada during that gun battle between your police and Mohawks. Those soldiers I repeat were in the United States of America when they were killed. Your police fired into our country and Americans died as a result. That Prime Minister in most cases could be considered an act of war! Add to that, over 100 US Navy sailors and Marines were killed on the USS Bataan when your ship opened fire while we were safely docked. Safely docked in your country and may I say, supposed to be under the protection of your military. Instead, your military attacks my ship! Just what in hell are you doing there? Are you looking for a war? Let me tell you, the American people will be looking for blood when this hits the news! So, let me make something crystal clear to you. Get your country under control and do it now. Not tomorrow – now!! I will NOT lose another American because you can't control your nation. Particularly people in uniform in your nation who are supposed to be trained and trustworthy."

Dion sat stunned in his chair. Almost hyperventilating, he struggled to answer the enraged President. "Madam President, you must know that these actions that were taken that negatively impacted your country were not the actions of the Canadian government."

"You call over 100 dead Americans, counting the sailors and soldiers your people killed "negatively impacted?"

"I don't mean to be insensitive, Madam President and, I assure you that there will be a detailed investigation into these terrible occurrences. "

"You're damn right there will be. And Americans will be involved in that investigation. That is not open to debate or discussion. And those responsible will face justice in our courts and may face the death penalty. I know that may offend your sensitivities but I don't care.

'I will leave you with this. I will try and calm down the American people. But I can't do this if there is chaos on our borders. Get your country under control and do it fast. I don't care how you do it. And in particular I don't want to hear and will not accept any excuses that your military is too small. That is your issue and you have to deal with that.

'Just so we are crystal clear. If you cannot stabilize your country so that is doesn't pose a threat to my country, then I will do it for you. I will not hesitate to order the Armed Forces of the United States to restore order in your country. Am I clear?"

Dion was shaking from rage and fear in his chair. He gasped out a response. "I assure you, Madam President, Canada will do whatever it takes to restore order and that in no way are we a threat to your nation."

"Prime Minister I'm holding you to that. You better be able to back up your words. You have 12 hours to ensure that your nation is under control and that there aren't any other actions that may threaten a single American or that may be perceived as a threat. Get it done now!"

With that the phone went dead. Dion then ordered Robert Lalonde to get Defense Minister Blais and General Tremblay on the phone.

When the two men were on the phone, Dion's orders were direct. "Gentlemen, I've just received a most disturbing call from President Morrison. She's threatening to send US troops into Canada unless we, as she puts it, restore order. As we already have some American forces in Canada, which I find intolerable, I believe she will do it. What I think we need to do is a bold action that will shock the other rebellious provinces into submission. General Tremblay I am ordering you to use Joint Task Force 2 [xxiv] (JTF2) and use it to seize control of Queens Park [xxv] and arrest Premier Cassidy and his cabinet.

'Are there any questions?"

There was shocked silence for a moment before Tremblay spoke up. "I understand your orders, Prime Minister. I will ensure that they are carried out. I have several questions for you."

"Yes? What are they," Dion impatiently asked.

"First, when do you wish this to be carried out? Immediately, tomorrow, etc? Secondly, do you want it done in public so the general population sees this being carried out, or would you prefer it to be done at night when it would be more discreet?

'Finally, sir, what are your orders if the reserve units surrounding Queens Park, and the Premiers' bodyguards resist? Currently, the Queens Own Rifles regiment has surrounded the legislature and have 'dug in.' My commandos will destroy them if need be. Reservists are no match for them. But are we ready to see Canadian soldiers fighting each other?"

"We have no choice, General," Dion responded. "We need to get control of this situation immediately. When the other provinces see that we have taken control in Ontario, then they will submit to the authority of Ottawa. We already have some American forces in Canada, and I will not tolerate any more coming in. This rebellion by the provinces ends today. As for your questions;

'Carry out the operation as quickly as possible. If not tonight, tomorrow.

'Second, by all means do it in public. Let the people see that their government is taking back the country.

'To reiterate – if I wasn't clear before then I will be now. Give the reservists the opportunity to surrender. If they will not, then carry out the operation, and whatever happens, happens. You have lawful orders and you and your troops are protected. "

"Yes, sir," General Tremblay replied.

"You are dismissed, General," the Prime Minister replied. "Good luck."

The following morning, as JTF 2 began their preparations, President Katherine Morrison called the Prime Minister of the United

Kingdom, Glenn McMillan.

"Good afternoon, Prime Minister," the President greeted the British Prime Minister. "Thank you for taking my call."

"Madam President, I'm always available for you. Seems as though there is quite a bit of excitement happening on your side of the Atlantic. Is there anything I can do to help out or calm things down?"

'Thanks for asking. And do you mind if I call you Glenn and you call me Katherine? I mean I know this is an official call and all but I'd be more comfortable as we are friends."

"That's a good idea, Katherine. Now what can I do for you?"

"Glenn, I'm calling you due to the deep respect the United States has for Great Britain and our history together. I'm also calling due to our own personal friendship. As you are aware things are turning into a mess in Canada. My government is furious at the actions of Prime Minister Dion and his government. His actions of seizing American property are outrageous as is the illegal manner in which he abrogated the NAFTA treaty. Add to all that the recent killings of American service men and women by Canadian military forces and police cannot be tolerated."

"Katherine, I agree things look bad in Canada, but surely you don't believe that the recent killings of American service personnel were a deliberate act by the Canadians, do you? I simply cannot believe that Pierre Dion would order that."

"I don't believe Dion ordered it. However, I have always viewed him as a weak leader and now even more so. He's clearly lost control of his country."

"I agree, Katherine," the British Prime Minister said. "What do you suggest be done, if anything?"

"Glenn, I may have to order US forces into Canada if this continues. The American public is up in arms over the death of our troops and the turmoil in Canada is getting very close to home for us. If I do so, this will be an attempt to restore order and bring calm back to Canada. I realize that Canada is no longer a British colony but she is part of the Commonwealth. I don't need to consult you on this Glenn, but my deep respect for the history between our two nations and for the history between the UK and Canada, tells me I should consult you."

"Thank you, Katherine; I appreciate you telling me this. And I agree that you may be left with no other option. If you feel you must in fact act in this manner, please do let me know before you send in troops and I assure you that His Majesty's Government will not oppose you."

"I appreciate that, Glenn. I understand you have some troops training in Manitoba currently. Would you be willing to use them to assist us if need be?"

The British Prime Minister paused for a moment before answering. "I don't believe so. So far, no British assets have been threatened and Canada is no longer a colony of ours. If our forces in Canada are threatened, I will direct them to defend themselves. But we will not be taking any action against the Canadian government unless we are directly threatened or unless there is so request by an official body for our help."

He paused and then continued. "What I will be prepared to do is send our Ambassador, Maureen Elliott, to see Prime Minister Dion. She's level-headed and might well be able to speak some sense into him. God knows somebody has to do it."

"Thank you, Glenn, I would appreciate that. I understand your position on the use of your troops."

Shortly after the call ended, President Morrison received another disturbing call. Secretary of State Youngblood was on the phone. "Good morning, Madam President. I am afraid I've some disturbing news for you."

"Good morning, Michael. Why I am not surprised? It seems that no news is good news anymore. What's up?"

"I am sorry to bring you more bad news. Our Chargé d'affaires in Ottawa, Sean Dillon just called me. It seems Canadian opposition politician Gurminder Grewal is leading a huge protest outside of our embassy gates in Ottawa. Dillon has doubled the Marine guard inside the compound and he advised me that both the RCMP and Ottawa police are doing an effective job keeping order. But they're very loud and angry. Grewal seems to have whipped them into a frenzy."

"I've met Grewal," President Morrison grumbled. "He's an anti-American horse's ass. Is there any fear that the embassy itself is being threatened?"

"I don't believe so," Youngblood responded. "The Canadian police are very effective and they know how to deal with such matters. One question however that Mr. Dillon asked, is does he have permission to issue live ammunition to the Marine guards, just in case the crowds get out of control?"

President Morrison sat back in her chair. Never in her wildest dreams did she ever imagine she would be asked such a question regarding the American embassy in Ottawa. She answered very carefully. "Sean is a level-headed man. If he feels it is necessary, tell him to go ahead. I am not going to have another Tehran[xxvi] incident with our embassy. But for god's sake tell him to use his head. Make sure he tells the Marine guards they are not to fire unless the embassy walls and gates are breached and they feel American lives are in danger. "

"I will make that very clear, Madam President. But as you said, Sean Dillon is a very level headed, calm man. He's exactly the right man to have in that situation."

As those words were being spoken, a mob scene was erupting outside the US Embassy in Ottawa. NDP Leader Gurminder Grewal, upon learning of US forces seizing control of the three Canadian ports, and entering Canada at Akwesasne had called upon all "traditional anti-American leftists" in the Ottawa area and had whipped them into an absolute furious mob. The mob seemed to symbolize the anti-American side of the political left that has been so prominent in Canadian history and amongst many Canadian politicians and intellectuals. For the left in Canada there was almost terror in their minds as they saw the possible collapse of the traditional "Laurentian Elite" that had ruled Canada through most of its' history. With the Western provinces now rebelling against the idea that Canada should be ruled only by Central Canada, their idea of an ideal liberal/left Canada was being shattered.

Before marching on the embassy, Gurminder Grewal addressed the crowd. "My friends, for the entire history of our great nation we have always battled against being swallowed up by the United States. Now, that threat has never been so clear. Yesterday US forces fired on our naval ships in Halifax and US troops have surged across the border at Cornwall Ontario – not far from here. They must be behind the attempts of several provinces to break up our nation. This is a clear attempt to begin their takeover of our beloved nation. We need to stop them now! Follow me to the lair of the imperialist Americans here in our city and show them and the world that we will not be cowed by them! Let us stand up for Canada!"

Led by Gurminder Grewal, the mob surged against the RCMP and Ottawa riot police who were guarding the embassy. Under international law, host countries are responsible for the safety and security of the embassies in their countries and the police were determined to do their duty and protect the American embassy. As the police pushed back against the mob, rocks and bottles began pelting the officers. They quickly responded with volleys of tear gas and rubber bullets. As the crowd fell back, a young left-wing radical student from Toronto's York University by the name of Jason Brandt, who had been firing rocks and bottles at the police suddenly collapsed with a geyser of blood erupting from his skull. A police rubber bullet had blasted through his left temple, shattering his skull and destroying his brain. Another radical from York, who was friends with Brandt, Abbad Hussein looked down at his obviously dead friend and screamed. "The Americans are killing us!! Let's burn the embassy!"

Nobody in the mob could know that it was not an American who had fired the deadly rubber bullet. It was in fact a terrified young Ottawa police officer named Andrew Ruskowsky. He had simply been following orders and firing into the crowd and trying to aim below chest level. He made a deadly error.

Fired up by Hussein's screams, the mob charged as one into the police. The outnumbered police officers went down swinging riots guns and batons. As the police lines collapsed, the mob began clambering up over the walls and gates. The Marine sergeant in charge of the embassy guard detail, Henry Bernstein frantically radioed Chargé d'affaires Sean Dillon. "Mr. Dillon, the mob is coming over the walls. What are your orders?"

Sean Dillon was horrified. He had seen footage of the US Embassy being taken over in Tehran in 1979. But he never imagined the scene would be repeated in Ottawa of all places. Knowing that Canadian police and military had already fired on Americans and that relations between the Canadian and American governments were becoming hostile, he made a terrifying decision.

He radioed Sergeant Bernstein and ordered. "Sergeant, you are authorized to use deadly force on the crowds entering the embassy grounds if that situation occurs. Tell your troops to fire into the crowd and retreat and secure the embassy building. Do you understand your orders?"

Sergeant Henry Bernstein was taken aback at his orders. Then he saw seemingly hundreds of rioters pouring over the walls and dropping onto embassy property. He quickly responded. "We will retreat sir, while using deadly force to repel the mobs and secure the embassy building."

"That is correct, Sergeant," Dillon responded.

With that, Sergeant Bernstein gave the orders over the radio to his troops. "Repel the mob with deadly force and retreat to embassy building."

The Marine guards were aghast at the orders. Then, as they saw the enraged mob advance towards them, they aimed their M16 rifles and opened fire as they slowly retreated. The hail of gunfire cut down the mob. Men and women hit the ground as the 5.56mm rounds ripped through their bodies. The barrage of heavy gunfire stopped the mob in their tracks and the ones who were unwounded retreated. The Marines stopped firing and fell back to the main building. Once inside, the doors were secured and the horrified Marines prepared for what they felt may be a long siege.

Ottawa police Chief Kristen Marshall was rushing to the scene when she heard the gunfire. She immediately knew from the distinct sound of the Marines' M16's that it was not her own police officers or that of the RCMP firing. She arrived at an absolute scene of chaos. She saw bloodied protesters and police officers and the heavy scent of tear gas and gunpowder hung over the mob. The officer heading up the RCMP embassy security contingent had been felled by a bottle thrown earlier by a protester so Marshall took control. She saw the casualties lying inside the compound grounds and grabbed a megaphone. She switched it on and spoke to the Marines now barricaded in the main embassy building. "Attention to the Marines inside the embassy. This is Ottawa Police Chief Kristen Marshall. May I have your permission to enter the grounds with medical personnel to care for the wounded? They need medical help. I will not allow anyone to advance towards the buildings and we will come in unarmed. May we enter to provide medical aid?"

Sean Dillon, horrified at the carnage he could see outside asked Sergeant Burnstein for a megaphone. When it was handed to him, Dillon responded. "Chief Marshall, you may enter the grounds with medical staff only. You may treat and evacuate the wounded. I warn you though we will resume firing on anyone who is armed and who enters the grounds. Only medical first responders may enter."

Pierre Dion had received reports of the demonstrations around the American embassy. He had given orders for the police to ensure the security of the embassy grounds. And now the word came to him about the soon to be called "Ottawa massacre." Robert Lalonde burst unannounced into the Prime Minister's office. "Pierre, my God. The protesters at the US Embassy breached the walls and gates of the embassy grounds and the Marine guards in the compound opened fire on them. As of right now, first responders have not been able to treat the wounded."

Dion reeled back in his chair as if he had been shot himself. He yelled in almost agonized fury. "What in the name of God happened with the police? How did they let the protesters breech the walls;" he yelled in French.

"I don't know, Prime Minister," Lalonde responded. "I've heard our officers used tear gas and rubber bullets but something must have happened."

"Take me there, right now," Dion snarled. "Get a driver and tell my security detail where we are going."

Moments after Lalonde ran out of his office, RCMP Inspector Brent Haldeman, who headed up the Prime Minister's security detail, entered the Prime Minister's office. The veteran Mountie walked stiffly up to the prime Minister's desk and said. "Prime Minister, I'm responsible for your safety and I won't agree to you going to the scene of the embassy shooting. We still don't know all that's happening or what has happened. It's still very dangerous and we cannot have you in physical danger."

Dion cussed violently in French and then muttered. "Fine, Inspector, I understand. But this is a direct order. I want you personally to head there and figure out what's going on and how this happened and report back to me. Am I clear?"

"Yes, Prime Minister. If you don't mind I'm going to increase the security detail around you. This could be the beginning of some type of anti-government insurrection for all we know."

"That's fine, Inspector. Just get over to the American Embassy and find out what the hell is happening."

With that, Inspector Haldeman hurried out. As he left the phone on his desk rang and Dion quickly answered it. On the end was Defense Minister Blais. "Prime Minister, I am alerting you that Joint Task Force 2 is boarding their aircraft at Canadian Forces Base Petawawa and will be airborne within 15 minutes on their way to Queens Park in Toronto."

"How will the mission be carried out?" the Prime Minister asked.

"The troops are going to deploy right from their helicopters. Some will repel into the grounds and others will land on the lawns and storm the buildings. The C130's will land at Billy Bishop Airport on Toronto Island, commandeer the ferries and bring their vehicles over to the mainland and move onto Queens Park. They should be deploying within 90 minutes. The RCAF is clearing the air space around Toronto as we speak."

"Make sure it works and get this done fast."

Inspector Haldeman arrived at a scene of complete carnage at the US Embassy. Ambulances and police cars were scattered across the road and up on the sidewalks with lights flashing and sirens blaring. Armed police officers were running "helter-skelter" not sure of where and if they should be forming a perimeter. Paramedics were frantically treating wounded and dying protesters within and outside of the embassy perimeter. Haldeman was quickly briefed by Ottawa Police Chief Marshall.

"Inspector, the shooting has stopped. From what I've found out, when our officers used rubber bullets on the protesters, one hit a protester and killed him. The mob thought it was American Marines firing at them from inside the embassy grounds and in a rage stormed the grounds overwhelming our officers. Once they got into the grounds the Marines opened fire on them."

Haldeman cursed and asked. "Do you have any idea how many causalities there are? And my god, if the Marines fired from their embassy grounds – do we have any jurisdiction on charging them? What a fucking mess this is."

Marshall replied. "Inspector, those people who were shot were on the grounds of the embassy. That's sovereign American territory. It was our job to keep those protestors out and we failed. The American guards were within their rights to fire on people entering their territory illegally. Plus, those guards and everyone in that embassy have diplomatic immunity. Don't even think about charges.

That mess Brent Haldeman referred to continued to grow. In Prince Albert Saskatchewan members of the Dakota Sioux living on the Round Plain Reserve rolled across the Diefenbaker Bridge and in a repeat performance of the Mohawks at the Mercier Bridge sealed it off at both ends. Prince Albert police officers responding to the situation were quickly staring down the barrels of various automatic and semi-automatic weapons. Having seen the results of the gun battle at the Mercier Bridge between the Mohawks and SQ the Prince Albert police wisely retreated and established perimeters at both ends of the bridge, without firing any shots. The Province of Saskatchewan's main North/South highway link was now blocked off.

That news was quickly reported by the local RCMP detachment to

166

headquarters in Ottawa and from there to Robert Lalonde. Lalonde, who was rushing to the Prime Minister's Office to be with the Prime Minister when the JTF2 assault started, stopped dead in his tracks at the news. He swore and rushed into Dion's office. "Prime Minister," he began. "Things aren't getting better. The fucking Indians out in Saskatchewan have now cut the entire province in half by barricading the Diefenbaker Bridget in Prince Albert. That is the main north/south highway route."

Dion erupted. "I'm sick to death of those ungrateful savages. We give them free education, don't tax them, brought civilization to them, and whatever else and still they turn on us. What do they want us to do – simply pack up and leave? Well we are sure not doing that. Just wait until JTF2 kicks ass in Ontario and then maybe I will turn them loose on those fucking animals."

JTF2 arrived like a thunderbolt at Queens Park. Operational security had been superb and the highly trained, elite, commandos arrived without warning. One moment the area was quiet with the soldiers of the Queens Own Rifles patrolling the grounds of the Ontario legislature. The next moment, helicopters arrived overhead. Emulating the tactics used by the US Green Berets at the Son Tay raid in 1970[xxvii] the choppers slammed down on the lawn surrounding the Ontario legislature and commandos leaped out. In an effort to avoid bloodshed they immediately began firing tear gas, rubber bullets and concussion grenades (known as "flash-bangs.) As this occurred and the young reservists began falling back in confusion more choppers appeared overhead and JTF2 commandos repelled out of them landing on the roof of the legislature and immediately blasted their way inside.

It was over quickly. No group of reservists is capable of standing up to an elite team such as JTF2. Knowing this, the officers of the

Queens Own Rifles ordered their troops to hold their fire. None of them would have hesitated to give their lives and/or ordered their troops to fight to the death against a foreign invader. But this scenario was something they had never dreamed of.

In less than ten minutes, Canada's top commando team had taken control of the Ontario legislature. The arrest of the Premier was done quickly and professionally. The commandos swarmed through the legislative building and approached the Premier's office. Cassidy seeing the commotion outside and wishing to avoid bloodshed stepped out of his office and loudly ordered his body guards to lay down their weapons.

"Nobody fires", he ordered. "All of you lay down your weapons and raise your hands. Do not resist the soldiers. You cannot defeat them and all you will accomplish by trying is dying. Nobody here is required to be a martyr."

Captain Patrick Keogh of JTF2 strode towards the Ontario Premier. In one hand he carried a Heckler-Koch 9-millimeter submachine gun. His face was covered with camouflage paint and various concussion and high explosive grenades hung off his belt. He had a handgun holstered on his right hip. He stared Cassidy in the eyes and asked. "Are you Premier Keith, David Cassidy?"

Showing no fear, the Ontario Premier looked Keogh steely in the eyes and responded. "I am."

"In the name of His Majesty, I am required to inform you that you are being placed under arrest for treason," Keogh stated.

"I understand, Captain. I'll go quietly and as you heard, I've ordered there be no resistance to your troops."

Keogh, who was born and raised in Ontario and was uncomfortable with this task took the Ontario Premier by his arm and led him away.

In Washington, Henry Stillman called Dr. Tucker and requested an immediate meeting with the President, Michael Youngblood and Robert Jackson. Upon Tucker's questioning Stillman gave her a quick update from Canada. Knowing how urgent the situation was, Tucker worked with her usual efficiency and slotted the Secretary of Defense and National Security Advisor into a meeting in the Oval Office with President Morrison. On her own initiative she also added Vice President Rafferty to the meeting.

The group gathered together and Secretary of Defense Stillman began his briefing. "Ladies and gentlemen, I know we're all very busy so I will be brief. Moments ago, Canada used its elite commando team, Joint Task Force 2 to capture the Ontario Provincial Legislative building in Toronto and place Ontario Premier Keith Cassidy and his cabinet under arrest. At the same time Sioux Indians in Saskatchewan have seized a bridge in a small city called Prince Albert. This bridge is on the main north/south highway in that province, so now the province is for all purposes cut in half with highway traffic stopped."

Vice President Joel Rafferty spoke up. "Henry, was there any resistance by the reserve troops who were guarding the legislature?"

"No, Mr. Vice President, there was not. By all accounts, they quietly put their arms down. They probably realized that they had not a hope in hell of successfully resisting the commandos. "

"Thank God for that," Rafferty answered. "Do you think with this move Dion will be able to get control up there in Canada?'

"I don't," Stillman responded. "I believe it's too far gone and too many of his military forces are rebelling and add to that, the various native groups that are flexing their muscles. I think Canada as a unified nation is now in 'terminal countdown.'"

President Morrison turned to her Secretary of State and asked. "Michael, if we have to send troops into Canada, what reaction can we expect from NATO, outside of the UK and from the UN? And will we face resistance from Canadians themselves? I know you have suggested these possibilities before. What do you think now?"

Before he could answer Vice President Rafferty spoke up. "I can't believe anyone in NATO or the UN would raise a peep about us moving in seeing as we have had our forces fired upon by Canadian forces and police. Good God that would be, in my mind anyway, simply ludicrous."

Michael Youngblood began speaking. "To Joel's point, I agree. Clearly the Canadians have crossed several lines, the ultimate being firing into the US and killing several of our soldiers. The usual leftist and Arab nations will condemn us. But who cares? Nobody whose relations we value will blame us."

President Morrison then said. "Let's wait another 12 or so hours and see if Dion is successful getting control of things. But let me make one thing clear. I want to be able to move fast if things continue to spiral out of control or if there is another incident of Canadians firing on us. I don't care how minor the incident is. If a single Canadian soldier or policeman passes gas in our direction, I want our forces to move in."

After a pause she asked. "Henry, are your people ready?"

"Madam President, we're ready to move. Just give the order. Troops are ready at Fort Drum, Fort Lewis-McChord, and Fort Devers. I have moved forces from Fort Custer in Michigan up towards Detroit and have various National Guard units along the border ready to deploy into Canada once the order is given."

"Don't deploy until I give the order, Henry," the President stated. "But I think it is pretty clear that this will be happening soon. I have no faith in Dion's ability to get this under control. None at all. And by the way, Henry, good work here."

"Thank you, Madam President," the Secretary of Defense answered.

"Any thoughts on your part, Bob," the President asked Robert Jackson.

"No, outside of how we may just see our Founding Father's dream of a united North America under the Stars and Stripes coming to fruition soon."

News of the JTF2 "assault" on Queens Park rocketed across Canada. At the Mercier and Diefenbaker Bridges First Nations warriors dug in behind their barricades waiting for the assault by police or military forces they felt would soon occur. In Edmonton, Banff, and St. John's the premiers of the rebellious provinces also waited for Dion's next move.

In Ottawa, Defense Minister Blais and Public Security Minister Oscar Redstone, briefed Dion, Lalonde, and Sara Freehan. Blais began. "Ladies and gentlemen, let me bring you up to speed on the ongoing situation. As you all know JTF2 captured Queens Park and has taken Ontario Premier Cassidy and his government into custody. They are currently being held under guard at the Moss Park Armory. The rebellious Queens Own Rifles have been disarmed and are also being held under guard at Moss Park. The other rebellious premiers are still being protected by troops who are disobeying federal orders.

'I have moved some units of the Royal 22nd regiment to the Three Nations Crossing to ensure the US forces that took control of the Canadian end of the bridge don't advance any further into Canada. Other units have been deployed around the Mercier Bridge as per your request keeping that area under control.

Oscar Redstone added. "I've ordered in RCMP tactical teams into the areas around those bridges as well. They have been ordered not to interfere with military units, but to support them in any way possible.

'As a quick update, the riots in Montreal didn't really take off. The Montreal police backed by the SQ were able to get things under control without help from the military. 'Now back to you Jean-Guy."

Blais continued his briefing. "Reserve units have deployed towards the naval bases currently being occupied by US forces in Victoria, Halifax and Newfoundland. These units are still following directives from Ottawa perhaps due to the fact that they are not being asked to take action against their provincial governments. I have also deployed some reservists into Prince Albert close to the Diefenbaker Bridge where the Sioux have taken control."

Sara Freehan asked. "Do you foresee any more violence or unrest with the First Nations?"

"It's very possible," he responded. "And god help us if there is more. At the best of times we don't have enough military forces to guard every bridge, power plant, and any other crucial piece of infrastructure across the country."

Dion suggested. "Minister Blais. It would stick in my craw to do so, but could we ask the Americans for assistance if we see native

172

unrest across the country?"

"Prime Minister, we could ask, but I doubt as if they would help us. First, they are very upset at our actions directed at their oil companies and at the unfortunate, recent incidents between our forces and theirs. Second, they are not having issues with their natives. If they supported us that could lead to unrest in their own country with their natives. I don't believe they would risk that. They would have nothing to gain and much to lose."

"You're probably right," Freehan answered. "I've always thought that the ugly racial issue here in Canada is our relationship with the First Nations."

"Sara, don't start," Lalonde snarled. "They have it good here and they know it."

"Give me a break, Robert," she snapped back. "If they have it so good why are they incarcerated at a rate double or triple that of other groups in this country? And why do we worry so much about preserving French in Canada and couldn't give a rat's ass about their languages? Languages that have been here probably thousands of years before French or English?"

Dion quickly stepped in. "We're not going to debate our policies towards the First Nations at this time. The country is in grave danger and that's where our focus must be. And we need to decide what our next step will be."

That next step was a national address by Dion. Using powers available to the government to compel the TV and radio networks to grant him airtime in a time of national urgency, Pierre Dion addressed the nation first in English and then in French. His speech was also live streamed over the internet.

"My fellow Canadians," he began. "Today I speak with you at a time of great national crisis and sorrow. As you are all aware, due to international circumstances my government was forced to take extreme actions to ensure energy security for all Canadians. These actions have had the unfortunate side effect of upsetting several provincial governments who are more interested in promoting their own self-interests, and those of multi-national energy companies whose only concerns are their shareholders. My duty and that of my government is to look out for the interests of all Canadians. And we have done that with the various actions of ensuring that Canada's energy reserves are owned by Canadians and available to Canadians. It is also to ensure the rule of law is supported. And that is why I ordered Canadian forces to take control of the Ontario legislature today and place Premier Keith Cassidy and his cabinet under arrest. I will be taking the same actions against all other provincial governments and political leaders who are rebelling against the rule of law in this country. I call upon Premiers Henderson of British Columbia, Van Pelt of Alberta, Craig of Saskatchewan, McNamara of Manitoba and Mountjoy of Newfoundland to cease their resistance immediately and submit to the authority of the Federal government.

'I also call upon members of the First Nations who are engaged in violent demonstrations and occupations to immediately and without delay lay down your arms and surrender to local police authorities. If you do not follow this directive, then I will take no pleasure in doing this, but I will use my powers under the Emergencies Act and the Peace, Order and Good Government clause of the Constitution to immediately abrogate all First Nations Treaty Rights with Canada and will order the military and police to take all appropriate actions against you. Consider yourself duly warned.

'I trust that my government will not be forced to take any more such

174

extreme measures and that Canada will return to being a peaceful and united nation.

'Thank you."

Shortly after Dion's speech, as shockwaves rolled across Canada, Melissa Calhoun the Secretary of the Interior received a call in her office in Washington. On the phone was Rick Volk, the head of the Bureau of Indian Affairs. He sounded very agitated. "Madam Secretary, I've some very disturbing news for you," he began, sounding out of breath.

"Calm down, Rick, and call me Melissa. For goodness sakes, you've worked for me for over three years. You know I'm not formal."

"Thank you, Melissa. I just got off the phone with Chaska Summers, the head of AIM[xxviii] a few minutes ago."

"Ahh yes, our dear friend, Mr. Summers," Calhoun responded. "What did he have to say to you today?"

"He said that AIM is calling for all American Indians to gather their arms and go to Canada to defend their Canadian brethren. He told me as well that the National Congress of American Indians is pledging support. He also said any attack by Canadian forces against Canadian Indians will be regarded as an attack on all Indians and will be responded to appropriately."

"Jesus Christ," Calhoun whispered. "You're sure?'

"Very sure, Melissa. Chaska was very direct and he wanted me to know that while AIM has no love for the US government, currently they have no beef with us. But as he pointed out, Jay's Treaty allows Indians to freely cross the border. Mr. Summers said in his mind that border only applies to whites and Indians don't recognize it. That being the case, an attack by the Canadians on Indians in Canada will be viewed as an attack against all Indians in North America and will require an active and violent defense. He also said warriors are gathering across the country and preparing to head to Canada. Finally, he warned us not to interfere, that this is no business of the United States. "

"I'd better call the White House," Calhoun responded. "This isn't good."

Moments later, Calhoun was on the phone with Dr. Kimberly Tucker requesting an immediate audience with the President. When Tucker pressed her for details Calhoun said;

"You remember the story of Custer's Last Stand?"

"Of course I do." Tucker responded. "But what on earth does that have to do with you needing to see the President right away?"

"If we don't act fast, then we may see a repeat of Custer's Last Stand soon. Our Indians are enraged at what is happening in Canada and are heading for the border."

"Oh shit," Tucker said. "Give me a few minutes and I will get something set up. Who else do you think should be at the meeting?"

"Bob Jackson and Henry Stillman for sure. And if he is available Vice President Rafferty as well. He has always had a good relationship with our Indians and made it part of the election platform to improve relations between the government and various tribes."

As the group was gathering in Washington, George Cross, the

Leader of the Assembly of First Nations put the phone back on its cradle in his Ottawa office. He had just spoken with Chaska Summers of AIM, who had informed him that AIM was sending help to Canada. Cross shuddered momentarily. He had been appalled at Dion's speech. While never having had the bloody battles with Canadian authorities as did their American brethren, Canadian First Nations did not have a trusting relationship with Ottawa and the Provinces. Treaties were routinely violated and/or ignored. Prime Minister Pierre Trudeau had first attempted to abrogate all treaty rights back in 1969, and then had attempted to ignore aboriginal rights when he repatriated the Constitution in the early 1980's. The Canadian Constitution recognized the "founding people" of Canada to be the First Nations, English and French. But then it ignored First Nations languages in favor of recognizing only English and French as "Official Languages."

In 1990, there was a violent clash between the SQ and Mohawks at Oka, Quebec that eventually involved use of the Canadian army. New governments came to office promising a new and more respectful relationships between the Federal government and First Nations. As always that turned out to be empty words. And now there was an overt threat to the Canadian First Nations from the Prime Minister. Cross knew he had to work fast. At that time Ottawa was hosting the International Federation of Indigenous People's conference. Aboriginal/indigenous peoples from across the globe had gathered in Ottawa to discuss various issues. Also present at that conference was Princess Alexandra, daughter of the current British monarch, Edward IX. The Princess was known around the world for her support of indigenous rights and condemnation of past colonial regimes. And Cross knew her. He picked up the phone and called her directly at her hotel on her personal mobile phone. Not even Prime Minister Dion had such direct access to a member of the

177

Royal Family.

Princess Alexandra was the most dynamic member of the Royal family since the late Princess Diana. When her mobile phone went off, she was in her hotel room. She glanced at the call display and answered. "George, so good to hear from you again. To what do I owe this pleasure?"

"Thank you, Your Royal Highness, for taking my call. Did you hear Prime Minister Dion's speech today?"

"I didn't," she answered. "I take it, though, by the fact you are calling me regarding it, that there was something in the speech you find upsetting?"

"Yes, there was, Your Highness. Let me explain."

With that Cross went through and briefed the Princess on Dion's remarks to the First Nations. He finished off by saying;

"Your Highness, if Dion uses the police or troops against us, we will fight. And Chaska Summers of AIM has promised to send us support. We may be looking at a race war here. And let me remind you we signed treaties with the Crown. Not with the Canadian government, but with the British Crown. We need you to protect us and our rights and help stop this war from starting."

The Princess stood there, dumbfounded. She quickly responded. "George, hang tight. I'll call my father. Perhaps he can put pressure on Prime Minister McMillan to pressure Dion into backing down."

"I realize I'm asking a lot," Cross asked. "I mean the Royal Family isn't supposed to get involved in politics."

"We make our opinions known at opportune times," she responded.

178

"And you raise a very good point about the treaties signed between the First Nations and the Crown. I agree we have a responsibility here. Let me make a call to my father and I will be back to you."

Moments later she had her father on the phone. The King, like his daughter, was an extremely intellectual man who took his duties very seriously. He heard her out and told her. "I will call the Prime Minister immediately and see if I can encourage him to call Prime Minister Dion and help him to see some sense."

With that, the King placed a call to British Prime Minister Glenn McMillan. McMillan was working at his desk when his direct line rang. The display told him it was the King calling which in itself was very odd. McMillan had an excellent relationship with his majesty however he couldn't remember if the King had ever called him directly before.

"Good afternoon Your Majesty," McMillan answered. "To what do I owe this call?

"Good afternoon, Prime Minister. Thank you for taking my call. Do you have a few minutes to discuss a matter of great concern to myself and the entire Royal Family?"

McMillan stiffened in his chair at the monarch's words. What in the name of God was going on to cause the Royal Family "great concern", he wondered?

"Of course, Your Majesty," the Prime Minister answered. "What can I or my government help you with?"

"Thank you, Prime Minister. I need to inform you I received a distressing call from my daughter a few minutes ago. As you are aware, she is at a conference in Ottawa, Canada for aboriginal groups. She informs me that she received a call from the leader of the Canadian Assembly of First Nations, Mr. George Cross. He told her that Canadian Prime Minister Dion just gave a speech to the Canadian public and in that speech, he threatened the use of military and police forces to stop native groups who are currently protesting."

McMillan was confused. He was aware that Dion had addressed the Canadian people but wasn't aware of everything in his speech. And why that concerned the King was beyond him. Carefully he probed the monarch. "I'm not aware of all the details of Prime Minister Dion's speech, Your Majesty. I take it you're disturbed at what he said about Canadian native groups?"

"Prime Minister, you could say I am 'disturbed', as is my daughter. Let me make something clear. Those 'native groups', as you referred to them, signed treaties with the Crown. Not with the Canadian government. With the Crown. I believe the Crown has responsibilities towards those people and I do not take those responsibilities lightly, Prime Minister. I rarely involve myself in politics as you well know. But today is different. I don't have confidence in Prime Minister Dion or his government. I think his Governor General Mr. Mancino is a most unprincipled man and do not trust him. I want you to inform Mr. Dion that I'm taking a very strong interest in this and I do not support any form of military or law enforcement action against Canadian aboriginals with whom the Crown has a treaty. I want you to make that very clear."

McMillan was dumbfounded. Never had he heard of a member of the Royal Family acting in such a manner. That being said, he didn't disagree with the message he had just received.

"Your Majesty, I understand what you are saying and I will ensure

180

the Canadian government of Mr. Dion hears it loud and clear. I will immediately dispatch my High Commissioner[xxix] Maureen Elliott to see the Canadian Prime Minister forthwith. Is there anything else I need to know?"

"No, Prime Minister that is it. I appreciate your attention to this matter and quick response. Please ensure you advise me as to what response Ms. Elliott receives."

"I will, Your Majesty. Thank you for alerting my government to this concern of yours."

The next call went from Prime Minister McMillan to his Canadian ambassador. It was quick, detailed and left no room for any ambiguities. After that High Commissioner Maureen Elliott called Robert Lalonde directly. When Lalonde answered she began. "Good afternoon, Mr. Lalonde, this is High Commissioner Elliott of the United Kingdom."

"Hello, Your Excellency. How can I help you?"

"Mr. Lalonde, I must see Prime Minister Dion immediately. It's urgent."

"Madam Ambassador, as you must know we're in a crisis here and the Prime Minister is quite busy. Today is not a good day."

"Mr. Lalonde, I understand. Let me be clear. His Majesty himself has commanded that I see Prime Minister Dion today and deliver to him a message directly from His Majesty. There is no debate here. I am seeing the Prime Minister today. The question is when."

Lalonde sat at his desk stunned. What in hell could be so important that the British government, on behalf of the King, insisted on seeing the Prime Minister that day? He answered carefully. "May I ask what this is in regard to? Knowing that may give me a better opportunity to schedule a meeting."

"Mr. Lalonde, all I am permitted to say is that I have a grave concern from His Majesty himself to bring to the attention of Prime Minister Dion. Please set the meeting up. I will make myself available at whatever time you can find."

"Let me see what I can do. How long do you need?"

"No more than 30 minutes, Mr. Lalonde. And thank you."

"I will call you back within an hour with a time."

The call was disconnected and Lalonde called Dion. He explained the unusual persistence of the British High Commissioner and her insistence that the King had directed her to speak with Dion.   Dion shook his head and said. "This is crazy. What possible reason would the King have to speak with us now? What could be so important? And why should I care?"

"I don't know what the reason is Pierre but he is the head of state. Like it or not we are not a republic. I think you have to see her and hear why the King is concerned about."

"Fine. Book her in and make sure you're present at the meeting as well."

Two hours later, High Commissioner Maureen Elliott of the United Kingdom entered the Prime Minister's office on Parliament Hill. As she was directed to a seat by Robert Lalonde, she stared across the table at Dion, and to her surprise, Oscar Redstone.

"Your Excellency, nice to see you again. I know you know Mr.

Lalonde, and I believe you have met Oscar Redstone, my Public Security Minister," Dion began.

"I have, Prime Minister, but I'm not aware of why your Public Security Minister is at this meeting," Elliott replied.

Dion answered. "Your Excellency, I'm sure you are aware that Stephanie Howatt, my Minister of External Affairs resigned. She wasn't able to agree with the actions of my government. I have asked Oscar to temporarily fill in for her until I can name a replacement."

"I was aware that Stephanie had resigned, which is why I called Robert to arrange this meeting. But that's fine. Mr. Redstone, I wish you well in your new temporary role."

"Thank you, Your Excellency," the Public Security and now Acting External Affairs Minister replied.

"Let's get down to business, shall we?" Lalonde said. "We are all very busy and it wasn't easy fitting this meeting in. So, Your Excellency if you would like to begin, we're all ears."

"Thank you, Mr. Lalonde," Maureen Elliot began. "I do appreciate all of you seeing me on such short notice. I'll be as brief and concise as possible. His Majesty has commanded me to inform you that he looks upon your statement in which you threaten to, and I paraphrase here, abrogate all treaties with the various First Nations and take military and police action against them, with the gravest of concern. He believes those treaties were signed in good faith with the Crown, and that the Crown has a duty to defend and uphold them. He wishes to convey that to you."

There was a moment of shocked silence. Dion clearly furious spoke first. "Your Excellency, you may inform the King that, with all due respect, since the Statue of Westminster of 1931 [xxx], Canada has been a free nation and has not been subject to the whims of shall I say, the British Parliament. As well, since 1947 or so, the Crown's powers have been transferred to the Canadian Governor General.

'And while I appreciate His Majesty's concerns, please tell him they are being dealt with by the proper Canadian authorities. And we would appreciate it if he would, as we sometimes put it, butt-out!

'As Mr. Lalonde has already indicated, we are extremely busy and I have no time to deal with the hurt feelings of His Majesty or anyone else in the Royal Family who want to try and intrude into Canadian internal matters. Good day, Your Excellency. Mr. Lalonde will show you out."

With that, Dion got up and indicated to Robert Lalonde to show her out of his office. Maureen Elliot's face was stiff with anger. She stood up and said;

"I can find my own way out, thank you very much. Good day gentlemen."

After she left, Dion erupted. "The nerve of her to show up here and expect this government to care about what the fucking King thinks! Who does he think he is that he feels he can influence how we run our country?"

"Well, Prime Minister," Oscar Redstone offered. "He is the legal Head of State for Canada. I mean it's mainly ceremonial but legally he is."

"Fuck him and his family, anyway," Dion raged. "I tell you the big mistake Pierre Trudeau made when he repatriated the constitution in the early 80's was not turning Canada into a republic. How we are

184

still under the sway of that family of inbred idiots is beyond me."

As she returned to the British Embassy, Maureen Elliott took stock of her meeting. To say she was aghast would be an understatement. The Royal Family rarely intruded into public affairs. However, when they did raise a concern or express an opinion it was listened to with great respect and usually acted upon quickly. For Dion to simply disregard the Monarch's concerns was unheard of and without precedent.

When High Commissioner Elliott returned to the British embassy, she quickly called Prime Minister McMillan and briefed him on her meeting with Dion. When she finished, McMillan was appalled. "Good lord, Maureen, he actually told you to tell His Majesty to "butt-out?"

"Yes, he did, Prime Minister. Never have I experienced such disrespect for the monarchy. That Dion is a most unprincipled man."

"I agree," McMillan responded. "I sure don't look forward to His Majesty's response when I tell him about your meeting. However, I suppose that is why I am in this job. Thank you, Maureen, I'll call the Palace right away and let him know. I'll get back to you with his response."

Back in Ottawa, Denise McLean headed to Rideau Hall for a meeting with Governor General Mancino. This was a "Hail Mary" attempt on her part. Canada doesn't have the legislated "checks and balances" that the American form of government has. What Canada does have, is the monarchy which in itself is a "check and balance." In the event of a Prime Minister using his/her powers in a non-democratic fashion, the monarch, represented in Canada by the Governor General, does have the constitutional authority to disallow legislation or even to remove a Prime Minister from office. It has been rarely used and at no time in Canadian history has a Governor General removed a sitting Prime Minister. But McLean was going to try and convince Mancino to use those powers and remove Dion from office. She knew it was a long-shot as the friendship between Mancino and Dion was very well known. However, Denise McLean truly believed that it was her duty as a Canadian to try.

When she arrived, Mancino kept her waiting for close to an hour. She felt that in itself was rather ominous. When she was finally ushered into the Governor General's office, she was surprised that Mancino was not even there yet. Five minutes later he arrived and sat down at his desk.

"So, Ms. McLean what can I do for you," he asked. "I was told that you urgently needed to see me."

"Your Excellency, I won't take up much of your time. I do appreciate you seeing me. I have come on behalf of Canadians to plead to you to use your Royal Authority to remove Prime Minister Dion from office. You are the final check and balance on a government that is a danger to the people. Please Your Excellency you must act while there is still a Canada to save."

"Ms. McLean, are you serious? Tell me what has the Prime Minister done that is illegal in your eyes?"

"Your Excellency, his actions under the Emergencies Act are outrageous. We have half the provinces in the country trying to separate, our indigenous peoples are taking up arms, our military units are in open revolt…"

The Governor General quickly cut her off. "Ms. McLean, it is my opinion that everything the Prime Minister has done is well within the legal authority of his powers. I understand your concerns however the issues you speak about are more due to various groups taking illegal actions against the lawful authority of the government. I would suggest to you that you use your efforts to convince the rebellious groups to accept the authority of the federal government and follow the law!"

"Please, Your Excellency, Canada is burning and only you can put out the fire," McLean exclaimed. "You're the only hope for democracy in our nation."

"Ms. McLean, what you're asking me isn't about saving democracy. What you're actually asking me is to remove the democratically elected leader of our nation with no legal or constitutional basis. There is a term for that, which you may have come across in your career as a politician. It's called treason, Ms. McLean! I'm going to do you a huge favor and pretend this meeting did not occur. I suggest you leave now."

Denise McLean gathered up her belongings and walked briskly out of Rideau Hall. She hadn't expected to get far with the Prime Minister's buddy; however, she didn't expect that Mancino would be so hostile either. She got back in her limo and ordered her driver to take her back to her official residence, Stornoway. [xxxi] When she arrived, she placed a call to Karen Van Pelt. After the JTF 2 assault on Queens Park, she had held a conference call with the remaining "rebellious premiers." On that call it was agreed she would approach the Governor General in a last-ditch attempt to "calm the waters" and avoid possible civil war. Now she had to advise that her attempt had been a disaster. "I'm sorry, Karen," McLean said. 'Maybe I wasn't the right person to approach Mancino."

"It's okay, Denise," Van Pelt responded. "We all know Mancino and Dion are buddies and neither would ever turn on the other. Jesus

Christ himself could have descended from the heavens into Rideau Hall and made the same request you did. And he would have ended up with the same result."

"What do we do now?" McLean asked.

"Let's set up another call with the group and put our heads together. Whatever we do we'll have to move quickly as I am sure Dion has further plans to take us down."

Dion was in a rage after getting off the phone with Governor General Mancino.

"Robert," he screamed to Lalonde in French. "That traitorous bitch McLean went to Rocco and pleaded with him to use his Royal Prerogative and remove me from office. I knew that NDP bastard Grewal couldn't be trusted but I did trust her to at least do the right thing."

Robert Lalonde tried to calm down the enraged Prime Minister. "Pierre, calm down. This was just a normal political ploy. My goodness how many times in our lifetime have we heard various opposition leaders use non-confidence votes and such. Sure going directly to the Governor General is an escalation. But it is simply politics. Remember everything we are doing is legal. And we are trying to save our Canada.

'Pierre, you must keep this in mind. Most people in Canada live east of Manitoba. I know I keep saying that but we must remember that. Our actions are in the best interests of the majority of Canadians."

As always, Lalonde was the voice of reason in Pierre Dion's life. He gradually calmed down and said in an angry tone. "I may just have the bitch arrested under the Emergencies Act. Maybe if she spent

188

some quality time in a jail with no access to a lawyer as we can do with our emergency powers, she may just remember who is in charge."

"A tempting thought," Lalonde responded. "But I wouldn't recommend it. It would look politically motivated. Let her do what she wants. Once we have control of the country again the people will see what we did was for the best and she and Grewal will pay the price next time we go to the polls."

"You're right. I believe our next move is to send JTF2 out west. We need to get control of those provinces. We sent a huge message to everyone when we took back control of Ontario. I think it's time we moved on the west, starting with Alberta. I believe if we capture Van Pelt and her government, the others will collapse and surrender to us."

In London, Glenn McMillan decided that it would be better to meet the monarch in person. During the drive to Buckingham Palace he reflected on his relationship with the King, Edward IX. The King was an extremely intelligent man, asked very good, and at times difficult, questions during his daily briefings where he was kept up to date on serious issues in the United Kingdom. He was also a very private man, and pushed back hard against media intrusions into his family life. McMillan couldn't really say that he "knew" the King well on a personal level. However, he admired and respected the King's devotion to the United Kingdom and its' people and subjects.

Edward IX, while always remaining "above politics" genuinely liked Glenn McMillan. There had been some previous British and other Commonwealth Prime Ministers that he didn't respect or care for. But he admired McMillan's work ethic and very high sense of duty and honor.

Upon arrival at Buckingham Palace McMillan was ushered into the meeting room where King Edward awaited him. The British Prime Minister sat down and said. "Your Majesty, thank you for seeing me on such short notice."

"Not at all, Prime Minister. I am always available for you. I take it you have some news for me regarding the meeting between High Commissioner Elliott and the Canadian Prime Minister?"

"I do, Your Majesty. I'm afraid it didn't go well. Ms. Elliott reports Prime Minister Dion was offended at your interest in the plight of Canadian indigenous peoples and, well there is no polite way to put this. But he said you should 'butt-out.' That is an exact quote."

The British King was shocked. In his entire time on the throne (and even in his earlier days as a prince) nobody had ever spoken to him or about him in that manner to his knowledge. His emerald green eyes blazed in fury. He then spoke in a clearly angered but controlled fashion.;

"I see, Prime Minister. I must say I'm upset he would take offense to my interest in my subjects! I'm not at all pleased with the actions I see him taking in Canada. In fact, I find them disturbing. What are your thoughts on the subject?"

"Your Majesty, like you I am disturbed. I must advise I've been in discussions with the American President. She's drafting plans to militarily intercede in Canada to restore order if necessary. She reached out to me to ascertain if we had objections to such actions and if we would assist. I thanked her for advising me but I did say that we would not assist in such an undertaking. On the other hand, we'd not oppose it either. I believe Canada could possibly be on the verge of a bloody civil war. And that US intervention may be the only way to avoid that."

190

The King asked. "May I ask why you declined to assist the Americans?"

Glenn McMillan was surprised at the question. He had almost "by reflex" declined to assist President Morrison out of concern that such intervention would be condemned around the world as a desire for Great Britain to return to its imperial/colonial days.

He replied. "Your Majesty, I believe such actions on our part would be viewed, especially by Third World nations, as rather imperialist on our part. Perhaps even many people here in Great Britain may view it the same way. "

"I see," the King replied. It was obvious to McMillan that in the manner in which the King had answered him that he wasn't in agreement with his Prime Minister.

King Edward then began speaking in more detail. "I agree from all appearances Canada is headed towards a nasty civil war. I also believe that we have a responsibility to try and assist in order to avoid that possibility.

'Now, I have a question for you. I have had my staff looking into what actions I can take to assist. I understand that, in 1947, King George VI signed the Letters Patent[xxxii] that transferred most Royal powers from the Monarchy to the Canadian Governor General. That being said I still have the power to revoke that letter and remove the Canadian Governor General and then the Canadian Prime Minister from office."

"Well, Your Majesty," McMillan responded. "I have never looked into that possibility as to be honest I never even considered that we would need to. But for now, I assume you are correct. Are you considering that action?"

191

"I'm considering it. I take my duties seriously. I have always considered the Crown to be the final check and balance on an anti-democratic or out of control government."

"I agree with your sentiment, Your Majesty."

"I'm glad you agree. That being said, I don't believe it would be proper for me to act in this manner without some form of request to do so from Canada. Do you agree?"

"I do, Your Majesty. Don't be too surprised if you do get such a request. As you are aware, we still have excellent intelligence in Canada. There is little that goes on in the Canadian government that we don't know about quickly. I'm sure President Morrison could say the same. My intelligence sources tell me the Canadian Opposition Leader Denise McLean has made an appeal to Governor General Mancino to remove Prime Minister Dion from power that was turned down immediately by Mancino."

"Mancino is quite unprincipled," the King grumbled. "In fact, he is nothing short of a common thug."

"I've only met the man once," McMillan responded. "I must say I'd not care to have him in my home for dinner. I don't like him at all and don't trust him."

"Prime Minister, please do the following. I want you to call the President of the United States and see if she has decided on interceding in Canada with troops. If she is going to do so, it's my wish we assist in some manner."

"So, you want to use British troops in support of the Americans in Canada," Prime Minister McMillan asked.

"That is correct," the King answered. "I want to send a very strong message that the Crown takes its treaty obligations with Canadian native peoples very seriously."

"That can be done, Your Majesty," McMillan replied. "In fact, we have troops training in Manitoba right now. I will need to speak with the Minister of Defense Christine Symington. I'll get her thoughts on how quickly those forces can deploy and where and be back to you. I will also have to brief Parliament fairly soon after our troops are deployed."

"Very well, Prime Minister, thank you for your time and good luck."

Once McMillan had left, King Edward reflected on the upcoming course of action. Some could argue that he had stepped into the realm of politics with his directive to Prime Minister McMillan. On the other hand, the King thought others would agree that what he had done was exactly what the role of the Monarch was supposed to be. That is to be a check and balance on a non-democratic government, which is how he viewed the actions of the Dion government now. He firmly believed that his action were democratic and legally sound.

As dawn came to Canada the following day, JTF 2 began final preparations for their next mission which would be an attempt to capture Premier Karen Van Pelt of Alberta and whatever other rebellious premiers were with her. The rebellious premiers were on a conference call scattered across various parts of Canada.

Premier Van Pelt began the call. "Ladies and gentlemen thank you for your time. I know for some us including myself, it isn't even dawn yet. But we need to speak quickly and frankly about our next steps as my sources tell me that Dion will be sending JTF 2 west and soon. Maybe even today. What are our next steps?"

Speaking from Banff, Alberta Neil Craig spoke up. "I think we publicly condemn Dion's actions and ask the United Nations for assistance. Perhaps they could send in peacekeepers."

Heidi McNamara who was with Karen Van Pelt in Edmonton responded. "Neil, I agree with the first part but disagree about the UN. They are useless. By the time the General Assembly and Security Council met and made a decision JTF 2 would have swept across Canada capturing us. Our only real option here is to ask the Americans for help. We know President Morrison and Dion don't get along and that the US has moved forces close to Canada. Morrison would be more apt to help us. They could move in far quicker than could the UN."

"I don't disagree that the Americans could move in far quicker than could the UN, Heidi but what if after they do so, they don't wish to leave," Carla Henderson asked.

"I believe that is a chance we have to take," McNamara answered. "But let me suggest that if they decided on staying, being part of the United States may well be preferable to remaining in a union dominated by one party and one province as Canada has historically been."

There was quiet on the phone line for a moment after that comment.

Premier Max Mountjoy then spoke up. "This may go over like a lead balloon but I've thought Newfoundland may well have been better off as part of the American union then the Canadian one. Hell, we had a long history of American military personnel being posted here. There were US Air Force bases here from WWII until the mid-1990's. Let me propose something even stronger here. Why don't we appeal for US troops to protect us and at the same time ask for admittance into the American union?"

194

There was excited chatter on the phone for a minute or so, led by Carla Henderson who was shocked by the notion. Karen Van Pelt got the call back under control and spoke. "Don't be too quick to discount what Max suggested. Think about this. Some of us here like Alberta and Carla you in BC and Neil you in Saskatchewan have to prop up provinces like Quebec with equalization payments. We have to support them – and yet we get very little say in how the Federal government works. Ottawa bends over backwards for Central Canada and especially Quebec. They are happy to take our money, oil and natural gas but not so happy as to make us true partners in the union. If we went to the Americans, I have no doubt they would accept us. They would love to have our natural resources and especially our oil and natural gas. I see no reason why they would turn us down."

Carla Henderson responded. "Look, I'm not Anti-American like so many Canadians. But the US has some serious issues that I am not so sure the people of British Columbia want to become part of. I'm thinking of gun crime, racial issues, income inequality, lack of medical care, just to name a few."

Heidi McNamara spoke up. "Carla, it's my understanding that each state controls the medical system. There is no federal law that makes it illegal for an individual state to adopt the same health care system as we have. We could simply join the American union and keep our health care intact. As individual states we would also have the authority to pass our own criminal laws and could have very strict gun control."

Neil Craig added. "Heidi is correct, Carla. But these are also all things that we would negotiate. I don't believe we have a lot of choice here. I say we go with Max's idea."

Karen Van Pelt responded. "We're heading towards a civil war. The only way out of it as I see is exactly what Max suggested. It isn't a perfect solution. I believe Alberta and indeed all of us would be better off in a nation that isn't dominated by a single province and a single political party obsessed with that one provinces' place in Canada. "

Carla Henderson then said. "I won't say no. But I will say I don't have the right to make such a monumental decision that would affect every person in B.C. I will reserve the right to think about this and try to make up my mind. And even if I agree I will insist that the question of being admitted into the United States will be put to a binding referendum in B.C."

Heidi McNamara spoke up. "Carla, that's a great idea. We can reach out to President Morrison and ask for protection by American troops and then negotiate terms to enter the United States. A condition of any province entering the US would be contingent on an affirmative referendum vote."

Henderson responded. "Look, everyone, let's sit on this for a day or so. Please this is so big. I need some time to really think about this. Canada has tried to be separate from the US for over 200 years. We can't simply do a 180 degree turn in a single phone conversation."

Neil Craig answered. "Carla, while I'm not against the idea of appealing to the Americans I do agree. Let's all agree to reconvene over the phone tomorrow at this same time. Let's use this time to really think about this."

After the call Carla Henderson called her father. Jack Henderson was a legendary former Canadian politician. After a stellar business career, he had entered federal politics, being elected as a Member of Parliament in a Vancouver riding. He later was named to Cabinet serving as Finance Minister, before resigning, returning home to British Columbia and being elected Premier. He served three successful terms as BC Premier before retiring. He always said his proudest moment was seeing his daughter Carla move into the same Premier's office where he had worked.

Carla Henderson had graduated with a Bachelor of Commerce degree from the University of British Columbia. She worked for ten years in the private sector, before following her father into politics. She had risen through the provincial Liberal party starting as a Member of the Provincial Parliament (MPP), then several cabinet roles, then party leader and finally Premier. She was considered a more "approachable" version of Karen Van Pelt. She had the same high intellect as the Alberta Premier but a far warmer personality. Carla Henderson was a lesbian and had been married to her partner Michelle for over 12 years.

Jack Henderson answered the phone in his Victoria BC home. "Hello, my beautiful daughter! It seems you're are involved in some interesting and troubling times."

"Hello, Dad. You can say that again. Do you have time to talk?"

"Of course, I do. How can I help you?"

Carla Henderson then went on to explain to her father the JTF2 "strike" at Toronto's Queens Park, and the gist of the conversation between the rebellious premiers. And most importantly the idea of reaching out to the United States for assistance and admittance to the American union.

"Dad, you've sat in my chair before. What would you do?"

Jack Henderson sat quietly. He was astounded and horrified by current events; in particular, the Federal governments military actions against the Ontario government. But now the news of approaching the US left him speechless for a moment.

He sat quietly and then responded. "Carla, part of me has always thought this day may come. We have worked hard in Canada to build a nation and in many ways, we did a great job. We are a kind, compassionate country that has struck a good balance between capitalism and government action and intervention. But the errors we have made are many. I saw this when I was in Ottawa and in your job. We built an imperfect union dominated by two provinces and unable to respond to the changing nature of the country. The Maritimes were given far more seats in both the House of Commons and Senate then their population would warrant. Ontario and Quebec have far more seats in the Senate than they deserve and to add to the oddness Ontario has less House of Commons seats then it deserves. Parliament was never really designed to change, based on changes in population across the country. Sit back as I give you a brief history lesson."

Carla smiled. Her father loved to discuss history and could never resist when he had a "captive audience."

"Go ahead, Dad."

"In 1974, the Trudeau government passed new legislation called the Representation Act, related to how the House of Commons would be elected. First, they confirmed that Quebec would be used as the basis for the calculations. Notice, my dear, once again this focus on one province. Then Quebec was guaranteed 75 seats. What if for example in 150 years Quebec's population had dropped significantly so that it didn't warrant 75 seats? It wouldn't matter. In that way the Canada of 150 years from now would be bound to the

Canada of 1974. Is this just? Is this right for the country as a whole?

'At the same time the legislation ensured no province could ever lose seats. No matter how small a region could become due to population changes it could never lose seats. Is that right I ask?"

"No, Dad, it doesn't sound like it to me," Carla responded.

The elder Henderson continued. "In the early 1980's when we created our new constitution nothing was done to correct this imbalance. The Western Premiers failed terribly to push the issue. I have always believed that if Peter Lougheed [xxxiii] had pushed the matter strongly with Prime Minister Trudeau we could have actually had a House of Commons elected through "true" Representation by Population and a 'Triple E Senate' [xxxiv] . However, I don't believe Mr. Lougheed wanted to push things, figuring the Maritimes and Quebec would balk at losing so much influence. It's too bad we didn't have a show- down then over this. It may have saved us from the situation we are finding ourselves in now.

'Anyway, we're in a bad spot. Pierre Dion is no friend of BC's or the west nor is his party. He is your typical easterner in the Liberal Party. Their world revolves around Quebec in particular and to a lesser extent Ontario and the Maritimes. That isn't going to change."

"Then what should we do, Dad," Carla asked. "What would you do?"

"Well looks like you have several options.

You can remove yourself from the group of Premiers that wish to leave and stay with Canada. That would leave you though geographically isolated and still dominated by the East.

You could try and take BC out of Confederation as a new, independent nation on its' own. I don't have to tell you how tough that would be. Creating your own currency, global trade agreements, an entire military, diplomatic relations, etc. It would be awfully hard.

Or stick with the group and approach the United States. The US may say no. We Canadians are always so worried that the Americans may take us over. If I were an American politician, I'd be thrilled at getting our natural resources but very cautious as the entire political balance in the United States will be upset. All of a sudden you may be getting millions of new citizens who demand public healthcare, maternity leave, among other things. I don't know what they will say.

'But if I were you, I think that last option is the safest for the people of British Columbia. BC may be able to join the largest democracy in the history of mankind. God knows the US has its issues. There are things about it I don't like. But there are many strong points there as well that we could learn from. And as I said, I believe it's the safest option."

"Thanks Dad," Carla Henderson responded. "You have given me much to think about."

Later that evening, she spoke on the phone with her wife Michelle and relayed what she discussed with her father. Michelle Henderson (she had taken Carla's name) was no dummy. She was a Canadian History professor at the University of Victoria and on a daily basis spoke to her students about Canada's efforts to build and maintain a nation. She listened carefully and said. "Hon, you were elected to take care of the best interests of the people of BC. What choice do you have now? Your dad is right, it isn't reasonable to stay in

Canada if the other Western Provinces have left. And we don't have the population to be a successful nation on our own. As much as it will hurt our pride, we are better off staying with Karen, Neil, Heidi, and Max and hopefully Keith and joining the US. If they will have us."

Carla Henderson smiled ruefully and said. "I guess it is decided, isn't it?"

The following day the "rebellious Premiers" reconvened over the phone. Carla Henderson began the conversation. "Okay everyone. I've thought about this idea of asking for admittance to the United States. I'm not happy about it but after some real soul-searching I don't believe we have any other realistic options available to us. So, I am in but only on the condition that if the US will agree to have us our people have the final say in a binding referendum."

Karen Van Pelt answered. "We agree, Carla. The people will have the final say on the future. We won't follow the example Pierre Trudeau set in 1981-82 and bring in a constitution with only the approval of Parliament and various Provincial governments. I'm comfortable opening the door to discussions with the United States on joining them; however, we will make it clear to all of our citizens that they will have the final say."

After more animated discussion, the question of how to brief their cabinets and caucuses on the idea of approaching the United States and asking to be admitted as states, while they were "in hiding" from the Federal government became first and foremost. The general consensus was the briefings would need to be done via conference calls however it must be done quickly. Delays could mean being captured by troops acting under orders from Prime Minister Dion, and thus disaster.

Max Mountjoy raised the next question. "How exactly do we go about doing this? I'm afraid I've never contacted another country to inquire about being admitted into it along with my province. And what about Keith in Ontario? He was joining us and now he is being held prisoner by Dion."

Neil Craig suggested. "I believe we need to agree on a spokesperson. I think it should be Karen. She's the most prominent Premier in the country and Alberta is the wealthiest province. Much of that is due to her and her government. People will take her more seriously than anyone else. If we agree on that, and if Karen herself agrees, then I think she should contact Secretary of State Michael Youngblood. I believe the process would begin with the State Department. At the same time, I'm sure Mr. Youngblood can ensure our request for military protection is directed to the correct people at the Pentagon and the President herself.

'As for Keith, I think we proceed in the same manner as if Keith was present on this call and had agreed with us. We know Ontario was joining us in our quest to leave Canada. Knowing Keith, I believe he would approve of our actions in asking the Americans for help and to join them. Again, let's remember that there will be a referendum where the people can give us their opinion on our actions. They will have the final say, not us."

After more conversation and debate, it was agreed that Karen Van Pelt would act as the spokesperson for the premiers and would initiate contact with the United States through Secretary of State Youngblood. It was also agreed that even though they didn't have approval from their caucuses to proceed with the request to join the United States, it was agreed to make that request at the same time as the request for military assistance. They all agreed they could "get the ball rolling" knowing their citizens would have the final say and could always stop the process.

That event happened very quickly after the premiers ended their call. Michael Youngblood was in his office at the State Department when the call came through. In his mind he wasn't shocked by it as with things "spiraling out of control in Canada he had thought there may be a request for American help. However, this would be a moment he would never forget. His chief aid Kathy Racey came into his office and said. "Excuse me, Mr. Secretary; Premier Karen Van Pelt of Alberta is on the phone requesting to speak with you regarding a matter of great urgency."

"Really? Okay, put her through and stay with me while I take her call. I'll put it on speaker. Please take notes. I have a feeling this may be a momentous occasion."

Once Ms. Racey had taken a seat the call came through. "Premier Van Pelt, this is Michael Youngblood. My aide, Kathy Racey, is also with me. What can we do for you?"

"Thank you for taking my call Mr. Secretary, I know you must be quite busy."

"We don't get too many quiet days here at Foggy Bottom,"[xxxv]Youngblood answered with a laugh.

Van Pelt smiled at Youngblood's humor. She had met the American Secretary of State the previous year when he had visited the oil fields near Fort McMurray, Alberta and found him to be a man of great intellect, with a fine sense of humor.

"I'll get to the point, Mr. Secretary," Van Pelt responded. "I know you are aware of the crisis ongoing in Canada due to the outrageous actions of Prime Minister Pierre Dion."

"Of course, we've been following it very closely," Youngblood answered. "The President and I are most concerned."

"Well, Mr. Secretary, I've been selected to be spokesperson for the premiers of British Columbia, my own Province of Alberta, Saskatchewan, Manitoba, and Newfoundland. I cannot speak for Ontario as Premier Cassidy has been arrested as I am sure you are aware.

'I have been empowered to do is to reach out to you and ask first and foremost for protection by the United States military from Canadian Federal authorities and in particular the Canadian military. Second we wish to begin negotiations with the United States to discuss the admittance of our provinces into the American union."

After a brief silence Youngblood answered. "Well, Premier Van Pelt, I must admit this isn't the type of call I receive on a regular basis. Are you quite sure about this?"

"We're very sure, Mr. Secretary. And we realize there will be a process to be followed before we could possibly join the union. But please, we are most anxious about receiving American military protection as quickly as possible. There is a real possibility of a civil war here in Canada and we believe the only way to prevent this is for your military to intervene."

"I understand, Premier," Youngblood answered. "Obviously we do not wish to see major civil unrest on our northern border. But we must also be careful not to be seen as interfering in the internal workings of Canada either. Would you be willing to make your request for American assistance in writing and in that request document your plans to request admittance to the American union? I would say unofficially that if you did so, both of your requests would be viewed very sympathetically by the current

204

administration."

Karen Van Pelt had anticipated such a response and quickly answered;

"Mr. Secretary, I was sure you would ask for that. I have a document ready to send you. I'd appreciate a swift response, respecting obviously that you have your own processes to follow."

"Premier, if you can send that document to me forthwith, I assure you I will contact the President as soon as I have it in my hands."

He gave her his State Department secure fax number. Moments after the call disconnected the document came through. He quickly called White House Chief of Staff, Dr. Kimberly Tucker, and informed her that he urgently needed to see the President along with Secretary of Defense Stillman and National Security Advisor Jackson. Knowing Michael Youngblood would never waste the President's time Dr. Tucker found room in the Presidents' calendar; 90 minutes later Youngblood was in the Oval Office with the President, Henry Stillman, Robert Jackson and Dr. Tucker.

President Morrison began the meeting. "Okay Michael, Kimberly told me this is most urgent. You have our attention."

"Thank you everyone for dropping everything and seeing me. I just received this communication from Alberta Premier Karen Van Pelt. It is signed by her, and the premiers of British Columbia, Saskatchewan, Manitoba, and Newfoundland. It reads;

To the Secretary of State of the United States of America;

We, the Premiers of the current Canadian Provinces of British Columbia, Alberta, Saskatchewan, Manitoba and Newfoundland respectfully request military intervention by your nation into Canada. In particular to avoid a civil war and the resulting loss of human life, we request the immediate deployment of American military forces into our before mentioned provinces and the Province of Ontario which was most recently the target of military action by the Canadian Federal government.

'   *We also request that the Congress of the United States of America consider admitting our provinces and that of Ontario into the American union as new States.*

"Well, then, this isn't something we regularly receive, is it?" Katherine Morrison stated. "What do we all think? And can we act on this request from Provincial Premiers as opposed to the head of government which is Dion?"

Henry Stillman spoke up immediately. "Canada is coming apart and we need to act. Legally, can we respond to their request? Maybe or maybe not. But remember that while this may be irregular, we have supported many groups in the past around the world that were seeking freedom from their government. So there is historical precedent for us to do so. However, as I said, things are coming apart there fast, we don't have time for a long debate. Now give me the word and I'll have our forces rolling within the hour. I also took the liberty of putting the 82nd Airborne at Fort Bragg, North Carolina, and the 101st Airborne at Fort Campbell, Kentucky on higher states of alert. The plans have been developed and the code name for the operation is 'Operation Northern Freedom.' I have placed General Jack Reynolds in overall command of our forces. You probably all remember him. He received the nickname 'Buzz saw' from the media when he led our intervention into El Salvador two years ago, and accomplished the mission in half the time we had predicted. There is no better man for the job. He has assured me that our troops can be ready to move very quickly."

"Does anyone disagree with Henry?" President Morrison asked.

"Henry is right," Robert Jackson stated. "If we don't intercede, we're going to see a bloody civil war up there. We will have major disorder on our border and we have already seen some of that slip into our nation. I say send in the troops. Just as our troops begin their movement into Canada, I think we need to bring the Canadian ambassador in and brief her on our intentions and let her know what the consequences will be if there is resistance to them."

"And what will those consequences be, Bob?" Dr. Tucker asked.

"I'll answer that," Henry Stillman responded. "Our troops will be authorized to defend themselves. We will, I am sure, make it clear this is not an invasion. We are coming into Canada to restore peace and order. However, if we are attacked, we will respond in kind."

"I agree," President Morrison added. "Michael, get hold of Ambassador Russo and set up a meeting with yourself, myself and her. And do it quickly.

'Henry, you're authorized to begin operations in Canada. I'll send you formal orders shortly, as soon as I get them drawn up. I want American forces to enter Canada, stop any actions by Canadian forces directed against the governments and peoples of the provinces we have discussed. I know it's a huge country but make sure all 10 Provinces and three Territories are occupied. I don't want our troops in one province being attacked by Canadian forces from another. Let's get this situation in Canada under control. I want to ensure that Native Communities are protected. Make sure there will be no actions taken against them by Canadian police or military.

'Are there any questions so far?"

Robert Jackson asked. "I have one. What in hell are we going to do with Prime Minister Dion when or if our forces capture him? "

Michael Youngblood answered. "We'll take him into custody and he'll be treated correctly. We should then consult with Prime Minister McMillan and see if the King has any thoughts on the matter. After all the King is Head of State in Canada."

Henry Stillman added. "Michael is correct. I am tasking Delta Team xxxvi with capturing Parliament Hill and Dion, along with the Canadian Governor General. They are our best troops and the best chance we have at taking control in Ottawa peacefully."

President Morrison looked around the room and asked. "Are there any other questions? If not, let's get moving. I want to see the Canadian ambassador quickly. Henry, let me know when the first troops cross the Canadian frontier. I need to speak to Prime Minister Glenn McMillan in London and let him know what we are doing. And finally, I need to address the nation. Get hold of the networks and tell them I have a major announcement to make. Get them here asap."

Within 15 minutes, President Morrison was speaking with British Prime Minister Glenn McMillan via secure telephone. Morrison outlined to McMillan what she had ordered the American military to do. When she finished the British Prime Minister replied. I'm very sorry to hear about this, Katherine, but I understand and support you. I don't believe you have any other choice. I should tell you His Majesty has also informed me that that it's his wish that the British forces training at Canadian Forces Base Shiloh in Manitoba should support your efforts. I just spoke with my Defense Minister Christine Symington and advised her to contact Henry Stillman. I doubt that has been done yet as I just finished with Ms. Symington less than an hour ago."

"Henry didn't mention any conversation with your Defense Minister, so I agree they have yet to speak. I really appreciate your help Glenn and we will let Henry and Minister Symington work out the details of how your forces can assist ours. Now you will forgive me as I must run. I am about to brief the Canadian ambassador as to your actions."

"Very well, Katherine. I suppose I'd better meet with the Canadian High Commissioner and let her know that my government will be cooperating with yours."

Less than an hour after the conversation with Prime Minister McMillan, Canadian Ambassador Maria Russo was ushered into the Oval Office. With her, were Michael Youngblood and Dr. Tucker. After very brief pleasantries President Morrison got to the point. "Ambassador Russo, I appreciate you coming on such short notice. I'll get right to the point. The State Department has received a formal request for military intervention and protection by the governments of British Columbia, Alberta, Saskatchewan, Manitoba and Newfoundland. As well these same provinces have formally requested to be admitted into the union of the United States of America. My government has decided to agree to the request of military protection and as such I have ordered the Armed Forces of the United States to enter Canada and restore order and to protect these provinces until their applications for admittance to our union has been dealt with by Congress. American forces will also enter Ontario, Quebec, New Brunswick, Nova Scotia, Prince Edward Island and the three territories, to ensure law and order remain in place and that there are no threats to American troops in the other provinces."

Ambassador Russo was astonished. Never in her life did she ever imagine she would be in a meeting in which a foreign government would inform her that they were for all intents and purposes invading Canada! Trying to contain her anger, she said. "Madam President, I'm well aware we have some challenges in Canada but these are internal matters that are the responsibility of our own government to deal with. You have no right to interfere in our internal affairs."

'Wrong, Ambassador," President Morrison thundered. "Myself and my government and the American people have been very patient waiting for the Canadian government to get its' act in order. And what have we seen? We've seen American sailors and Marines murdered by your navy in Halifax. We've seen American soldiers who were in the United States, for god's sake murdered by your police whose shots came into my country and killed my soldiers! We have seen your government steal American property! And still I waited for you to show that you could get things under control. But no more! You have provinces in open revolt, your natives who I may remind you are also Americans as per Jay's Treaty, in rebellion and my citizens are furious.

'Let me be 100% clear. My troops are coming into Canada. There will be no resistance and if there is, they will take whatever action they need to, in order to protect themselves. You would be wise to tell your government to stand down."

There are few if any organizations able to communicate with the speed that the Pentagon is able to do so in times of crisis. Minutes after Defense Secretary Stillman had left the Oval Office orders to the US forces massing near Canada and the two Airborne divisions at Fort Bragg and Fort Campbell had gone out;

210

"Execute Operation Northern Freedom immediately. This is not a drill."

As soon as the order was received, US forces for the first time since the War of 1812 began their movement to the Canadian border. The 10th Mountain Division based at Fort Drum in upstate New York moved with lightning speed. Units made up of armored vehicles including M1 tanks rumbled across the Ivy Lee Bridge as Canadian border guards stood in shock. These armored units then swung both east and west along Highway 401 heading towards Toronto, Ottawa and Montreal. Troops in Blackhawk helicopters supported by Apache helicopter gunships seized control of the RCAF base at Trenton Ontario, and the city of Kingston Ontario, including the Royal Military College based there[xxxvii].

US military cyber warfare units took over the radio and television signals from Canada and began broadcasting the following message on a repeating loop;

"To all Canadians; Under orders from the President of the United States, and upon the request of some Canadian Premiers, United States military forces are entering Canada. We come in peace. We are here to restore order and peace. Remain calm and do not resist and no harm will come to you. Again, we come in peace and will not harm you. More instructions will follow later."

With their car radios broadcasting that message all along the eastern portions of Highway 401, Canadians pulled over at the sight of convoys of American military vehicles carrying heavily armed soldiers rumbling along the freeway. Kingston, Ontario resident Heather Evans told the Kingston Whig Standard newspaper;

"My God, it was something like 'War of the Worlds! All of a sudden, we see these convoys of huge trucks and armored vehicles with the

American white star on them and soldiers openly carrying guns riding in them. It was terrifying. We are being invaded!"

The Canadian and American militaries have a long history of cooperating in the mutual defense of North America. To try and ensure there would be little or no blood shed, many senior American military officials quietly gave a "heads up" to their Canadian counterparts of the impending US "invasion" and warnings not to resist. Most Canadian officers were shocked at their allies' movement into Canada and stood down as no orders were received from Ottawa and they knew resistance was suicidal.

In the air above Canada, US Air Force fighter planes roamed the skies. Radio messages and directives had gone out to RCAF bases at Bagotville, Quebec, Trenton, Ontario, and Cold Lake, Alberta ordering Canadian fighters to remain on the ground or be considered hostile. As an ominous show of force, 18 massive B52 bombers thundered into the air across Canada and simply circled, reminding Canadian authorities of how much destructive firepower could be delivered upon the nation if there was resistance. And with the B52's came the terrifying threat of the possible use of the B2 Stealth bombers if Canada resisted and B52's were not enough.

JTF2 was at Canadian Forces Base, Petawawa when 2 B52's began to ominously "orbit" the massive military base. Along with the B52's were escorting F15 Strike Eagles. Already the elite Canadian commando team had heard over the communications net that US forces were rolling into Canada. Major General Peter O'Reilly, the commanding officer of JTF2 looked up at the orbiting "angels of death" and swore. "We're trapped. We can't get off the ground and if we tried, those boys up there would blow us to bits."

With that, he was alerted to an incoming message from American

General Jack Reynolds.

"This is General O'Reilly," the Canadian officer answered.

"Hello, General, you're speaking to General Jack Reynolds, United States Army. I'm reaching out to you directly, General O'Reilly, in the hope they we can spare a lot of lives tonight. I'm sure you've have looked overhead and see what is circling your base."

"I can see what you're speaking of, General," O'Reilly carefully answered.

"That's good. General O'Reilly, I had the pleasure of working with JTF2 in Afghanistan. Your boys are really good. I know that. But let me tell you, I have six companies of the 101 Airborne Division coming straight towards you. They are backed by Apache gunships as well as what the Air Force has flying over your head right now. So, I am advising you now to surrender. Put down your weapons and don't resist us. If you fight us you will hurt us. Like I said I know how good you are. But we are just as good and are packing way more firepower. You can't win this battle, General. And you owe it to your troops not to throw their lives away."

General Peter O'Reilly had proven his courage fighting in the dusty hills of Afghanistan. And he knew General Reynolds was 100% correct. His troops would put up a fight, and a damn good one. And they would be annihilated in return. This was a battle that could only end one way. He quietly responded. "General Reynolds my troops will not resist you. When your helicopters arrive tell them to land and we will great them peacefully. Just treat my soldiers correctly."

"You're an officer and a gentleman General O'Reilly. Your men will be taken care of properly. I guarantee it."

As this was occurring, the Western Premiers and Max Mountjoy took to the airwaves urging the various reserve units that had supported them along with the police to lay down their weapons and not to resist. Across the Prairies, Army and National Guard units from Minnesota, North Dakota, Montana and Idaho rolled into Canada. They quickly moved along the highways and began taking control of various towns.

Green Beret units moved by helicopter to the sites in Banff and Edmonton where the western premiers were "holed up". In Edmonton, US Army Major Donald Kennedy landed at the grounds of the Alberta legislature with a unit of Green Berets. Above them were four Apache helicopter gunships circling the area waiting to pour destruction on any force that would resist them. Major Kennedy was ushered into the office where Premiers Van Pelt and McNamara were. He snapped to attention and saluted them and said. "Madam Premiers, I am ordered to tell you the President of the United States has agreed to your request of military protection. American units are moving through Canada restoring order and will protect you."

There were similar such "meetings" in Banff and in St. John, Newfoundland. The reserve units that had mobilized to protect their Premiers offered no resistance to the Green Berets.

In other parts of Canada, Green Berets and Navy Seals (Sea Air Land) roaring in by helicopter captured the airports in Toronto, Montreal and Vancouver.

In Toronto, a unit of Navy Seal commandos had moved across Lake Ontario via helicopter from Buffalo and stormed the Moss Park Armory freeing Premier Cassidy and his cabinet.

The 82nd Airborne Division in a spectacular operation seized the

RCAF base at Bagotville, Quebec. This mission however was not without bloodshed. Unlike other military units that were "frozen" waiting for orders from Ottawa that would not arrive, the RCAF security forces guarding the air base were always on alert. Thus, they put up a short but furious battle leaving 67 Canadian, and 54 American personnel dead, (the majority of the American dead came when two Black Hawk helicopters carrying a total of 30 crew and combat troops were shot down by RCAF security forces) and over150 wounded. Along with the human casualties was the destruction of the control tower and 14 CF 18 Hornet fighter jets destroyed in the fighting on the ground.

At Cheyenne Mountain, Colorado at the NORAD defense headquarters, Canadian military personnel on duty were quietly and politely asked to move away from their posts and then placed under guard in their quarters. The NORAD secondary command post at North Bay, Ontario was quickly taken control of by another contingent of Green Berets. Elsewhere in Southern Ontario, Canadian residents were awed to see US military vehicles rumbling across bridges into Fort Erie, Niagara Falls, Queenston and Windsor. In the Canadian border towns, people stared silently as the endless stream of American military vehicles drove past. More American troops poured through the Detroit/Winsor tunnel and along with the forces that had come across the Ambassador Bridge quickly seized control of Canada's "Motor City."

On Huron Church Road in Windsor, which links with the Ambassador Bridge, spanning the Detroit River, Windsor Star photographer Jeanne Manchester snapped a picture that would go on to nominate her for a Pulitzer Prize that year. The photo was of a retired middle-aged Canadian Afghanistan war veteran by the name of Steven McLeod, who had put his army uniform on for the first time in over ten years and stood on the sidewalk watching the

215

endless line of American troops rolling into Canada. As he watched, he slowly waved a Canadian flag and his body was wracked by sobs. He was devastated at the sight of the country he bled for in Afghanistan ending. The picture would appear on the front page of the Windsor Star and other papers across Canada.

There was a brief flurry of violence in Hamilton, Ontario. As US Army units rolled into this industrial city, less than 60 miles from Buffalo, Hamilton resident Horace Ivey decided to make "a last stand." A long time alcoholic with a pathological hatred of the United States, Ivey had been working on a case of Molson Canadian beer supplemented by shots of Bushmills Irish whiskey, all the while grumbling and cursing the Americans. When he heard the rumble of American vehicles along Main Street East, he took out his Weatherby Vanguard Series 2, 308 caliber deer rifle. As the first Humvee with troops riding on it rumbled by his home, Ivey sighted in on Sergeant Gail McLintock who was riding outside and put a bullet through her left eye, blowing her clean off the vehicle. She was killed instantly. He then put two rounds into Private Quadarius Jones's chest. The private's body armor stopped the rounds; however, he was still catapulted off the vehicle, slamming into the road.

Private Jose Aguilar screamed "we are under fire" and then swung the 50-caliber machine gun around and fired over 300 rounds into Ivey's home. Over 30 of the rounds ripped into Ivey as they blasted through his windows and walls, shredding his body in the process. More troops dismounted as the convoy stopped and they surrounded the house, firing their rifles, while tossing grenades into it. The little home exploded into flames. A harsh lesson had just been sent and received. Resist and you will die.

In Ottawa, there was chaos. At first Defense Minister Blais and

216

Public Security Minister Redstone began receiving calls from Canadian border posts reporting US military personnel "crashing through" barriers and taking Canadian border guards prisoner. The calls received were mostly brief. From the Peace Bridge in Fort Erie, Ontario across the Niagara River from Buffalo, New York, personnel at Public Security headquarters in Ottawa received a panicked call from a Canadian border guard. "Sir, I have American Marines who have taken control of the Canadian end of the Peace Bridge approaching my booth and I now see US tanks and other vehicles coming across the bridge and entering Canada. What do we do?"

With that, the phone went dead and the Canadian guard, looking down the barrel of a M16 rifle came out of his customs booth with his hands up. It was the same story across the US-Canada frontier. Canadian border guards are not cowards. But nor are they equipped or trained to repel a military invasion.

As American forces began their relentless march into Canada, President Katherine Morrison began an address to American and Canadian citizens.

"To the people of Canada and the United States. Today, I made a very difficult decision. The most difficult decision I have ever made as President. Today, I ordered American military forces into Canada. At this same moment British military forces who were training at the Canadian military base in Shiloh, Manitoba are coordinating with American forces to support our efforts. I have been informed that the British Prime Minister will be giving a press conference shortly to explain their decision.

'My decision to use American military forces in Canada was made upon the request of the Premiers of five Canadian provinces. These provinces are; British Columbia, Alberta, Saskatchewan, Manitoba and Newfoundland. In this request they asked for American protection for what they feel is illegal actions by the government of Prime Minister Pierre Dion. This decision was also brought about in part due to the actions of some, not all, Canadian military and police personnel who have attacked innocent American service men and women. In one particular incident, innocent American soldiers were shot dead by Canadian police officers, while our troops were within the boundaries of the United States. No country can tolerate actions such as these.

'To add to this, we have grown steadily concerned at Prime Minister Dion's rhetoric as it has been directed at Native Canadians and their communities. I remind everyone that under Jay's Treaty, Canadian born natives with at least 50% aboriginal blood are entitled to live and work in the United States. In other words, they are indirectly American citizens and thus entitled to protection by the United States military.

'I want to make clear to the people of Canada. American forces are not entering your country as invaders or conquerors. They are entering at the request of some Canadian provincial governments, to restore law and order. How long they remain depends on circumstances and how quickly peace can be restored. I ask all Canadians to treat the American military personnel that they encounter with respect. I assure you all American military personnel will respect all Canadians, and their property. They are here to protect you, not to subjugate you. Any Canadian who feels they have been treated improperly by any member of the Armed Forces of the United States need only report it to any American military officer and I assure you it will be investigated thoroughly.

'As far as how people should live their lives during this time. My directives to you are clear. Go to work, go to school, and live your lives as you normally would. American military forces will not interfere with that. You should simply go about your lives as usual and in peace.

'Thank you."

As she spoke, British forces based in Manitoba, working in coordination with American military forces, moved into Winnipeg taking control of the legislature and the police headquarters as well as forming security perimeters around nearby native reservations. British Defense Secretary Christine Symington had worked out details with Henry Stillman in a call that began right after the conversation between President Morrison and Prime Minister McMillan. The two of them had a long, warm working relationship that had developed over the years through their work with NATO, and various other joint defense initiatives.

"Hello, Henry, this is Christine Symington calling from London. I trust you are well in this rather exciting time."

"Thank you for calling, Christine. And yes, it is exciting. I understand we're going to be working together on an operation in Canada."

"Yes, we are. We currently have the 7th Infantry Brigade training at a Canadian base in Shiloh, Manitoba. About 5,000 combat troops in total. In fact, I believe there are more British troops in that part of Canada than Canadian troops. A sad reflection of the terrible neglect of their armed forces since the late 1960's. Our forces there are equipped with Apache and Wildcat helicopters so they are mobile. I can deploy them quickly.

'One thing we must ensure, though," she went on. "We cannot allow a situation where British and American forces accidently meet. We don't want any friendly fire incidents. I don't want a situation like what happened in World War II when German and Soviet forces who had invaded Poland in 1939, slammed into each other starting a massive battle, causing huge casualties on both sides. That would be disastrous. I believe it would be best if we have the troops on the ground there coordinate their actions and movements to avoid such a situation."

"I agree, Christine," Henry Stillman said.

There was further discussion with an agreement that the commanding officer of the 7th Infantry Brigade would coordinate directly with the US command center at the Pentagon to plan how and where British forces would deploy.

In London, Prime Minister McMillan had a short, stormy meeting with Canadian High Commissioner Michelle Sweitzer. He went through the King's concerns over Dion's threats to the native groups in Canada and the British decision to cooperate with the American militaries' move into Canada.

High Commissioner Sweitzer was flabbergasted. She had just received reports of American troops entering Canada and was already reeling from that. She viewed the British Prime Minister's news as a "stab in the back" to Canada.

"Prime Minister," she began. "Words cannot begin to describe how utterly appalling I find your words to be. This is an utter betrayal of your oldest ally. Canadians joined Great Britain in the World Wars and we were always loyal. And now you turn on us?"

"Commissioner Sweitzer, I hate to say this, but since the Middle East war that lead to the current oil crisis, the actions of Mr. Dion's government have not been particularly friendly towards your traditional allies. And let me remind you, your natives have signed treaties with the Crown. We must honor them."

Sweitzer snapped. "May I remind you, Prime Minister, that in Canada the Crown is represented by the Governor General? The King is Head of State; but his power has been delegated to the Governor General. I've not heard that the Governor General agrees with your actions."

"I believe this meeting is over, Ms. Sweitzer," the Prime Minister responded. "You will be shown out. Good day."

In Ottawa, there was complete pandemonium. As soon as the US forces began their move into Canada Defense Minister Blais and Public Security Minister Redstone had alerted the Prime Minister's Office. Pierre Dion exploded at Robert Lalonde, who as usual was with the Prime Minister. "Robert, what in God's name is happening? Are we being invaded?"

Lalonde's mind was racing. He quickly said in French. "We need to get Blais in here and find out what exactly is going on and what the military can do to help us."

Minutes later an obviously harried Jean-Guy Blais hurried into the Prime Minister's office. He spoke quickly also in French. "Gentlemen, we are being invaded. I'm getting reports across Canada of American military forces crossing the frontier into our nation. I've lost contact with our personnel across the country and NORAD bases in Cheyenne Mountain, Colorado and North Bay. I've heard brief garbled reports of a firefight between our security forces at RCAF base Bagotville and invading US forces. I also heard from our base at Shiloh that the British forces training there have taken control and disarmed our troops on the base. There are reports from the RCMP that British military units in armored vehicles appear to be heading towards Winnipeg and other communities. We are certainly being invaded gentlemen. I must advise you we cannot hold out for long."

"We will fight them," Dion bellowed.

"With what," Public Security Minister Oscar Redstone retorted as he walked into the room. "We always assumed the Americans would protect us. So, we cut our forces so drastically that there is no way we can defend Prince Edward Island let alone the rest of our country. Now the Americans have turned on us. May God have mercy on us. We're screwed."

Dion glared at Redstone in absolute rage. He then snarled. "Oscar, get out of here. You're fired. I have no need of you or your anti-Canadian attitude."

With that, the Prime Minister's RCMP security detail deployed by the door escorted Redstone out of the office. As they did so a roar of helicopters became deafening and the building containing the Prime Minister's Office began shaking.

Dion, wild eyed, now yelled. "What's that?"

Before Blais or Lalonde could answer, the sound of helicopter blades filled the air. Then the windows in the Office of the Prime Minister and Privy Council Building began shaking from the thunder and vibrations of the helicopters and the crash of gunfire. Then came the booms of "flash bang" concussion grenades and those windows then blew in. Across Parliament Hill more gunfire and explosions erupted. Delta Team had arrived, roaring into Ottawa in massive Black Hawk helicopters with Apache helicopter gunships in support. They were in for their toughest test. Delta

Team had proven their fighting capability against poorly trained, suicidal terrorists and third world militaries around the world. But the tough, well trained Royal Canadian Regiment (RCR) troops surrounding Parliament Hill were anything but that. Days earlier, they had been reinforced by the 3rd Battalion – Canada's only paratrooper unit. As Delta Team swept in the soldiers of the RCR opened fire. Delta Team operatives repelling out of their choppers were cut down by automatic weapons fire. Some of the Delta troopers were able to blow in windows with flash bangs only to be torn to pieces from heavy gunfire by RCMP SWAT team members who had deployed as part of the security detachment for Prime Minister Dion.

One Black Hawk helicopter loaded with commandos was struck by a Stinger missile fired by a RCR paratrooper, and exploded into flames, smashing into the Peace Tower on Parliament Hill bringing that Canadian historical landmark crashing down in a blazing inferno. As that fireball spread, another fully loaded Black Hawk and then an Apache chopper were brought down by Stingers.

By now, any hope of a peaceful mission had ended. Delta Team commander Colonel Patrick O'Connor ordered the Apaches to open fire in support of his commandos. The Apaches laid down a destructive fire with their M230 chain guns, and Hellfire missiles ripping apart defensive positions and shredding any Canadian soldier caught in their horrific paths of fiery death.

Dion's security detachment rushed into his office and Inspector Caroline Carter grabbed Dion screaming. "Sir, we have to go now."

She began physically dragging and pulling him out of the room. As she did the main window blew in and two Delta Troopers rappelled into the room. Carter had her Glock handgun already out and immediately pumped six rounds into the chest of one trooper. Although his body armor absorbed the impact of the 9mm rounds, the force of the bullets slamming into him knocked him back out the window and to his death below. The second trooper riddled Carter with his H&K submachine gun, instantly killing her. As she collapsed in death, she pulled the Prime Minister to the floor. Two RCMP SWAT team members came through the door and blowing away the surviving Delta trooper, grabbed Dion dragging him out of the office.

As Parliament Hill turned into a cauldron of fire and death, Colonel O'Connor turned to his second in command Major Robert Hays and muttered. "Those Canadians are some tough bastards. Thank God, there aren't many of them and that their equipment sucks. Otherwise, we'd really have our hands full."

As bravely as the Canadians fought, the numerical and technical superiority of the American Delta Team and their air support could not be resisted for long. The Delta troopers swarmed in past the burning RCR positions, past the dead Canadians and began entering the burning Parliament buildings. Surviving RCR soldiers backed by RCMP officers and SWAT members fought bravely as they retreated into the shattered Prime Minister and Privy Council building but were steadily cut to pieces by the Delta soldiers now enraged at the huge casualties they had suffered.

In the upper floors, Dion, Robert Lalonde and Jean-Guy Blais huddled with the RCMP SWAT and Security Detail members protecting them. The sound of gunfire and exploding missiles echoed through the walls. In the lower floors, they could hear the screams of the wounded, the orders bellowed by officers and curses of the soldiers and police officers as they fought to the death. And always the sound of bullets hammering into human flesh and walls.

224

And that sound was getting closer. Inspector Peter Albert the commander of the RCMP SWAT detachment said urgently to Dion. "Prime Minister, we can't evacuate you safely. The Americans have the building surrounded and we could never get a vehicle or helicopter in to get you. You have two choices. We can surrender or we can fight and die. But you have to decide now. The Americans are getting closer. A lot of people are dying as we speak."

"Can't you get a helicopter here to rescue the Prime Minister." Robert Lalonde asked.

"No, we can't. As soon as the fighting here started, I got word that American forces have captured the airport here and at RCAF Base Trenton," Minister Blais responded. "There are no choppers to be found."

As Albert was speaking to the Prime Minister, Colonel O'Connor decided on a new tactic. Delta was involved in its toughest ever battle and were taking casualties at a rate never seen before. They were giving as good as they were taking but O'Connor wanted to stop the slaughter. Over the radio he ordered his troops to cease fire. As the Delta troopers stopped their fire the Canadians followed. O'Connor then got on the radio to Canadian General Andre Fortier, commanding officer of the Royal Canadian Regiment.

"General Fortier, I'm requesting a cease fire and wish to discuss terms for you and your brave troops. May I come out safely and speak with you?"

Andre Fortier was one of the Canadian Army's rising stars. A native of Rimouski, Quebec and graduate of the Royal Military College St. Jean, Fortier had risen steadily through the ranks. He was well respected by his troops for being a tough but fair officer who believed in sharing his troop's hardships. When they were in the

225

field, he was with them as well living in the same conditions and eating the same food. He had fought a superb battle here against Delta Team but he knew it couldn't go much longer.

"Affirmative, Colonel O'Connor. You may approach with a white flag. You and your aides will not be harmed."

O'Connor's aide, Lieutenant Jeremy Kreiger, fashioned a white flag, and he and Colonel O'Connor, while waving it, walked towards the shattered Prime Minister's Office and Privy Council Building. Bullet riddled corpses of US and Canadian soldiers and police littered the ground everywhere they looked. Canadian General Andre Fortier, the commander of the Royal Canadian Regiment came out of his defensive position and met Colonel O'Connor. O'Connor saluted the Canadian general and said. "General Fortier, my compliments on a well fought battle. Your troops are magnificent. That being said, you realize you cannot win this battle, don't you? The 101st Airborne Division captured the Ottawa airport and I got a battalion of those troopers on the way here. The only thing you will accomplish by continuing to fight is just killing people."

Fortier looked around at the hellish scene around him. He knew O'Connor was right. There was no chance that any reinforcements would be coming and even if he kept fighting all it would do was buy some time for Prime Minister Dion to try and escape. And it would also cost numerous precious lives. Fortier and his troops were willing to die for Canada. But he didn't see any sense is throwing away lives in a useless cause.

"Colonel, what are your terms," Fortier asked.

"Your troops will be taken into custody for now and treated honorably. We will ensure the wounded get the same medical care

226

that my troops will get. They won't be treated badly, General. We are after all supposed to be allies. Hell, I believe we still are. We sure didn't pick this fight with you nor did your troops with us. Once the politicians sort this cluster-fuck out, I'm pretty sure your troops will be released and be able to go home."

Fortier could see in O'Connor eyes that the American officer meant what he was saying. Fortier turned his back momentarily to think. He looked at the wreckage of battle surrounding him. Burning Canadian LAV III armored personnel carriers, blazing American helicopters that had been shot out of the air, and American and Canadian dead littering the ground. Medics worked frantically on the screaming wounded trying desperately to save them. He then turned back to General O'Connor and said. "General, normally I would need to check with my superiors but I don't know if they are even alive now. Nor do I know how to reach them. I accept your terms. Let me return to my command post and send the order to my troops and tell them to put down their arms. May I suggest a permanent cease fire take effect in 60 minutes?"

"That sounds acceptable General," O'Connor replied. "But let's be 100% clear. The temporary cease fire will be in effect for the next 60 minutes and then a permanent cease fire will take effect. During the temporary cease fire, I will have my medical personnel work with yours to care for the wounded. When the permanent one takes effect, my troops will advance and disarm your troops, and take control of Parliament Hill. Are you in agreement?"

The Canadian General looked sadly at his American counterpart and replied. "That is affirmative, General. And please remember to take care of my troops."

"Absolutely, General Fortier. You can be very proud of your troops.

They fought magnificently."

With that, both officers strode away. Fortier returned to his command post and alerted his forces that a permanent cease fire would be in effect in 60 minutes and the temporary cease fire would continue until then. He also ordered his medical corp. to cooperate with the American medical personnel. On the US side, General O'Connor gave similar orders with the difference being his men were ordered to advance in 60 minutes and disarm the Canadian forces.

Within the bullet riddled Prime Ministers and Privy Council Office Building, the Prime Minister, Lalonde, and Blais huddled with the RCMP SWAT team. They heard the guns go quiet and Inspector Albert got on his radio and was shortly afterwards patched into the RCR's command post. Albert was alerted to the cease fire and the decision of General Fortier to surrender. When Albert informed the Prime Minister, Dion erupted. "That fucking coward! How dare he simply roll over and play dead? Strip him of his command and have him arrested for treason!"

Blais lost his own self-control at Dion's rant. He laid into the Prime Minister. "Prime Minister, how dare you! General Fortier has been a brave and dedicated officer all his professional life. And from the sound of all the firing it is clear to me that his troops fought very bravely. I am appalled at you."

Inspector Albert interrupted. "Excuse me, but what are your orders" he asked staring at the Prime Minister. "We can't simply stay here. The building is burning and all of our lives are in danger."

"Get me out of here," hissed Dion.

"Sir, we can't," Albert snapped back. "I don't know how many more

228

times I can say it or how much clearer I can be. We have two choices. Stay in this building and die as it is burning. Or we surrender with our troops. Those are the only options."

Dion simply sat there, with a wild look in his eyes unable to give a directive. Blais then took over.

"Give me your radio, Inspector," he said. He then got on the air and reached General Fortier at the RCR command post. "General, this is Minister Blais. With me is the Prime Minister, Mr. Lalonde and an RCMP Security Detail. We are coming out of the Prime Minister's Office building on the east side. Please send an escort there to bring us to your command post. We will surrender with your troops."

Dion exploded. "How dare you, Blais! You are not authorized to give such orders. You're fired!"

Sergeant-Major Christine Fobert, Inspector Albert's second in command with the SWAT detachment had enough of Dion and snarled. "Are you fucking going to fire everyone", she yelled. "When the hell are you ever going to show some leadership? We have brave women and men dying to protect you and you couldn't lead a pack of winos to a liquor store! You disgust me and everyone here."

"That's enough, Sergeant-Major" Albert quickly interceded. "You're out of line here big time, l will deal with you once we are out of here and hostilities cease. Until then keep your mouth shut and do your job."

Fobert glared at Albert and then back at the Prime Minister and then moved back to her defensive flanking position in the formation the SWAT team had set up. Slowly, amidst the rising heat and smoke from the fire the SWAT team and their "VIP's" moved through the building. When they reached the exit, they shoved it open and two SWAT members burst out in a crouch and panned the area with their submachine guns. Captain Richard Thornton of the RCR had come forward with an escort to lead them to the RCR command post and he bellowed. "Stand down, troopers! We are from RCR command post at the request of your commander. We have been ordered to escort you all there."

The RCMP SWAT members lowered their weapons and with the military rushed Dion, Lalonde and Blais to the command post. Once there Dion implored to General Fortier. "General, please get me out of here. Surely there is a way to get a helicopter into here and use that to get me out of this area."

General Andre Fortier looked at his Prime Minister with a look that was a combination of contempt and disgust. He responded in an icy tone. "Prime Minister, it's impossible to get a helicopter into this area. And even if it was not, I don't know where we would get one. The United States Air Force controls the air and all nearby military bases are under American control now. As the leader of the country Sir, I would think you would want to share your troop's dangers as they march into captivity very shortly."

Dion didn't respond. He simply stared blankly at the ground. Robert Lalonde "shook off" some of the shock he was feeling and stood up and faced Fortier. "Thank you, General. You're correct. We'll be honored to stand with you and your gallant troops when the American forces come to capture us. And the story of your epic and courageous stand here on Parliament Hill will never be forgotten by Canadians."

Moments later, US troops showed up at the command post. Colonel

230

Patrick O'Connor led the American forces in. He walked towards General Fortier, stood at attention, and snapped a sharp salute. Fortier returned his salute and then handed over his personal sidearm and said. "Colonel, you're an honorable and brave opponent. I surrender my troops to you and ask that you treat them fairly and honorably. As well, the Prime Minister of Canada is here and we expect that he will be treated with the correct diplomatic respect."

O'Connor looked startled. He wasn't aware that Dion was in the command post but he recovered quickly. He walked over to the Canadian Prime Minister, stood to attention and saluted and said. "Prime Minister, what an honor to meet you. I'm Colonel Patrick O'Connor, United States Army. Let me congratulate you on the superb performance of General Fortier and his troops. You can be very proud of them. I'll ensure the White House and State Department are aware you are now under our protection. And please know you and all of your aides and troops here are quite safe. We will protect you and ensure to your well-being."

Prime Minister Dion seemed to rally at Colonel O'Connor's kind words. He replied. "Thank you, Colonel. And with that I deliver myself, my aides and these soldiers into your hands."

CHAPTER VIII

In the White House Situation Room, President Morrison sat down with Henry Stillman, Robert Jackson, Michael Youngblood, and Kimberly Tucker. British Prime Minister Glenn McMillan was on the speakerphone in the middle of the table where they all were sitting. She turned to the group and asked. "Okay, everyone what's going on in Canada? I've heard that there has been some fighting in areas."

"Madam President," Henry Stillman began. "Let me bring everyone up to date. First our forces, including the British forces that assisted us in Manitoba, have achieved all of their objectives. Every major city and military base in Canada is under our control. We have also taken control of all 'traditional media sources' such as radio and television stations. The Federal government and all provincial governments are also under our control.

'We did see some fighting. The RCAF security forces at the RCAF base in Bagotville, Quebec put up a fight when the 82nd Airborne troops arrived. We lost slightly more than 50 men, most of who died when two Black Hawk choppers with our troops in them were shot down. We got a real bloody nose in Ottawa. Delta Team stormed Parliament Hill and the Royal Canadian Regiment along with RCMP SWAT teams, put up a hell of a fight. Those Canadians are tough. I haven't received confirmed causality figures but I'd say both us and the Canadians lost over 200-300 troops each. This was our bloodiest battle since Vietnam. Overall, it was fairly peaceful. We moved so fast that their national command structure wasn't able to react and get orders out and even if they had, we took control of their bases very quickly. I wouldn't be surprised either if somehow some warnings slipped out to the Canadians before we moved in an effort to avoid bloodshed. In all, I would compare our operation in Canada to what the Germans accomplished when they overran Holland in 1940. Very fast and with relatively little bloodshed."

Michael Youngblood spoke up. "Canada has traditionally been a peaceful nation. But they also have a long history of being outstanding soldiers. At D-Day in 1944, they took Juno Beach on their own. People forget how long and brave a history they have as warriors."

"Okay, so what's next?" Morrison asked.

Glenn McMillan joined the conversation. "Hello, everybody. First let me say good job everyone. It was a very difficult decision we all made to intercede into the affairs of a longtime ally and friend. But we did what we had to do.

'Now as far as what we are to do next, I have an announcement to make. King Edward is flying to Canada tomorrow. The Canadian Opposition Leader Denise McLean flew to London and met with His Majesty and myself and formally requested that His Majesty act to remove the current government. His Majesty has agreed to her request. We kept her visit very quiet for fear that it would stir up more problems in Canada. Ms. McLean reached out to me after her very unsuccessful meeting with Governor General Mancino and asked me to arrange for a meeting with the King. Even though it was highly irregular for a foreign opposition politician to seek and be granted an audience with His Majesty, in this case I thought it was

234

proper. His Majesty also agreed.

'Once His Majesty reaches Ottawa, he will be meeting with Governor General Mancino and will formally revoke the 1947 Letters Patent which transferred most royal powers from the Monarch to the Governor General. After he has done that, he will be removing Rocco Mancino from his office as Governor General and Pierre Dion from his office as Prime Minister and then meeting with Parliamentary leaders to select a new interim Prime Minister and Governor General until a new election can be held."

Dr. Tucker responded. "That is huge. I'm sorry to sound ignorant, but is it legal?"

"Good question." Prime Minister McMillan answered. "And, yes, our constitutional experts assure us that this move is legal. It's highly irregular or maybe a better way to put it is 'unusual', but it is legal. Remember in our system we don't have the legislated 'checks and balances' that you do in your constitution. Instead, the Monarchy acts as a final check on a government that is stepping beyond its proper limits. And the King is the Head of State in Canada as he is of course here in the United Kingdom."

Robert Jackson then spoke up. "I think that sounds very positive. I don't believe Dion or his government have any credibility within Canada or internationally anymore. But I want to emphasize something here. Canada is an enormous nation physically. While traditionally peaceful, as Michael pointed out they also have a history of being very tough warriors. We do not want to get into a situation where we have guerilla style attacks against our forces there. There is simply far too much land for us to try and successfully fight any sort of insurgency."

"What do you suggest, Bob" President Morrison asked.

"We need to make sure we avoid the errors that we made in places like Vietnam, Iraq and Afghanistan. We must ensure people feel safe and secure. And that means having enough "boots on the ground" to ensure guerilla warfare doesn't begin. It also means ensuring our troops follow and respect Canadian laws. Make sure life continues as normal for them, until we can sort out if and what provinces do in fact join our union and help what is left of Canada move on. But we can't do any of this if people are resisting us.

'I have one other idea that I will raise while we have everyone here together. People in Canada are going to be very frightened over recent events – and rightfully so. They have gone from one of the world's most admired, peaceful and stable nations to a nation wracked by civil war. I believe we should offer to admit all the provinces and territories of Canada into the union. We make it clear that they will be free to enter the union and keep such policies as public healthcare, and such. We make it as palatable as possible. And in return they join the most powerful and wealthiest nation in the world."

Dr. Kimberly Tucker interjected. "Bob, I like your ideas. I have to say while much and perhaps even most of Canada would be very desirable to have as part of the USA; I don't believe any Americans would have the stomach for dealing with Quebec's incessant whining and bitching about their distinct society and language laws. And there is no way in hell any American government would agree to bilingualism just to keep Quebec happy."

President Morrison asked. "What about our people? Does anyone have any idea of what most Americans would think about Canada joining us?"

Michael Youngblood answered. "Madam President, I don't think it

236

will be a massive issue. Americans have always had positive thoughts on Canada. Most Americans don't know very much about Canada in so far as how the government works and such or its' history. They do tend to believe it is very left wing, much like some of the more socialist nations in Europe. But they are considered our friends. The biggest concerns will come from the Republicans. They'll be worried about how the political balance here will be upset by 40 million new, and in their minds, very liberal voters coming into the country. And to be honest I'm am sure many regular Americans may be concerned about what will happen to their tax rates if they have to support Canadian style social programs, many of which are far more generous than our current ones."

"Thank you, Michael that was very interesting. I believe we'll make the offer to all the provinces and northern territories to join us. As far as I can see, there are no legal or constitutional barriers to any state wishing to adopt publicly funded healthcare – it is just none have had the common sense or courage to fight the medical insurance companies so far. We can work out other ways to merge their employment insurance into our unemployment insurance schemes, and the Canada Pension Plan into Social Security. Both countries have enough smart people to figure this out. The three big sticking points that will affect everyone in both nations as I see it will be our gun laws, the systems of measurement, and bilingualism.

'Regarding gun laws this is our opportunity to bring some badly needed common sense to our country. Canada has fairly rational gun laws, which allow for private ownership but do a pretty good job of keeping guns out of the hands of nuts. This would be a good opportunity to look at the best of our laws and the best of theirs and come up with something that works. I'm ready to take on the NRA to do it!

'As for measurements. Metric is legal here in the US; it's just nobody outside of some scientists likes to use it. Canada has a hodge-podge system of both metric and imperial. Canadians use metric for the weather – but they cook using Fahrenheit temperatures. They measure themselves in pounds and feet and yet use metric distances for a road trip. As Canada uses a lot of imperial already, we will stick with the imperial system for government use. In so far as the market I think it is fair if stores and such use both. For example, if a gas station in Toronto has gas prices posted in gallons and liters nobody is hurt by that. Maybe road signs could be in both metric and imperial. We can see.

'Bilingualism is a no go for the Federal government. If Quebec joins us, they can absolutely continue to speak French and offer provincial or I guess it will be state services in French. But we'll deal with residents there in English. I know we do serve people in Spanish in many areas as customer service requires it. There are no legal obligations to do so, so I'd be prepared to try and do the same in Quebec in French. But nothing official or legal. I have never agreed with Canada's bilingualism. They accepted the English, French and Indians as "founding nations" but only recognized English and French languages. Sounds pretty racist to me. It makes sense to use the language of the majority."

Henry Stillman spoke up now. "What about any provinces and territories who don't want to become part of the United States?"

"Then we will wish them well, and support them as being part of an independent Canada. What's left of it," Morrison replied. 'Trust me Henry I have no imperial aspirations, nor does our country.

'What do we believe our next steps should be?"

Michael Youngblood answered. "You need to address the peoples
238

of Canada and the United States and describe what will be happening and when."

Across Canada, an eerie calm descended upon the nation. Fires still burned on Parliament Hill. The Ottawa Fire Department, assisted by the Canadian and American military, were getting it under control. Most people stayed inside their homes watching military vehicles and police cars patrolling the streets. A few wandered close to Parliament Hill and looked in awe at the smoking ruins of the shattered Peace Tower. The greatest symbol of Canadian Parliamentary democracy was gone.

President Morrison again addressed the people of North America. Before the address she had reached out to the rebellious Premiers and suggested that their spokeswoman Premier Van Pelt join the address with the President. Her suggestion was quickly accepted. President Morrison began.

"My fellow Americans and Canadians, I am coming to you now to update you on the situation in Canada. When I am done, the Premier of Alberta Karen Van Pelt will then speak.

'I realize all of you are probably concerned and even scared. But you have nothing to fear. Currently the situation across Canada is peaceful. We did see some unfortunate, short-term violence in two particular areas but that is over now. American and British military forces, along with your local police, are ensuring peace and security for everyone. And let me assure you all, that peace is the primary goal of all of us. I urge all of you to go about your regular lives. Attend school, go to work, shop in your local stores and live your lives.

'Going forward the following will occur. The five Canadian Provinces who requested American military aid have also requested to be admitted as states into the United States of America. Those provinces are; British Columbia, Alberta, Saskatchewan, Manitoba, and Newfoundland. I am now also inviting the remaining five provinces of Ontario, Quebec, New Brunswick, Nova Scotia, and Prince Edward Island, as well as the northern territories of Yukon, North West Territories, and Nunavut to also apply for entrance into the American union. There is a process for doing this that must be followed and acceptance is not guaranteed. However, I believe it is safe to say that such an application to join our union would be viewed very positively.

'For any province that declines this invitation or is not accepted, we will wish them well and fully support them as independent nations. But I say to you all now. Let us take this opportunity to finally create a true North American single great nation. We Americans can learn much from Canada in ways of building a strong, compassionate nation and you Canadians can also learn from us. Together we can build the finest nation there is that will be the envy of the entire world.

'Thank you."

At this point Premier Karen Van Pelt spoke from Edmonton.

"Thank you, Madam President.

"To all Canadians and Americans, thank you for letting me speak with you tonight. I was part of a group of Provincial Premiers who initiated the process of beginning to discuss separation from Canada due to the outrageous actions of the Federal government and Prime Minister Dion. We then were forced to seek aid from the United States due to the decision of Prime Minister Dion to attempt to use military force against us. Something I will point out was never used or attempted in Quebec during both of their referendum campaigns.

240

It also became very clear to us that through the entire history of Canada, numerous Federal governments favored central Canada in decisions of great magnitude. Other provinces in particular in Western Canada were not treated with respect and quite frankly were taken advantage of. This must stop immediately and separation appears to be the only way for that to occur.

'We took the very large step of asking that the process of our provinces being admitted into the American union to begin. It is a detailed process but I wish to assure all Canadians, that there will be a binding referendum that will be held. The decision of Canadians on this will be final. This will not be something that Canadians should feel is being forced upon them. One admirable aspect of the United States is their system of government is not dominated by a single state or region as is the current case in Canada. We believe our provinces would more easily thrive in that system then in the current Canadian system.

'There will be more details to follow.

'Thank you.”

The following morning, a Royal Air Force (RAF) Airbus VIP Voyager touched down at MacDonald-Cartier International Airport in Ottawa. King Edward, surrounded by members of the Royal Protection Squad (RPS) emerged from the aircraft. Along with the RPS were two troops of Squadron B of the 22nd Special Air Service (SAS) Regiment as further protection for the Monarch. On the ground was an honor guard of RCMP officers with soldiers from the US 101st Airborne Division also very visible securing all areas of the airport.

The King was taken by motorcade through the streets of Ottawa to Rideau Hall. All along the route, the streets were lined with RCMP and Ottawa police officers along with more troopers from the 101st Airborne. Nobody was taking any chances on the safety of the King during this time. Upon arrival the RCMP officers snapped to attention as the King was ushered into Rideau Hall to meet with Governor General Mancino. It wasn't a pleasant meeting.

"Good morning, Your Majesty," Mancino began.

"Good morning, Mr. Mancino," the King responded coldly. "Mr. Mancino, I will be very quick and to the point. I am most disappointed in your behavior and performance of your duties during this crisis. You blindly followed the Prime Minister's lead and allowed Canada to plunge itself in a virtual civil war forcing the Americans and us to intercede. You had the power to stop Prime Minister Dion and you didn't. So, as of now, I am hereby revoking the 1947 Letters Patent and firing you. I am taking back the Royal powers that had been assigned to the Canadian Governor General. My security personnel will supervise you removing your personal effects from here and escort you off the property. "

"Can you do this?"

"I assure you, Mr. Mancino, I can do this. Just because it has never been done before, doesn't mean that it cannot be done. I suggest you begin removing your personal effects from here and leave as soon as possible."

Rocco Mancino stared at the King and could see he was deadly serious. He could also see that the SAS soldiers and other body guards with the King were also deadly serious, and so an argument with His Majesty would not be wise.

"Your Majesty, I understand. I'll start moving out."

From there, the King was taken to 24 Sussex Drive, where Pierre Dion was being held under house arrest. It was another short meeting.

"Prime Minister, it is my duty to inform you that I just left a meeting with Mr. Mancino, at Rideau Hall."

"You mean Governor General Mancino, don't you, Your Majesty?" Dion responded.

"No, I don't, Prime Minister," King Edward snapped back. "I told him that I have revoked the 1947 Letters Patent and reclaimed the Royal Powers that had been delegated to the Canadian Governor General. Then I fired him. I am here now to fire you. Effective immediately, you are no longer Prime Minister of Canada. My security detail will allow you and your wife to remove your personal belongings from here and we will make arrangements to transport you safely anyplace you would like to go. But there is no debate here. You are finished as Prime Minister."

Dion was stunned. Even though he knew with the military intervention by the United States and Great Britain that he had little hope of retaining power, he never dreamed that he would be personally fired by the King himself. He quickly responded. "You can't do that. King or not, you don't have the authority to fire a Canadian Prime Minister," he yelled leaping from his chair.

SAS Lance Corporal Nolan Cromwell reacted instantly. He grabbed Dion and hurled him back into his chair which toppled backward throwing the Canadian Prime Minister on the floor. Cromwell then stood over him and snarled. "Now, mate, understand that you're talking to His Majesty the King. Show some respect and if you jump up again, I may just have to put a bullet into you. Do you understand?"

Dion standing up slowly nodded his head. He looked into the icy, slate blue eyes of Cromwell and knew right away that the young SAS trooper wouldn't hesitate to back up his words. Dion slowly stood up and said. "Your Majesty, may I ask who is replacing me?"

King Edward glared coldly at the former Prime Minister. He waited before answering. "You may ask. I will be meeting with Denise McLain, your Leader of the Official Opposition and your House Leader Gilles Tardif. I will discuss with them who may be able to form a government that would command the confidence of the House of Commons. Now, you can start removing your personal effects from this house. My security personnel will assist you and they will arrange to get you safely back to your home wherever that is.

'I'll add something else now. Your performance during this entire crisis, from the war breaking out in the Middle East to this moment, was a disgrace. You turned your back on half of Canada, its' indigenous population and your closest, most historical allies. History will damn you for what you did. Now do Canada a favor and leave quietly. Let Canadians figure out exactly what they want to do with their nation."

With that, King Edward turned around and strode out of the room. He was taken by motorcade to Stornoway there to meet with Denise McLean and Gilles Tardif. After a day of discussions, it was agreed by McLean and Tardif and supported by the Monarch that a coalition government made up of Liberals and Conservatives would rule Canada until issues related to the possible separation of provinces was finalized.

Once that agreement was made, King Edward spoke to Canadians.

"Good evening my fellow Canadians[xxxviii]. This is the first time I
244

have ever directly addressed the people of Canada. Thank you for taking the time to hear me.

'I come to you tonight to inform you that after detailed discussions here in Ottawa, an interim coalition government has been created. Ms. Denise McLean will serve as the Prime Minister and her cabinet will be made up of Conservative, Liberal and NDP Members of Parliament. This government will provide effective government to all Canadians while the process of possibly joining the United States is being undertaken. During this time the government will operate in the traditional Westminster fashion.

'As well I have named former External Affairs Minister Stephanie Howatt to the office of Governor General. She will be my representative here in Ottawa.

'I know you will all join me in wishing them the very best in this most momentous time in Canada's history.

'Thank you."

CHAPTER IX

Three months later in Philadelphia, leaders from the United States Congress, President Morrison, Vice President Rafferty, Secretary of State Michael Youngblood, new Canadian Prime Minister Denise McLean, Deputy Prime Minister Gilles Tardif, George Cross of the Assembly of First Nations, and the ten provincial Premiers, three territorial leaders, as well as numerous other aides sat down to discuss the future of North America. Philadelphia had been chosen due to its historical role in the creation of the Declaration of Independence.

When the talks began, Quebec Premier Nicole Ouellet announced. "Quebec wishes the very best to everyone here. We take this opportunity to finally achieve independence. We are forming the Republic of Quebec and will be an independent French speaking nation. We will be a friend and ally to all here, and wish to remain as free trade and military partners to everyone as well. But we do not feel that a French speaking Quebec can survive in a new much larger, English speaking nation.

'With this I will take my leave. Quebec will formally leave this meeting and begin the process of building our new independent nation."

Premier Ouellet then left the room and headed back to Quebec City.

The general consensus in the room was relief. There was some sadness as Quebec had always had such a strong presence in Canada however nobody had been looking forward to the perceived difficult negotiations that would have occurred in trying to meet all of Quebec's concerns.

With Quebec having left, negotiations to form a new North American nation began in earnest. Vice President Joel Rafferty who had been appointed by President Morrison to be the US "lead negotiator" stood up to speak. "Ladies and Gentlemen, thank you all for coming on this momentous day in North American history. We Americans are very flattered that our friends from Canada have expressed interest in joining our great union. We are happy to negotiate and try to make this work so that everyone here and across our two great nations are happy with the results.

'One point I must make first is this. While we are willing and quite happy to consider the idea of all current Canadian provinces entering our union, one thing we will insist on is there must be changes to the current provincial boundaries if they are to become states in our union. It has never made economic sense for New Brunswick, Nova Scotia and Prince Edward Island to be separate provinces. The populations there are simply too small nor are they culturally diverse from one another. We will only consider admitting that region if they are one state. They must merge together. This doesn't include Newfoundland which is very distinct and to which we will consider as a separate state. We feel the same of Saskatchewan and Manitoba. They must also form one single entity and apply as such. We have had top State and Treasury Department economists and analysts 'crunch the numbers' in regard to this as the duplication of government services across multiples provincial boundaries is outrageously expensive and serves no purpose outside of guaranteeing a large number of duplicate government jobs. We are happy to share the data with you.

248

'As well, we believe the current Territories of Yukon, North West Territories and Nunavut are currently too sparsely populated to consider as states. We will consider them as an unincorporated territory in the same manner as Puerto Rico. The residents there, if this merger goes through, will be considered US citizens with all the duties, responsibilities, and benefits associated with that.

'I will also say that the union between our two nations, if it goes forward, will lead to major benefits for Canadians. But one enormous benefit that will be seen immediately is that no longer will Canada's political system be dominated by two provinces and in particular, the interests of one province. We will all know that since the 1960's and possibly before that Quebec and its' interests dominated Canada. In our system with each state receiving Members of the House of Representatives based on representation by population, and each state receiving two Senators regardless of population, larger states cannot dominate smaller states. The interests of smaller Canadian regions will be better protected joining the American union.

'And one final, and may I say, very critical point. We Americans learned a very valuable lesson during our Civil War. Never again would we allow our nation to be broken apart. So, please understand that the road you are traveling on here is one way. If we accept you into our union it is forever. There is no possibility, whatsoever of leaving. So, as we negotiate here please understand that. There is no trial period or get acquainted or anything of the matter. Once you are in our union it is forever."

Prime Minister McLean then asked to address the meeting. "Ladies and Gentlemen, thank you for allowing me to address this most momentous meeting in our two great nations' histories. We Canadians like you Americans are willing to discuss a merger of our nations together into one great North American nation. However, we have some issues that we will state up front that are not negotiable from our end. They are;

Any Canadian province or territory that joins the United States must be able to keep its publicly funded medical care system. This cannot be open to challenge from the current American health care insurance industry. Canadians from coast to coast firmly believe that it is a basic human right to have affordable and accessible health care. We are open to changes that make our health care system more efficient and indeed more accessible. But we start all such negotiations with the premise that all citizens must be covered and guaranteed, public affordable health care.

There must be some form of change to the current 2nd Amendment to your constitution in order to protect all our current citizens from gun violence. We are not asking or advocating for the 2nd Amendment to be repealed. We are aware and sensitive that there is a strong cultural connection to guns in the United States. Many of you probably are not aware of this but within many parts of Canada, mainly our rural areas; there is a very strong tradition of gun ownership as well. Canadians don't have the constitutional right to bear arms however we do agree that firearms are part of the way of life in many of our communities. That all being said we also are aware that the majority of Americans and Canadians want to see common sense gun laws that protect all people. Let us use this opportunity to face these problems and amend the 2nd Amendment so that the scourge of gun violence is finally abolished across North America.

Finally, I must ask everyone here to consider the Indigenous peoples of North America. Both Canada and the United States have a shameful record when it comes to the treatment of our aboriginals and respecting treaty rights. Part of the Canadian negotiating team is George Cross of the Assembly of First Nations. We urge our American friends to bring in aboriginal representatives from your nation and let us all work together to create a brand new nation that is also a true partnership with the First Nations of North America.

With that, we can begin negotiations to begin the process of merging our two great 'into a single entity that will be the envy of the world."

Over the next year, the most intense negotiations ever seen in North America were held. To ensure that they appeared fully "fair and inclusive" the negotiations rotated on a monthly basis from an American city to a Canadian city. That also ensured negotiators from both nations became familiar with the people and cities of both countries. In a landmark move, one set of talks was held at the Six Nations Mohawk Reserve outside of Brantford Ontario and then followed by another set of talks at the Pine Ridge Oglala Lakota Reservation in South Dakota. Pine Ridge was also a very symbolic locations as it marked the site of the 1890 Wounded Knee Massacre in which the 7th Cavalry Regiment (General Custer's unit that had been decimated at the Battle of Little Big Horn in 1876) slaughtered Oglala Lakota people practicing the Ghost Dance Religion and the 1973 shoot-out between FBI agents and members of AIM. For most of the "white negotiators" these two months of talks were brutally uncomfortable and eye opening. The depth of poverty and despair among the aboriginal peoples was "in the face" of negotiators every day. President Morrison and Prime Minister McLean, who were both strong advocates for aboriginal justice and rights had both insisted on these two locations being included.

As negotiations went on, Prime Minister Denise McLean worked hard to repair the damage created by Prime Minister Dion and his government. The Emergencies Act was withdrawn. Ottawa returned management of the oil sector back to Alberta, Saskatchewan, and Newfoundland. There was also tense at times negotiations with Quebec on its separation from Canada.

Everything that nations use to govern themselves was up for negotiation. What health and safety regulations would be adopted in the workplace, would American cars be forced to adopt daytime running lights (they were), what would happen to the publicly funded Canadian Broadcasting Corporation (it would be turned into a model similar to that of the US Public Broadcasting System PBS). Another huge issue was what would happen to the thousands of Canadian federal civil servants. Logic would dictate that most of them would be "surplus" and have to be "packaged out." The overall list of issues they worked on was simply exhaustive.

One high profile issue was the death penalty. Even though most Canadians, according to polls, supported the death penalty in certain cases no politician would reopen that debate. [xxxix] The issue was resolved when Canadian negotiators were reminded that each state had the ability to use or not to use the death penalty and that the US federal law did have the death penalty "on the books" and that it wasn't going away. Canadians opposed to it were somewhat satisfied that they would have the ability to block it in their regions.

Another "sticking point" that came up during the long negotiations was the legal drinking age. In 1984 Congress had passed the National Minimum Drinking Age Act, which forced states to raise their legal drinking age to 21 or lose 10% of their highway funding. All Canadian provinces had drinking ages below that. Most had a drinking age of 19, while Alberta, Manitoba and Quebec had drinking ages of 18. The Canadian negotiators were unbendable on this issue. As Prime Minister McLean stated. "If a young person is old enough to die for their country, vote and get married they are old enough to have a drink. A drinking age of 21 is idiotic. The roads in Canada are not covered in blood due to a lower drinking age."

The compromise that was worked out was the current US law would apply to the "original 50 states" and would be reconsidered over time and the incoming new states would be free to set and enforce their own drinking ages.

Another area of controversy that arose that caught people off guard was football. Especially in Western Canada, Canadian football is almost a religion and the thought of adopting US rules was unthinkable. When told of this "obstacle" President Morrison exclaimed. "We're not going to have negotiations upset or stalled over something as trivial as football. I know Canada has their own league. Get people involved in football in both countries, sit them down and knock their heads together until they come up with a solution!"

Officials from both the National Football League (NFL) and Canadian Football League (CFL) were brought into the negotiations. It was finally agreed that the two leagues would remain separate and football in the new states would continue to play by "Canadian rules." A task force however would be created to come up with ideas whereby a new professional league would be created and would play by a hybrid of US and Canadian rules.

After 15 months of negotiations, the President Morrison and Prime Minister McLean came together in Washington for a joint address to the people of both nations.

President Morrison began. "To the people of the United States and Canada, I am very pleased to announce that our two governments have reached an agreement for the admittance of the nine Canadian provinces and three territories into the American union. The official name of this agreement is the "North American Unification Treaty or NAUT." The name of our newly united great nation will become the United States of North America. The acronym for this nation will be the USNA. This agreement however is contingent on approval by the American Congress, the Canadian Parliament and a binding referendum in Canada. The referendum must receive a "yes vote" by a margin no less than 50% plus one for it to be approved. The normal approval rules of both Congress and Parliament will dictate approvals in those bodies."

Prime Minister McLean then spoke. "Thank you, Madam President. I know for Canadians this is an exciting day and very a sad day. We love our nation and are proud of it. But I want you to imagine the future that we will be leaving for our future generations. We will be leaving them a future as part of the largest and most powerful nation on earth. And I remind all of you. We are not turning our back on our past by joining the United States. North America was one undivided land mass when European colonists arrived. It wasn't the First Nations that felt the need to create artificial barriers across North America. It was the European colonists. A merging of our two nations would simply return North America to its' traditional manner.

'As for the highlights of the negotiations let me discuss the areas in which Canadians have insisted is most important to them.

'The first is health care. I want all of you to know our health care system is protected 100%. Many of you do not realize that any state in the American union can create publicly funded healthcare available to all. They have simply chosen not to do so. Our healthcare system will continue. The only change one will see is people will be able to purchase private coverage to supplement their public coverage. This is the same as is done across Western Europe.

Nobody in the Canadian provinces and territories will lose their coverage.

'A large number of hours of negotiations involved the First Nations and treaty rights. We have agreed on a newly expanded concept of "Dependent Sovereign Nations" across our new nation. What this will mean is First Nations will have the complete right to pass any and all civil and criminal laws on their territories. Federal and state law will not apply on their lands. The only rights that they will not have involve relationships with foreign nations. That will still be the responsibly of the Federal government. There will also be a special conference that will be held within six months of the ratification of NAUT to deal with all outstanding treaty claims across our new nation. There will be two new seats in the Senate created for members of the First Nations and at least one Supreme Court Justice will be aboriginal. This is far greater representation for First Nations peoples in government then has ever before been seen in Canada or the United States.

'The President will outline the deal we have struck on firearms shortly.

'Another highlight is citizenship. All current Canadian citizens will be granted American citizenship and be considered Natural Born American citizens. This means they will have every right and responsibility of a person born in the United States including the right to run for any elected office."

President Morrison then took over. "Many Americans are very concerned about both the high rate of gun violence in our nation and the 2nd Amendment. Our Canadian friends are deeply troubled by our rate of gun violence. We believe we have a proposal that we will introduce into the normal constitutional amendment process that is reasonable and protects all rights. Currently the 2nd Amendment states;

"A well-regulated Militia, being necessary to the security of a free State, the right of the people to keep and bear Arms, shall not be infringed."

Most Americans believe in the 2nd Amendment however they also support common sense gun laws that will assist us in keeping our communities safe. Therefore, we propose the following addition to the 2nd Amendment;

"Reasonable laws passed by any State or Federal government that has the purpose of protecting society from firearms violence, shall not be unreasonably impeded."

'We believe this is a common-sense approach to the scourge of gun violence that has plagued our society for decades.

'We are using this time to make a final effort to have the Equal Rights Amendment (ERA) passed. As you may or may not know the ERA was first introduced into Congress in 1921 and again reintroduced in 1971. Its' aim was to ensure the equality of women across our great nation. It has been stalled since the early 1980's although Nevada in 2017 and Illinois in 2018 have brought it back to life with successful ratification votes. We will now take the opportunity brought about by amending the 2nd Amendment to finally ratify the ERA."

Prime Minister McLean then spoke again. "There have been agreements on many other fronts related to this process. I will outline just a few of them. More details will be released to the media after this joint address.

256

'The Canadian Armed Forces will be merged into the United States Armed Forces. Current members of the Canadian regular and reserve forces will be assigned the equivalent American rank.

'Currently, the United States doesn't have and has never had a national police force unlike our RCMP. What has been agreed upon are current members of the RCMP will be merged into the state police departments that will be required in each new state. As well, current members of the RCMP in administrative duties in Ottawa at RCMP headquarters will be offered jobs with either the new FBI 'Northern Administrative Office' in Ottawa or at various other FBI offices.

'There will be some duplication of services in the Federal governments. American and Canadian civil servants who may be impacted will be offered generous early retirement packages or severance packages.

'Our current social benefits such as the Canada Pension Plan and Employment Insurance will be merged into the current US Social Security and Unemployment Insurance systems. The current Canadian equalization systems of where wealthier provinces help to subsidize less wealthy provinces will be phased out over the next two years after ratification of the NAUT.

'As for the metric system and bilingualism, it has been agreed that Canada will return to the imperial system, but unlike in the past where we used the British imperial system, we will use the American imperial system. Metric may still be used as many businesses require it to do business with other countries. However, imperial will be the official system. In addition, to avoid confusion our road signs will be converted to reflect both imperial and metric speeds and distances. Metric, however, will be in smaller letters and numbers on the signs and the Imperial numbers will be the legal distances and speed limits. Gas stations will be required to sell fuels by the gallon. They will have the freedom to also use liters however gallons will be the official measure. Grocery stores will sell meat and produce by imperial measures.

'Official bilingualism will be over. Government offices will provide services in languages that best allow them to serve their customers. For example, many US Federal government offices in Southern California offer services in Spanish. They are not legally obliged to do so but they choose to do so. In what was Canada, the same model will be used in offering services in French and First Nations languages. The official language of government however will be English."

Prime Minister McLean spoke for an additional 25 minutes outlining the main points of the NAUT before giving away to President Morrison who wrapped up the joint address. The next steps would be the approval/ratification processes in each nation.

The process within Canada was painful. Gurminder Grewal led a small but vocal anti-American protest group and did his best to whip up hysteria claiming that Canadians despite the clauses in the NAUT would lose their healthcare and be overrun by guns and violence. The forces aligned with approving the treaty responded by pointing out that Canada for all intents and purposes had "outsourced" its national defense to the United States decades ago and they had deeply integrated economies. This would simply be a natural extension of that.

The Maritime Provinces of Nova Scotia, New Brunswick, and Prince Edward Island staged referendums to merge their provinces into one entity. Despite protests by civil servants who at times violently protested the loss of public sector jobs that would occur with such integration, the referendums did pass and the new entity was formally called "Acadia."

Next came the mergers of Manitoba and Saskatchewan into the new entity to be called "Assiniboia."

From there, the terms of the NAUT were introduced into each provincial legislature and the Federal Parliament. Debates in all the houses were emotional and at times stormy. Still, even politicians opposed to the treaty admitted that their opposition was based mainly on emotional grounds as opposed to objective evidence. They admitted that the Canadian negotiators had done such a fine job with the treaty negotiations that most of their fears related to such matters as health care and guns were positively addressed. The approval for the new treaty was passed by all the houses within eight months.

The final step for Canada was the national referendum. Prime Minister McLean had proclaimed. "Back in the early 1980's, the Canadian constitution was re-written and brought home from the United Kingdom by Prime Minister Pierre Trudeau. When he did that, he relied on the approvals of the provincial legislatures and Parliament. All of these bodies were controlled by strict party discipline that dictated how members of each body would vote. Prime Minister Brian Mulroney attempted to do the same with the Meech Lake Accord only to see that it was defeated, in Manitoba, by one courageous aboriginal MPP, Elijah Harper, and in Newfoundland in 1990. Prime Minister Mulroney did put the 1992 Charlottown Accord [xl] to a national referendum where, again thank god, it was defeated. The people need to have a final say that isn't dominated by political parties that dictate how politicians will vote. So we will follow the example of Charlottown and put it to the people directly for their approval."

The referendum was held in October, just as Charlottown had been, but unlike the unpopular 1992 constitutional accord, this vote was approved by Canadians by a margin of 57% voting yes, and 43% turning it down. Over 90% of eligible Canadian voted.

With the successful referendum, Canada officially petitioned Congress to join the American union. Now the question of Canada joining the United States was up to the United States Congress.

As Congress debated the Canadian petition, the United States was also involved in the process to amend their own constitution with the proposed change to the 2nd Amendment and the addition of the ERA. Finally, after tremendous wrangling across the nation both amendments were passed by 39 states and Congress. Congress also approved the Canadian petition for statehood. The main stumbling block in Congress in regards to the Canadian petition came from conservative Republicans. Many of them were deeply concerned about how the dynamics of the US political order would be changed by the influx of close to 40 million new citizens most of whom would tend to be quite liberal and would thus vote Democrat. The majority of them were convinced that the positives such as the oil fields in Alberta, Saskatchewan and Newfoundland would now be part of the United States and not to mention the huge amounts of natural gas in Canada, and deep water harbors such as Halifax and Victoria, that would now be part of the United States, would outweigh the huge increase in liberal voters.

The final step was approval by the President. And on April 16th President Morrison signed the petition that would merge Canada into the United States on July 1st. That date was chosen on purpose to coincide with Canada Day.

EPILOGUE

On the night of June 30[th,] dignitaries gathered in Ottawa. President Morrison and Vice-President Rafferty were there along with various Congressional leaders. Prime Minister McLean, along with King Edward IX, Princess Alexandra and the various Provincial Premiers, who the following day would become State Governors, gathered. Aboriginal leaders from both nations were also present.

Various galas were staged across the city and there were colorful fireworks displays. At the bridges crossing the Ottawa River which separates Ontario and Quebec US Customs and Immigration officers prepared to man newly constructed customs booths. It had been agreed that the Republic of Quebec having turned its back on the new "super nation" would be treated as an independent nation with no economic or political ties to the newly enlarged United States of North America. As well, people who had opted to remain in Quebec would not have access to American citizenship. Most English-speaking Quebecers used this time to move to regions of Canada that were joining the United States. Now a person who wished to cross the river from Quebec into Ottawa (or anyplace else along the frontier between Quebec and new American states) would be forced to present a valid passport and clear customs. The same was true for someone going in the opposite direction.

At this time, negotiations were ongoing between Quebec and the United States of North America as to if and how Quebec may be included in the free trade agreement with the USNA and Mexico. Until then all good travelling between both nations were subject to tariffs and duties. As well public servants who had lived in Quebec and worked in Ottawa had been advised well before this time, that if their job still existed upon the beginning of the USNA, they would be forced to move their residence to the USNA or be terminated. No "foreign" workers would be allowed to work in the new government.

Across Canada, road crews had moved out to remove metric road signs and replacing them with the new road signs with imperial measurements in the forefront – the exact opposite of what was done during Labor Day weekend of 1977 when imperial road signs in Canada were replaced by metric signs. Most of the new states decided on maximum speed limits of either 65 MPH or 70 MPH. Most gas stations had by now converted their pumps to gallons.

At midnight, the various dignitaries and thousands of onlookers gathered on Parliament Hill. There, two honor guards were present. One made up of officers of the RCMP and the other a United States Marine Corp honor guard. At midnight, the RCMP honor guard lowered the Maple Leaf for the last time. The flag was carefully folded and would be placed in a display of honor at the Smithsonian Institute in Washington. Then the Marine honor guard slowly and solemnly raised the flag of the new nation with its 50 stars and nine maple leaves on it. President Morrison had insisted that the new additions to the union have specific place of honor on the flag.

As the flag began blowing in the breeze, now former Prime Minister Denise McLean turned to President Morrison and said. "Part of my heart is breaking looking at that flag but another part is beating proudly as I think of our exciting future."

President Morrison smiled and responded. "Our children will thank us for the great future and opportunities we have now given them. North America should always have been one nation. Our ancestors created unnecessary divisions where they should have worked harder to find ways to bridge them."

"I agree," McLean responded. "And let our daughters in particular rejoice and be proud as it was two women who made this happen! For over 200 years men kept our nations apart and emphasized our differences. We brought everyone together."

"Here's to women and the new United States of North America," Morrison said with a huge smile.

The nine Maple Leaves on the flag represent the original nine Provinces before the amalgamation votes that joined the United States.

END NOTES

---

[i] From the beginning of Canada, through most of its history the direction that country would take was determined by the economic, academic, political and cultural elite who were in Ottawa, Toronto, and Montreal. They became known as the Laurentian Elite, due to the nearby St. Lawrence River and Laurentian Mountains.

[ii] In Canada, the House of Commons is elected on a very "rough" Representation by Population principle. The reality is provinces such as Alberta and British Columbia are badly under-represented and Maritime Provinces such as Prince Edward Island and New Brunswick are overly represented. This all came about due to historical compromises decades ago, that current politicians are loath to reopen and fix.

[iii] NORAD is the North American Air Defense Command. It is a joint operation between Canada and the United States.

[iv] Question Period is the daily 45 minute segment where opposition politicians are free to ask questions of the government. Its purpose is to "hold the government accountable." Sadly over the past few decades it has become more a "media circus" where both the opposition and government simply recite "canned talking points."

[v] The RCMP is responsible for security on Parliament Hill but may not enter the House of Commons unless directed to do so by the Speaker of the House.

[vi] Read more at: https://www.brainyquote.com/quotes/robert_mcnamara_564189

[vii] The Quiet Revolution refers to Quebec's metamorphosis in the 1960's from a society dominated by the Roman Catholic Church, and where the English elite controlled the economy, to a cosmopolitan, urban society where the French took control of the economy.

[viii] Princess Patricia Light Infantry

[ix] Canadian Forces Base Edmonton

[x] Royal Canadian Air Force

[xi] International Monetary Fund

[xii] In October 1970, Prime Minister Pierre Trudeau invoked the War Measures Act in response to the kidnapping of Quebec Labor Minister Pierre Laporte, and British Trade Commissioner James Cross. The result of this was Canada was placed under Martial Law and such rights as Habeas Corpus was suspended.

[xiii] CEGEPS are a unique Quebec educational institution. Quebec high schools only go to grade 11. If a student wishes to go to university they then must

complete a two year pre-university course of study at a college (the French acronym is CEGEP.)

[xiv] The "Byng/King Affair of 1926 occurred when Prime Minister William Lyon Mackenzie King asked Governor General Lord Julian Byng to dissolve Parliament and call a general election. Governor General Byng refused the request from Prime Minister King and asked Opposition leader Arthur Meighen to form a government, which he did. This marked the last time in Canadian history that a Governor General refused a request from a Prime Minister.

[xv] Merde is a common French Canadian cuss word.

[xvi] In the early 1980's it was common to see bumper stickers in Alberta with this phrase on it. It was in reaction to the National Energy Program imposed on Alberta by the government of Pierre Trudeau.

[xvii] Sovereignty Association was a concept or idea used by Quebec separatists to convince Quebecers that they could separate from Canada and yet still receive benefits from Canada.

[xviii] In Canada, the federal government makes equalization payments to less wealthy Canadian provinces to equalize the provinces' "fiscal capacity or their ability to generate tax revenues. A province that does not receive equalization payments is often called a "have province", while one that does receive them is called a "have not province".

[xix] Mohawk Culture is Matrilineal in nature.

[xx] In Canada unlike other nations such as the United States, members of the armed forces reserves are not obliged to join their units unless the Federal government passes an Order in Council activating the reserves. Outside of that, any action taken by reserve units is carried out by members of those units who have volunteered.

[xxi] Câlice is another common French Canadian cuss word.

[xxii] In the summer of 1990 Mohawk Warriors seized the Mercier Bridge over a land dispute with the Government of Quebec. The crisis last all summer and involved a shoot out between the Warriors and Quebec Provincial Police and an intervention by the Canadian Army.

[xxiii] Tabernac is a common French Canadian cuss word.

[xxiv] Joint Task Force 2 or JTF 2 is the Canadian version of the British SAS or US Delta Team. It is a group of superbly trained commandos who are trained to handle the most difficult and dangerous missions. It is currently based at Dwyer Hill a facility near Ottawa.

[xxv] Queens Park is located in Toronto and is the site of the Ontario Legislature.

[xxvi] Referring to the takeover of the US embassy in Tehran in 1979.

[xxvii] Operation Kingpin was carried out on November 21, 1970. Green Berets crash-landed a helicopter in the grounds of the Son Tay prison camp in North Vietnam. The Green Berets destroyed the watch towers and stormed the prison hoping to rescue American Prisoners of War. Unbeknownst to them the prisoners had been moved just weeks earlier and the camp was empty.

xxviii Aim is the acronym for American Indian Movement, an American indigenous group that has had a troubled relationship with the US government for over 50 years.

xxix In the Commonwealth, the most senior diplomat is referred to as a High Commissioner.

xxx The Statute of Westminster was passed by the British House of Commons in 1931 and essentially said that Canada was free to pass its' one laws and was no longer subject to British laws.

xxxi There are several Official Residences in Ottawa and the surrounding area. The Prime Minister has 24 Sussex Drive and a country home known as Harrington Lake. The Leader of the Official Opposition has Stornoway. The Governor General has Rideau Hall and the Speaker of the House has "The Farm." There are several others.

xxxii The 1947 Letters Patent turned over most of the Monarch's power to the Canadian Governor General except in "exceptional circumstances." The Letter Patent may be revoked at anytime by the Monarch.

xxxiii Peter Laugheed served as Alberta Premier from 1971-1985. He was a well-known advocate for Western Canadian rights.

xxxiv The concept of the Tripe E Senate came from the United States. That is a Senate that is Elected, Equal, and Effective. Currently the Canadian Senate is made up of Senators selected by the Prime Minister. Western Canada is badly under-represented in this legislative body.

xxxv Foggy Bottom is the nickname for the State Department.

xxxvi Delta Team is the US Army's elite commando team.

xxxvii The Royal Military College or RMC is Canada's version of West Point.

xxxviii The British Monarch is a Canadian citizen.

xxxix The death penalty was abolished in 1976 by Parliament.

xl The Charlottetown Accord was a series of amendments to Canada's constitution that were defeated in a national referendum in October 1992.

AUTHOR'S BIOGRAPHY

Craig Wallace was born and raised in Toronto, Ontario and is a graduate of the University of Western Ontario with a BA in Canadian and American History. He has worked extensively in the United States and Canada and is blessed to have friends and family in both nations. He is the father of two daughters and currently lives in Hamilton, Ontario with his partner Maria.

Craig is the author of four previous history books. "Canada in Pieces" is his first novel.

Craig can be reached at craigwallace@bell.net